The Evan Myers Series
The Ledge

Bryan Loveless

LIBRARY OF CONGRESS CATALOGING-IN-PUBLICATION DATA AVAILABLE

ISBN 9798569826575

TO MY FAMILY WHO MADE THIS DREAM
POSSIBLE

Contents

Chapter One

Devil's Chute

Several major highways were blocked by almost two feet of snow that had pounded Colorado the last several days. The hordes of people who normally crowded to the ski resorts in their fancy SUVs and name brand clothing were stuck in Denver leaving the ski resort almost completely empty for the local skiers to enjoy. Shielded from the cold by thick ski coats, snow pants and goggles Evan Myers, his kid brother Jackson and the twins, Brady and Brian Miller were taking full advantage of the nonexistent ski lift lines and the fresh powder which Evan tossed high in the air as he dug the edges of his skis deep into the snow.

Evan led the small group onto a narrow trail lined with pines drooping from the weight of the snowfall. The trail led to Mother Lode, a black diamond run on the North Slope. The fresh blanket of powder on this side of the mountain had not been touched since the storm and it glistened invitingly under the sun. Skiing on fresh powder was the group's favorite way to get down the mountain. There were days they would search all day looking for a virgin slope. Today they didn't have to search long because every run had plenty of the best powder Colorado had to offer. They worked their way down the steep terrain effortlessly. At the bottom of the run, the group cheered as Evan attempted a back flip off of a large jump. The cheering, however, was quickly replaced by laughter as the best skier in the group belly flopped into the powder, not having finished his rotation in time and buried himself completely.

"I'll give him a five for effort," Brady announced as he laughed hysterically, slapping his leg for effect.

"A five Brady? Are you blind? He deserves at least a seven for a flop of that magnitude!" Brian said as he pulled off his goggles and helmet and raised his arms high in the air as if he were holding up a giant score card.

Brady and Brian were twins, but they couldn't have been more different and disagreed about almost everything. They didn't look anything alike either. Even with his thick ski coat, Brady looked skinny, like a starved ally cat. Brian was the tallest one in the group standing six feet tall with a head full of thick red hair that almost doubled the size of his already large head.

"What do you think Jackson?" Brady asked disgusted by Brian's inflated score, as he turned to Evan's kid brother, the youngest one in the group, who looked like he was in deep concentration.

"The effort was definitely there and the takeoff flawless," Jackson answered as if struggling to give his brother a meaningless score.

"Will you guys just get me out of this hole?" Evan complained as he struggled in vain to dig himself out of the snow.

"Doesn't mom always say that patience is a virtue?" Jackson said calmly.

"Brady, Brian, help me out so that I can teach my kid brother to respect his elders. Another one of our Mom's great lessons."

Although Evan was three years older than his kid brother, Jackson was tall for his age and was just an inch or two shorter than Evan and catching up fast. With Jackson's broad shoulders and large frame Evan guessed that one day soon he wouldn't be able to threaten Jackson into submission anymore.

"I'll give him a two. I was going to give him a three, but not with an attitude like that." Jackson said jokingly as he dodged a snowball from Evan.

Evan and Jackson both had brown hair and blue eyes, although Jackson's eyes were a much darker shade than his brother's. Even though they were similar in appearance Evan and Jackson's personality were very different. Evan always tried to please everyone around him, especially his parents and ski coach, while Jackson really didn't care what other people thought and did what he wanted most of the time.

"A wipeout like that makes for a grand finale for the best day of skiing this year so far. Don't you think Evan?" Brady said laughing as he toyed with his friend. He knew Evan would never call it a day until the ski lifts closed.

"If you wimps want to go home and eat peanut butter sandwiches with the crusts cut off by your mommy, then go ahead and go. Jackson and I are going to get in one more run before they close the lifts," Evan said as he struggled to free himself from the powder.

The twins laughed as they pulled Evan out of the snow. Evan stretched out his back and removed his goggles. Evan was average size for a fifteen year old kid with an athletic build and contagious, giant smile. His blue eyes lit up with excitement as he searched for Jackson, who was already skiing towards the lift.

"It's on!" Evan yelled as he pushed himself towards the lift with Brady and Brian following close behind. "You might as well give up now Jackson. You know I can catch you."

"We'll see," Jackson said as he was whisked out of reach by the chair lift.

Evan had been skiing with the twins ever since they were eleven year olds, just over four years ago. Brady and Brian had accidentally skied down a black diamond run their first time ever skiing down the mountain. Evan found them hugging at the base of a pine tree and crying for their mom. That was the beginning of the endless mom jokes that Evan never grew tired of delivering. He had helped them down the mountain, teaching them the finer points of the snow plow method of skiing that day, and they had been friends ever since.

Brady and Brian's family lived just outside the city limits of Steamboat Springs, Colorado for part of the year. Here they had their family's second house, which they only used during holidays and for a few weeks in the summer. Their primary residence was in New York City, where their dad worked as a doctor and their mom as an attorney. Evan could never understand why a family with two kids needed a nine thousand square foot house on twenty acres, but hanging out at their house had its perks, so he never asked questions. Evan and Jackson loved spending time with the Millers. They were not stuck up like most of the rich people they had met, and growing up in a resort town, they had met plenty.

Riding the high speed ski lift, it took no time at all to reach the top of the mountain.

"Last run, boys," Jerry, the chair attendant, and ski bum for life, told the group of boys as they exited the chairs.

"We'll have to make it count then," Evan yelled back as they headed down the hill.

Everyone who worked at the resort knew Evan and Jackson. Their family lived at the base of the mountain in a three story building built in the mid 1800's. His parents had purchased the building when Evan was too young to remember, before the town had boomed into a true winter paradise for the wealthy. Evan's parents had spent close to ten years renovating the old log building which was rumored to have housed the town's first saloon and brothel. After the renovations Evan's parents nicknamed the building The Lodge, since it resembled a small, quaint European ski lodge you would find in the middle of the Alps. They turned the basement into a small studio apartment which they rented out during the ski season to help finance the renovation. The apartment was booked solid from the end of November to the first week of April by some of the best skiers in the world. They came every year for the inexpensive apartment, the amazing skiing and Evan's mom's home cooked meals.

The ski resort was like a second home to Evan and Jackson. Nightly they received expert skiing tips during family dinners, from the best skiers in the world who were staying in his family's apartment. That combined with their season passes, which the brothers spent all year saving for, Evan and Jackson had turned into the best skiers the town had produced in years. As a freshman at Steamboat High, Evan was already skiing on his school's varsity ski team and was considered to be one of the best young skiers in the state.

Evan smiled as he led the twins after Jackson, who had a head start. Evan knew exactly which run Jackson was headed for. Jackson turned sharply off of the groomed trail and onto a narrow trail, where Evan would have a hard time catching him. Evan tucked lower in an attempt to gain more speed. Jackson anticipated Evan's move and did the same as they raced dangerously between trees and over fallen logs. They were getting close to Death Valley. The name was appropriate for the jump. If you didn't hit the take off with enough speed, you would end up in the deep ravine that you were trying to jump over. Evan reached forward. He could almost grab Jackson's coat. Jackson swerved to the right and Evan missed.

Evan positioned himself for another attempt when Jackson screamed.

"Watch out!"

Evan looked up just in time to see something blocking the trail, Jackson jumped sideways digging the edges of his skis deep into the snow. Evan did the same as they both skidded sideways towards the object blocking the narrow trail. Jackson lost control and flew off the trail and into the trees, missing a large, jagged rock by inches. Evan continued sliding sideways, digging the edges of his skis deeper and deeper into the powder until finally he stopped. Evan heard the twins coming and ducked as Brady sent a large wall of snow flying towards his head as he tried to stop and Brian went flying off the trail in the same direction Jackson had just gone.

"You look like the abominable snow creature," Brady laughed.

Evan shook his head disapprovingly as he brushed the snow from his coat and straightened his hat and goggles.

"Why did you stop?" Brian asked as he followed Jackson back onto the trail.

"Because I made him," a sarcastic voice announced from the other side of Evan. The voice belonged to a large, pimpled faced snow boarder who was blocking the trail.

"You think you could waddle out of our way Mark?" Evan asked politely referencing the snowboarder's low hanging snow pants. Evan knew the punk from Steamboat High.

"Sure I'll get out of your way as soon as you each hand over ten bucks for trespassing on our turf."

"This isn't your turf," Evan responded, growing more irritated by the second.

"Shut up freshman!" Mark ordered. "My friends and I are hungry and you and your ski bunny pals are going to buy us dinner."

Mark pointed to the three other boarders at the bottom of the hill guarding the takeoff to the Death Valley jump.

Evan recognized them. Mark and his gang of losers. The only reason they got away with half the crap they did was because they were seniors and bigger than everybody else.

"As soon as you pay up, my friends will move out of the way and you will be free to snow plow down the mountain."

Brady hated bullies more than anyone, probably because he was small for his age and had experienced his fair share of encounters with kids like Mark. "You didn't plan this very well," Brady said mockingly. He turned his skies down the hill and gained just enough speed to slam his right shoulder into Mark's ribs, knocking him off his feet and into some deep powder on the perimeter of the trail.

"Now you've done it," Brian said while he watched the struggling snow boarder thrash in the powder.

"I'm going to kill you!" Mark yelled.

"Yeah, he looks mad," Evan said looking at Mark's beet red face.

"Are you two always going to be chickens?" Jackson asked as he used his ski to kick some snow on Mark's head.

"Not always," Evan said with determination.

Before the other boarders could form a plan to retaliate, Evan started down the hill towards the group of snowboarders, tucking in to get maximum speed. "Follow me! I'll clear the path for you to hit the jump," Evan yelled back, toward the small group of skiers standing motionless next to Mark who was yelling insults at the top of his lungs.

As he gained speed, Evan glared at the roadblock with determination, daring the boarders to call his bluff. At the last possible moment, two of them dove out of the way, but the third boarder, a chubby kid with apparently no brains in his head, stood firm blocking the entire trail. Evan had to move to plan B. He quickly pulled out of his tuck and into a jump turn digging his edges so deep into the fresh powder that it sent a small avalanche directly at the lone boarder's face. The kid jumped out of the way to avoid the wall of snow, allowing Jackson and the twins their opportunity to escape up the take off and over Death Valley landing victoriously on the other side. This left Evan alone with the four irate boarders. Mark had already pulled himself out of the powder and was racing down the hill directly towards Evan. Evan pointed his skis downhill and used his poles to help pick up speed as he skied parallel to the ravine, in no time he was flying down the mountain with enough speed to barely stay in front of the boarders.

"What are you going to do now?" Jackson shouted at Evan from the other side of the ravine.

"Ski fast!" Evan yelled back.

Jackson and the twins disappeared behind the thick pine trees on the other side of the ravine leaving Evan alone to deal with the boarders. At this point, Evan had two options to get down the mountain to safety. Option one, he could stay on the catwalks, wide trails with little to no slope all the way down the mountain. The catwalks usually small kids to avoid which meant the boarders might catch Evan. The risk of capture was too great to consider option one and without a second thought about the dangers associated with option two, Evan took a sharp left jumping off a small cliff and into the trees on a trail leading to Devil's Chute, the only double black diamond on the mountain.

Evan's mind raced a hundred miles an hour. He had never attempted to ski this run before. One wrong choice could land him at the bottom of the large cliff. Evan had been obsessed with this run for years, studying and planning his own descent down the double black, but he still had not mustered up the courage, or stupidity, to try it. Evan's thoughts were coming quickly but not clearly. Most skiers never attempted to ski down Devil's Chute and of the few who had, some came away with broken bones or even worse.

Evan burst out of the trees and skidded to a stop next to a sign which read in thick, black letters, "Devil's Chute. WARNING: Expert Skiers Only!" Evan shivered with anticipation over what he was about to attempt as he looked out over the valley from the top of a three hundred foot cliff. He shook his head and stared back in the direction he had just come as the angry boarders emerged from the trees. Like a pack of wolves cornering their prey, they formed a semicircle around Evan.

"Not so cocky when you're trapped?" the chubby boarder said as he inched closer.

"The avalanche sent at your head was nothing personal," Evan said with a nervous smile. Four against one, Evan didn't like the odds.

"You should have given us the money! When we're done with you, your friends aren't going to recognize you!" Mark taunted, as he edged closer to Evan.

From Mark's reputation at school, Evan was certain it was not an idle threat. "I'm afraid I won't be around for that," Evan said as he pointed his skis down the mountain towards the edge of the cliff and skied slowly pass the sign. Evan skidded to a stop at the top of the deep, almost vertical chute. Using his poles for support Evan leaned out over the cliff, his heart skipped a beat as he looked down at the solid rock on either side of the snow covered chute.

"He's bluffing," Mark told his friends. "There's no way he's stupid enough to ski the chute."

"I don't know," the chubby boarder replied. "I think he might actually do it."

Evan shifted his weight nervously sending several small snowballs rolling down the chute. He had never felt this much fear in his life. He regretted not paying the ten dollars to Mark or taking his chances down the catwalk. At least on the catwalk there would have been witnesses. If he died in the chute no one would know what had happened to him. He was sure the kids wouldn't confess to forcing him down the chute. Evan looked back at Mark and was about to beg for forgiveness and take his chances with the kids when the snow under his skis suddenly gave way sending him into the chute.

Evan struggled to control his descent as the small avalanche he had triggered carried him down the narrow ravine. His skis and legs were covered in moving powder. Evan was sure that if he fell the avalanche would cover him completely and he would die of suffocation. Evan tucked low to get more speed and in a matter of moments he was ahead of the accelerating snow. Pure adrenaline coursed through Evan's veins as he regained control. He had never felt more focused in his entire life. Every detail of the run replayed in Evan's head as he strained to stay in the Chute and ahead of the wall of snow. One wrong move, one missed turn and Evan would ski out of the chute and right off of the cliff or be buried by the snow chasing him down the mountain.

Devil's Chute had been chiseled into the cliff surface by water rushing down the mountain during the spring runoff, creating a deep, narrow ravine which was slightly less vertical than the towering cliffs on both sides of Evan. The chute was about five feet wide and was filled with fresh powder, covering most of the logs and debris that littered its bottom. The chute was steeper than any black diamond run he had ever attempted, and its narrowness gave Evan little possibility to slow his descent.

Evan dodged a large boulder, and then dropped off of a 10 foot cliff. The chute was getting narrower and he was beginning to feel claustrophobic. He started to question his memory of the terrain. Deep in the ravine the avalanche gained momentum as its decent triggered other avalanches. The snow sounded like an earthquake threatening to tear the mountain apart as it rushed down the mountain feet behind Evan's skis.

Am I going to die and not be found until next spring when the snow melts? Maybe they would name this death trap after me in memorial. Evan thought to himself as he rounded a small bend which gave him a clear view of nothing but blue sky ahead. Directly in front of him was Steamboat Falls. If the falls had been on an actual river, it would have been a class 10 with a sign at the top reading "You're Nuts!" Steamboat Falls was a 50-foot drop that in early spring was an actual water fall from the winter runoff. If a skier landed correctly at the bottom of the falls, they could only survive because of the steep slope which they landed on allowing their momentum gained from free falling to continue to carry them down the mountain. If the landing was flat, Evan was sure he would break every bone in his body.

The avalanche had caught up with Evan and covered his skis completely. He had to get out of the chute. His mind raced as fast as his heart, as he emerged from the chute. His skis met nothing but air as the avalanche dropped over the cliff creating a white waterfall. Evan looked down, he could see the entire valley with the small resort town of Steamboat Springs nestled at the base of the mountain. His claustrophobic feeling while in the chute was replaced by a terrifying sensation of free-falling. He could see the ground approaching fast and was anticipating the pain, but forced himself to keep his eyes open.

Evan hit the deep powder at the base of the cliff with such force that his legs crumbled beneath him, and his body was thrown backwards into the snow. In seconds he was buried in the snow that poured down from the top of the cliff as the avalanche followed him down the mountain. The moving snow pulled Evan down the hill blindly as he struggled to ski out of the avalanche. The snow pushed him into a grove of thick pine trees. The giant trees pushed against the wall of snow and Evan could feel the snow around him slowing. Evan burst out of the avalanche and missed a large pine tree by inches. Evan tried to stop by grabbing on to anything he could, but the steep hill continued to pull him down the mountain. Evan's skis hit a stump sticking out of the snow, but instead of stopping him the stump propelled Evan into a series of summersaults, during which his skis and poles were ripped away. Completely out of control, Evan screamed as he bounced down the mountain and right into the branches of a large pine tree, which stopped him abruptly.

The thundering avalanche had stopped and the mountain was completely still. Evan was still shaking and his insides felt like they had been tied in a knot. Evan moved his arms and then his legs. He couldn't believe that he was alive and from the looks of things not injured. Evan stared up at the chute through the pine branches expecting to see Mark and his friends at the top staring back at him. Evan quickly gave up looking, even if the kids were still at the top, he was too far away to see them. Exhaustion set in as the adrenaline released its grip. Evan climbed out of the pine branches and after searching for some time he found his skis and poles and skied slowly down the rest of the mountain.

Evan reached the trail leading to the back of his house a few minutes later. He still hadn't seen the twins or Jackson. It was almost dark, as he followed the trail around a pine tree just off of his family's back porch. As Evan prepared to stop he was unexpectedly grabbed from behind and thrown into the deep powder off to the side of the trail. Powder covered Evan's face making it impossible to see his attackers or fight back.

"Leave me alone!" Evan yelled out as he flung his arms blindly in front of him, hoping to hit something. He wouldn't give up without a fight.

Evan was stunned by a snowball that smashed him in his face, knocking his goggles halfway off.

Evan thrashed side to side in the powder trying to avoid the next snowball or fist that came his way, but it was no use he was trapped, not able to move with his skis still attached. Then as quickly as the attack had started it was over and Evan heard laughing.

"Your flopping around makes you look like a fish out of water," Brady said still laughing. "Remind me that if I ever get into a fight to call for your kid brother to come and help me. All you would do is flop around on the ground and hope that no one would hit you."

"Ha, ha, very funny. Is this the thanks I get for saving your butt?" Evan retorted, too tired to pull himself out of the snow.

"We thought you were done for," Brian admitted as he pulled Evan out of the snow and back onto the trail.

"How did you get away?" Brady asked.

"I skied Devil's Chute," Evan replied.

He proceeded to tell them the entire story from when the boarders cornered him to his run down the chute and finishing with his spectacular landing off of the falls.

"I can't believe you survived," Brian said.

13

"I would have taken them all on instead of running away," Brady boasted as he tried to flex what muscles he thought he had.

Evan was about to make him prove how tough he really was when they heard a honk coming from the front of Evan's house.

"Mom's here," Brian said.

"Saved by your mommy again," Evan shouted after his friends as they ran to the front of the house.

"See you tomorrow, Evan," they called out in unison.

Before Evan went inside, he looked up at the mountain one last time, taking a deep breath of fresh mountain air. He felt relieved to be home. He could faintly smell smoke from the fire his dad started every evening around dinner time. He suddenly felt very tired and very hungry.

Chapter Two

Big News

Evan walked through the back door of The Lodge and into a small mudroom where they kept their ski gear. Exhausted from the physical demands and excitement of the day he quickly put his skis by the back door next to Jackson's and hung his snow gear on hooks to dry. The faint aroma of his mom's famous spaghetti greeted him as he hung up his last item of clothing. His stomach grumbled in response.

"Wash your hands, Evan! Your dad will be down in a minute," Evan's mom called from somewhere deep inside the pantry as he walked into the kitchen.

She emerged a moment later wearing a sweater, jeans and tennis shoes with her black hair pulled up in a ponytail. She was holding a package of noodles in her hand and wore what briefly appeared to be a worried expression on her face. Upon seeing Evan, however, her expression quickly dissipated into an easy smile.

"Sure thing mom," Evan replied as he headed to the only bathroom in The Lodge to wash up.

"I wouldn't go in there if I were you." Jackson said as he walked out of the bathroom wearing nothing more than his worn out long johns and wool socks.

Jackson was moving his hand in a fanning motion behind himself. Evan shook his head in a disapproving manner and, holding in a deep breath, opened the door and went in to wash his hands.

Emerging moments later from the stench Jackson had left behind Evan found his latest ski magazine. It had been buried underneath several of his mom's home decorating magazines lying on the coffee table in the middle of the great room. Exhausted, Evan settled down into one of the overstuffed chairs and propped his feet up, facing the fire. This was his favorite room in the house. Several chairs and a large sofa lined a plush rug which faced a fireplace big enough to roast an entire pig in it, which Evan's family had tried only once followed by a visit from the local fire department. The room had 20 foot cathedral ceilings held up by giant timbers, original wood floors and four huge windows facing the mountains. There was a kitchen attached to the room, with a portion of the old saloon bar still used for morning breakfast, new appliances and a large wooden table that Evan's dad had built. In fact, Evan's dad had built most of the rustic furniture in the house according to his mom's specifications. Evan could always imagine several saloon tables full of miners gambling away their hard work, listening to the music on a player piano, trying to get warm around the fireplace. There was a loft over the kitchen, where the family slept, with two bedrooms and a small library with thousands of books Evan's dad had collected throughout the years. The warmth from the fire felt nice, and Evan's eyelids started to droop. He was tired after a hard day of skiing.

"How was skiing today?"

Evan opened his eyes and saw that his dad had just emerged from the loft carrying a book with a map of the United States on the cover under his arm. Evan's dad was kind of a geek, but in a good way of course. He was wearing a V-neck sweater and worn jeans.

He had majored in engineering and was constantly offering explanations about how the world worked. At one time, he had shaggy brown hair just like Evan's and piercing green eyes. He now sported a shaved look to compensate for his receding hairline and although he wore glasses now, his green eyes were still filled with life and excitement.

"The powder was amazing," Evan answered, half conscious. "Are we going on a trip?"

"Why do you ask?" Evan's dad replied with a nervous hint in his voice.

"The map," Evan said as his gaze fell upon the Atlas that his dad was now trying to conceal.

"We'll talk about it after dinner," Evan's dad replied as he walked into the Kitchen and kissed Evan's mom on the cheek. "Dinner smells amazing, J."

J was short for Jacqueline. Evan always found it interesting that his Dad never used his mom's full name, but his mom would always call his dad by his full name James, instead of Jim which is what everyone else called him.

"You must be hungry if you think spaghetti smells amazing" Evan's mom replied.

They gave each other a smile that Evan had seen a hundred times. His parents were definitely in love and had no problem showing it. Evan didn't mind. In fact, he couldn't imagine anything more perfect than living in The Lodge with his close-to-perfect family and endless ski opportunities nearby. Evan's eyes closed again, succumbing to the warmth of the fire. Jackson suddenly appeared out of nowhere and tackled Evan right out of the chair, throwing him to the rug. Evan had no trouble restoring the right of power as he threw Jackson off of him like he was nothing but a rag doll and pinned him to the floor.

"Give up?" Evan taunted.

"Never," Jackson answered with a look of defiance. His brother was the most determined kid Evan had ever met. No matter how much he tortured his kid brother, Jackson never surrendered.

"Evan wait, wait I need to tell you something," Jackson pleaded just as Evan was about to execute one of his favorite brother torture techniques.

"What is it?" Evan asked annoyed, being familiar with Jackson's delays.

"I saw someone go down Devil's Chute this afternoon," Jackson said with excitement.

Evan froze. "Did you see who it was?" he asked quietly, not wanting his parents to overhear the conversation.

"I was too far away to tell. It was probably some professional," Jackson said. "By the way, how did you get away from the boarders?"

"It's nice to know that my brother cares so much about me. I noticed that you didn't wait with Brady and Brian to see if I needed help."

"Oh, I knew you would be okay, you can ski faster than anyone on the mountain and besides, when you have to go, you have to..."

"I know, I know," Evan said cutting his brother off before he went into details.

Evan liked his younger brother, but he'd never admit that to Jackson for fear it would just go to his head. They spent hours on the slopes together, and at night, when they were supposed to be sleeping, they would talk about their plans to someday ski every resort in the world as professional skiers. Evan would eventually tell Jackson tonight about his trip down Devil's Chute. He just had to get through dinner without his mom and dad finding out about his dangerous run.

"Dinner is served," Evan's mom announced with a fancy voice as if she was serving filet mignon at a five star restaurant.

A second later Evan released his grip on Jackson and they both raced to the table. Evan loved his mom's cooking, and his favorite dinner was her spaghetti. She boasted that it contained a secret ingredient from an old family recipe which made the marinara sweeter than any other marinara he had ever tasted. The combination of the sauce and her fresh French bread which was lathered in butter and garlic, was better than eating at the fanciest restaurant in Steamboat Springs. At least that is what Evan's dad had always told them. Evan or Jackson had never actually eaten at a fancy restaurant.

Dinner conversation consisted of small talk about the day's happenings, with Evan trying to steer clear of any discussion about his day on the slopes. Jackson, however, was making this difficult, as he went on and on about the boarders and a mysterious skier he had witnessed plunging down Devil's Chute. His parents seemed distracted throughout the meal, often exchanging mysterious glances between each other. Finally, as dinner ended and Jackson finished off his third helping, Evan's dad reached for the book that he had brought down from upstairs, which he had left on the floor during dinner, and nervously cleared his throat.

Evan's mom jumped up quickly as if she had been expecting this, "Before you do that, dear, I made carrot cake". She rushed away from the table before Evan's dad could respond.

Something fishy was going on this evening, Evan was sure of it. Jackson didn't seem to notice anything as he finished mopping up the last of the marinara sauce with his bread. Evan loved his mom's carrot cake. It ranked right up there with the spaghetti as one of his favorites. In fact, come to think of it, this was his and Jackson's favorite dinner menu; one that his mom always cooked on his birthday or when his family celebrated a special occasion of some sort. His suspicions that something was going on increased.

Evan nervously glanced at the map his dad was still holding and the knots in his stomach that he had felt at the top of Devil's Chute returned in full force. Six months ago, Evan's dad had announced the possibility of his company closing some of their smaller offices and the Steamboat Springs office had made that list. Evan's family had hoped for the best, but if the job left Steamboat Springs, the family would have to follow. Evan had pushed that possibility from his memory and had almost forgotten the conversation altogether, until now.

"I have been offered a new position at work," Evan's dad said with guarded excitement.

Evan didn't say a word, expecting the worst.

"That's great news, Dad," Jackson said, his mouth stuffed full with a large piece of the carrot cake his mom had just served him.

"I've been promoted to Director of Engineering," he began.

"We can't leave Steamboat," Evan blurted out.

"What? We are leaving? Why?" Jackson asked, confused by what was happening.

"We don't want to leave Steamboat Springs either," Evan's mom said, a tear forming in her eye.

"But sometimes, change finds us. It may be hard at first, but together as a family we will get through this," Evan's dad said as he took Evan's mom's hand in his.

"I have friends here! A life here! You can't rip us away from everything we know," Evan pleaded.

His mom looked heartbroken.

"We don't have much of a choice Evan. Besides you and Jackson will find new friends," Evan's dad said as he opened the map on the table.

"Where are we moving, Dad?" Evan asked bitterly. He was angry and not trying to hide that fact. His parents were going to ruin his life.

Jackson was starting to understand what was going on. "We're moving? Where, Hawaii, China, Siberia?"

They all looked at Jackson incredulously. If the situation had been different, they might have all laughed at the crazy ideas coming out of his mouth.

Evan's dad turned to a page in the book and then slowly turned the book around so that Evan and Jackson could see the page clearly. A lump formed in Evan's throat as he silently read the words on the top of the page in front of him.

"Rhode Island," Jackson read out loud.

"It's a small state on the East Coast," Evan's mom explained.

"Are there even mountains in Rhode Island?" Evan asked.

"Not really, but the house we found is right on the ocean and I've heard all the kids down there like to surf in the summer," Evan's mom explained.

Evan had heard enough. Before his parents could explain further, he stood up so fast that he knocked his chair to the hardwood floor with a loud bang. Without picking up the chair Evan ran to the stairs leading to the garage. He heard his mom call after him, as the door slammed shut behind him, but he didn't care. He hated his parents. They were going to ruin his life. He had to be alone. When he reached the mudroom, he grabbed his ski gear and ran out into the frigid night air.

— · — · · — · · — · · — · ·

Evan silently skied to the only lift on the mountain, designated for night skiing. Distracted by the news his dad had just delivered, Evan almost ran directly into Mark, the boarder who Brady had buried in the snow earlier that day. Luckily Mark and his friends were too exhausted after their hike down from the top of Devil's Chute to notice Evan.

Evan started to regret his response at the dinner table as the lift slowly took him up the mountain. Snowflakes fell around him and by the time he reached the top of the mountain his coat was covered in a white dust. Instead of heading down the illuminated run with the other skiers, he clicked on his head lamp and turned his skis toward a hidden trail that only he, Jackson, and the twins used.

As his skis found the worn grooves under the deep powder, he picked up speed, quietly darting carelessly between thick snow covered evergreens. The trail led him away from the groomed runs of the ski resort, and soon he found himself enveloped in a deep canyon. Evan traveled for several minutes, hearing only the sound of his skis swishing through the snow, until he skidded to a stop in a small opening in the pines. Directly in front of him, nestled in the pines and buried in the snow was an old miner's cabin, deserted and weathered. He, Jackson and the twins had discovered the structure two years ago while skiing through the trees and it had become a hideaway for them; a place to rest from their long hours on the slopes.

The mountain was full of old mines and the memories of men who had lost everything in the pursuit of riches. In the case of Steamboat Springs, the boom had lasted only a few years before the silver and gold supply veins ran out. The town had all but died until the ski industry moved in. There were still several old buildings left in the town, like the one Evan's family owned, but this was a 10 foot by 15 foot, one room cabin with a steep roof, one door and no windows, situated adjacent to an old mine whose entrance had long ago been sealed off by falling debris. It looked like the owner had left in a hurry leaving everything behind. Brian imagined that the old miner, while tending to his rich silver vein, had been trapped in the mine after a violent cave in and had been forgotten, never to be seen again. The most interesting clue they had found in the cabin was 400 white marks on the wall of the cabin just above the door. Brady believed the miner had been tracking how many days he had worked his silver mine. Brian believed that on the 400th day the mine caved in. The boys had always hoped to solve the mystery by researching city mining records, but had never gotten around to it.

The small group had spent weeks during the summer repairing the holes in the roof and stocking it with firewood and supplies. They took breaks from skiing to visit the cabin, which they named Cave Inn, in honor of the lost miner, and spent nights sleeping there whenever the twins visited. Tonight, Evan looked at the dark outline of the cabin, as if seeing it for the last time, sad that the mystery of the lost miner would never be solved.

Without dwelling on the task ahead of him, Evan grabbed the shovel they kept stashed under a pine tree and started to dig out the entrance. After a half hour of vigorous digging, Evan threw the shovel to the side in frustration, exhausted by his labors after what had already been a long and taxing day.

Before opening the freshly uncovered door, he looked down at the lights coming from Steamboat Springs. He could see the entire town. His whole life was changing. This town was his home. From the winter festival held during the month of December to the rodeos, fairs and kayak races in summer. This was his life. Everything he had ever loved.

"Is there even snow in Rhode Island?" Evan yelled into the darkness.

"Yes," came a ghostly reply from behind him.

Evan jumped into the air. Shaking, he slowly turned his body in the direction of the reply, fully expecting to find himself looking into the face of the old miner's ghost, but instead he was looking at three figures covered in snow.

"You're as white as a ghost," Brady said laughing uncontrollably as he fell backwards into the snow.

"It looks like you need your mommy," Brian joined in as he removed his skis, attempting a mama joke, which he could never pull off.

"What are you doing here?" Evan asked.

"Your mom called. She said you might need a friend tonight," Brady responded.

"Why would I need a friend tonight," Evan replied unconvincingly.

Jackson walked up to Evan without saying a word, looking almost as depressed as Evan felt. Evan was about to reach out to comfort his brother, when a large grin spread across Jackson's face and he tackled Evan, knocking him off of the small porch and into the deep powder. Evan struggled to throw Jackson off as the two wrestled in the snow, dealing with the problem the only way boys know how.

Brady took out his cell phone and dialed Evan's mom's phone. "Yeah, we found him at the cabin," he reported, like he was some big hero. "I'll tell him," he said before hanging up.

"Tell me what?" Evan asked as he finally succeeded in throwing Jackson off of him.

"That she understands why you are upset."

"She said that?" Evan said in shock. After the way he had stormed out of the house he figured he would be grounded for a month.

"She also said that she wants you home before breakfast and that if you and Jackson aren't home before breakfast, she will not hesitate to ski up here and pull you off of the mountain herself."

"Were they mad?" Evan asked Jackson.

"Let's just say that tonight mom and dad referred to me as their favorite son," Jackson said with a smile.

Evan knew Jackson was kidding, but there were surely going to be consequences for his actions tonight.

"It's freezing," Brian said, taking Evan's mind away from the punishment that he was certain awaited him at home. Brian opened the door and walked into the cabin.

Before long, the cabin lit up with the glow from the fireplace.

"I'm cooking s'mores," Brian called from inside the cabin.

Jackson wasted no time in joining Brian in the warm cabin.

"Rhode Island isn't that bad," Brady reassured Evan, before they headed into the cabin for the night.

"How do you know? Have you been there?" Evan challenged.

"Not exactly, but it's only a couple hours to New York City by train. You can come and visit"

"I guess there's that," Evan agreed, as he headed into the cabin for a s'more.

Brady, Brian and Jackson always had a way of cheering up Evan. They talked for hours, sharing facts about the east coast and planning Evan and Jackson's first trip to the Big Apple. As the fire died down and the twins' faint snores became audible, Evan stared up at the rafters of the cabin, unable to fall asleep. There was so much Evan didn't know about what his life in Rhode Island was going to be like, but there was one thing that he knew for certain, and that was that his life was about to change forever.

Chapter Three

Niagara Falls

Evan felt chilled as he stood next to the metal railing separating him from an almost 170 foot drop into the mist below. In late December, the crowds at Niagara Falls were sparse. Freezing weather, combined with the mist from the falls made for an almost unbearable cold; the kind you felt all the way to your bones. The few people brave enough to endure the frozen misery long enough to gaze at the wall of water, were adjusting their coats, hats, and scarves, trying to fight off the bitter cold. Evan felt the cold, but to him it was more refreshing than miserable. For the first time in two weeks, he didn't feel like he was dying inside. The sadness that had set inside him ever since his parents had dropped the bomb about moving to Rhode Island was starting to lift.

Evan's family had enjoyed Christmas together at their home in Steamboat Springs before embarking on their new adventure. The family's annual Christmas party had felt more like a goodbye party, dampening the normal seasonal merriment. His parents had insisted on decorating the 10 foot-tall Christmas tree and making their own eggnog, even though they had been waist-high in boxes. The lodge had never looked more festive with Christmas lights strung to the top of the cathedral ceilings and frosted covered windows overlooking the beckoning slopes. All of their friends had shown up to say their goodbyes: friends from school, church, Dad's friends from work, and Mom's friends from the various committees she was involved with. Even Evan's ski coach had made a showing, expressing his regrets at losing his most promising skier.

On Christmas morning, Evan's parents had given him brand new skis. The ones he had begged for, for months (long before he knew his life was going to turn upside down). When he told them that the skis wouldn't work for water skiing in Rhode Island, his dad ignored Evan's sarcasm and explained that they hadn't had time to exchange them for a more appropriate gift.

Evan had attempted, in between packing his belongings into boxes and making his final runs on the slopes, to research his new home state of Rhode Island online. His first search was on skiing in Rhode Island. The only ski resort the state had to offer boasted a meager 245 foot-vertical rise, which put it slightly smaller than the bunny hill at his home resort, or what used to be his home resort. That day, out of frustration, Evan sold his new ski gear to a friend, vowing to give up the sport forever. He didn't want his gear around to remind him of his home or of his trip down Devil's Chute. After being so disappointed with his first search results, he gave up on any further searches and spent the remainder of his time on the slopes. After all, he would learn all about his new home state soon enough.

Unlike Evan, Jackson greeted the new adventure with pure excitement. He enjoyed skiing but wanted to get out and experience more than just what the mountains had to offer. He was excited to surf and fish in the ocean. He wanted to go to New York City and see his first professional baseball game. Evan would just walk away or start brother-torture sessions whenever Jackson started telling him something interesting about the state. His parents seemed equally excited about the move. It was three against one. In fact, Evan had not spent a lot of time at The Lodge during his last two weeks in Steamboat Springs. He didn't want to hear about his dad's new job, all of the great house renovation ideas his mom had for the new house, or Jackson's surfing plans. He wanted them to understand that this move was going to ruin his life. Even Brady and Brian were not very sympathetic. Brian had sent Evan a copy of the train schedule into New York City, along with a round trip train ticket to New York for a Christmas present. They were constantly discussing Evan's first day in the Big Apple. Before Evan knew what had hit him, he was cramped in the family's rusted SUV, headed for Rhode Island.

Evan's parents decided to turn the drive to Rhode Island into a cross country adventure. They stopped the SUV at every monument and historic site from Colorado to Rhode Island. They would arrive at their new house tomorrow.

Evan had seen pictures of the new house, and lacking his mom's vision, all he saw was a broken down piece of junk, built way before his grandparent's generation. He wondered if the old relic was home to any ghosts from the people surely buried in the basement. His mom, on the other hand, was more excited than Evan had seen her in years. She told him that the house had been vacant for a decade. It was built by a wealthy merchant back in the 1700's and sat on top of a cliff overlooking the bay leading to the Atlantic Ocean. She admitted that it needed a lot of work but then gushed that she was glad to have two strong boys big enough to help with the project.

Evan stared out into the heavy mist of Niagara Falls, lost in his own thoughts. Coming from the high desert country of Colorado, he had no idea so much water existed. Evan's dad, who was somewhat of a history buff, interrupted his thoughts throwing him back into reality.

"Did you know that the first person to ever go over Niagara Falls in a barrel and survive was a woman by the name of Annie Taylor in 1901?" Evan's dad read out loud from a pamphlet he had picked up from the visitor center. "Says here that she came away from it with only a small cut on her head. I guess people can survive a lot worse than a move across the country," Evan's dad added as he looked up from his pamphlet and raised his left eyebrow.

Here we go; another dad lecture about my attitude, Evan thought. "Dad, I don't want to talk about it right now," Evan shot back.

Frustrated, Evan navigated his way through the heavy mist and fog, away from his family and closer to the falls. He looked back in the direction he had just come, but could no longer see his family through the thick fog nor hear their conversation over the roar of the falls. He moved farther along the railing, edging closer to the falls.

Evan abruptly stopped to avoid colliding with a young girl who must have been around five or six years old. The small girl's long scarf trailed behind her as she excitedly rushed to the railing to get a closer look at the falls. Evan smiled as he noticed the young girl's two pigtails sticking out from her pink hat, which matched her pink outfit. She reminded Evan of Jackson when he was about five years old, full of energy and excited about everything.

Ignoring the little girl, Evan continued to follow the railing until he came to a large tree, which had probably been there when Annie had gone over the falls so long ago in that barrel. The withered leaves still clung to the tree's crooked branches long after they should have fallen to the ground.

"That would have been some ride, maybe like going down Devil's Chute," Evan said to himself. Although he was mad at his parents, he did think that a ride over the falls in a barrel made for a great story.

Evan leaned against the tree and put his ear phones in as he took his phone from his pocket. He cranked up his favorite band to hear the beat over the roar of the falls and was again lost in thought as he watched the water from the falls disappear into the mist below.

Evan looked back towards the little girl dressed in pink. She was now recklessly climbing onto the top of the railing, which was coated in ice.

Where are her parents? What is she thinking? Evan thought to himself.

Frustrated Evan turned back towards the falls. He wasn't her babysitter, why should he care? Evan thought back on his parent's decision to ruin his life by moving across the country. They didn't care about him, why should he care about others, even a little girl? After a moment, however, Evan was drawn back to the little girl. He needed to make sure she was okay, even if he was still mad at his parents and trying to play the part of not caring about anybody but himself.

What Evan saw was like a scene in a horror movie, and Evan could only watch helplessly. Without warning, the girl slipped off the rail and disappeared without even a scream. Evan couldn't believe it! The spot where the little girl had been playing moments before was now empty. He ran to the railing and looked over. Instead of a straight drop into nothingness, there was a small ledge about five feet down that sloped towards the falls. The little girl was clinging onto a crack in the rock, her legs dangling over the edge. Somehow, she had managed to grab hold of the crack as she tumbled over the ledge.

"Help! Help!" Evan yelled as loud as he could, hoping that someone, anyone, would hear his cries over the roar of the falls.

Evan looked down at the 170 foot drop. The girl would not survive if she fell. Evan looked back into the fog, hoping to see others running to help, but no one came. Nervously, Evan climbed over the railing. His body trembled as he dropped himself onto the ledge below. The ledge was slick. His feet slid over the surface as he tightened his grip on the railing, causing several small boulders to dislodge, narrowly missing the girl and disappearing into the mist. He clung to the railing, struggling to regain his footing under him. At last, he was able to plant his feet firmly on the ledge and release his death grip on the railing.

The girl was only a couple of feet away now, but Evan still couldn't reach her. He could see the fear in her eyes, but she did not scream. Slowly, Evan lowered himself down onto his stomach. He grabbed onto a jagged rock with his left hand and then reached out for the girl with his right hand. He grabbed her wrist just as her grip failed. Her body slid from the ledge. Evan held on, but the added weight of the girl caused his fingers to slip and he started sliding. He was going over the edge.

"No! No! No!" Evan yelled as he slid towards the ledge.

Just as his head cleared the ledge and he could see the mist below him, his left hand caught a crack in the rock. He yelled out in pain as he took the girl's full weight in his right hand, smashing his arm against the jagged ledge, but he held on. He tried with everything his body could muster to pull her up, but he didn't have the strength. His only option was to wait, to hold her until someone came along. Evan shifted his body slightly to look back up at the railing, hoping to see someone, anyone, but no one had come to help. Evan was alone.

The girl's wrist started slipping through Evan's grip and pain shot through Evan's arm. He gripped tighter and his concentration returned to the girl. He had to save her life! Evan looked into her frightened eyes, but he couldn't reassure her. His tongue was paralyzed. He wanted to tell her that it would be okay, but at that moment, he felt her wrist start to slip again through his tired and frozen fingers. He held on tighter, willing his hand to not let go.

"Don't let go," Evan's dad said softly. His dad was right next to him on the ledge. He must have heard Evan's yell for help and had already climbed over the railing and was next to his son.

"Dad, I can't hang on much longer!" Evan cried through clenched teeth.

The little girl looked more terrified than ever. Frozen tears cascaded down her flushed cheeks. The mist was causing Evan's hand to go numb and his grip started to fail again. He could feel the girl slipping. He closed his eyes and concentrated on his failing grip. This time Evan could not stop it!

With indescribable horror Evan felt the little girl's wrist slip from his hand. He opened his eyes certain that he would watch her disappear into the mist below.

Evan's dad's hand shot forward at that moment, catching the girl's arm before she could disappear into the midst. His dad pulled the little girl up to the ledge and then helped Evan to his feet. On the ledge, no larger than a small kitchen table, he and the girl huddled in the safety of his dad's arms. They stood there in silence hugging the back wall of the cliff, each of them breathing deeply.

"Everything is going to be all right," Evan's dad told the girl as he looked at Evan. "We are not going to let anything happen to you. You are safe."

The little girl calmed down and clung to Evan's dad. Although they were still inches from death, Evan knew that everything would be okay. His dad would never let him down.

A small crowd of concerned onlookers gathered at the top of the cliff next to the railing a few feet away, watching the drama unfold. Several men helped pull them over the railing to safety. Evan moved back from the edge and breathed a sigh of relief. He sat down with his back leaning against the tree he had been standing by only minutes earlier. Evan watched as his dad tried to return the still terrified little girl back to her mother. She was refusing to leave her hero, clinging to him with her arms wrapped tightly around his neck. Reluctantly the girl let go of Evan's dad and returned to her mother.

Evan could see Jackson and his mom struggling to get through the crowd. As Evan adjusted his body to stand, he felt warmth on the cold ground where he had positioned his hand. Looking down Evan saw a puddle of blood. He struggled to maintain consciousness, as his world slowly darkened and he fell to the ground.

— ·· — ·· — — ·· — ·· —

"Evan, Evan!" Evan's mom said, the second time more desperate than the first.

Slowly Evan opened his eyes. He was lying flat on his back. His surroundings were illuminated by a bright light directly above his head. At first all he could see was a blurred figure standing over him.

"Is he alive?" Evan heard Jackson ask.

"He's coming to," an unfamiliar voice announced.

Evan's eyes focused on the inside of an ambulance, with a paramedic wearing a blue uniform standing over him.

"Can you hear me?" The paramedic asked as he shined a flashlight in Evan's eyes.

"What happened?" Evan asked, still unsure as to how he got into the back of the ambulance.

"You lost a lot of blood and passed out," the paramedic said. "You sustained a large gash in your arm from a sharp rock on the ledge. It looked as though you had been sliced open by a knife."

Evan reached down to his bandaged arm and instantly cringed.

"It will be sore for a while, try not to move it to much."

Slowly Evan tried to sit up.

"Careful," the paramedic warned, bracing Evan, who was on the verge of falling off of the stretcher.

Evan's family sat next to him inside of the ambulance. The doors were closed against the cold, but through the partially fogged windows he could see the flashing lights of other emergency vehicles and the large number of people who had gathered outside of the ambulance.

Evan's parents both had worried expressions on their faces, but Jackson was grinning from ear to ear.

"The paramedic said that you might be weak for a while, and that I should go easy on you," Jackson said. "I told him that you were weak before you cut your arm open."

Leave it to Jackson to attempt sarcasm at a time like this.

"You doing okay?" Evan's dad asked.

"I'm fine, just a little light headed."

"I was so worried," Evan's mom said, tears flowing down her face.

— ·· — ·· — ·· — ··

"Did you see the girl slip and fall?" a reporter wearing white earmuffs asked a half hour later. Evan had just finished off a package of cookies, drank two juice boxes and was declared healthy enough to leave the ambulance by the paramedic.

He had already been asked this question by the police and park rangers.

"Yes, I saw her slip," Evan answered simply.

"How do you feel about being called a hero?" another reporter asked.

Evan didn't answer. His bad attitude had almost cost the little girl her life. Evan shifted awkwardly. He was no hero, he didn't deserve any attention.

"I was just in the right spot at the right time. Anyone would have done the same," Evan replied to the group of reporters before turning and walking back to his family.

Chapter Four

The Merchant's Mansion

Evan unfolded his legs as he climbed out of his family's packed SUV. A day had passed since their visit to Niagara Falls and they had driven continuously since waking up in a second rate motel that morning, with only one unplanned stop to let Jackson sprint behind a bush to pee.

Their realtor, who they recognized from her website, stood stiffly by the front door of their new home. She was dressed in a long, fancy-looking, designer coat and stilettos which she tapped on the wooden porch as she looked impatiently at her watch. They were almost an hour late, but in Evan's dad's defense, the house had been almost impossible to find as they had snaked their way along the coastal highway. The entrance to the narrow dirt road leading to the house was hidden by snow covered trees and bushes. Evan's dad had unknowingly passed by the entrance twice and would have missed it a third time had Jackson not spotted the tire tracks left in the fresh snow by the realtor's car.

Evan let out a long sigh as he breathed in the frigid air. They had finally arrived in Rhode Island, and as much as Evan hated to say it, they were home. Evan's mom and dad wasted no time rushing inside the house with the realtor. Evan and Jackson, on the other hand, stood by the car for several minutes surveying their new surroundings and the decrepit, sad structure that loomed in front of them. The only interesting feature about the house was its location on top of a cliff, overlooking the ocean.

The wood shutters and roof shingles of the colonial-style house had long ago lost their color and looked rotted, the result of many years of neglect. A fresh coat of paint was badly needed. It had two stories and a large porch, but in its current state, Evan wondered if it was even livable. He half hoped to see his parents come running out of the house disgusted that they had been tricked into buying this relic, but he knew that his mom would never be discouraged by a few shattered windows and a leaky roof. Evan had not seen the lodge before his parents renovated it, but he had heard the stories and knew that this house was probably in no better condition. This was going to be his home and he would need to make the best of it. Evan closed his eyes and imagined the house to be a majestic structure, which only lasted until he opened his eyes again.

"I hope this place has heat," Jackson sprinted for the front door. "First one in the house gets first pick of bedrooms." Jackson disappeared into the dark house.

Evan zipped up his coat to protect against the stiff breeze blowing in from the coast, but he didn't rush inside. After four days of being crammed in the SUV with his family, he was glad to finally be alone. He followed a snow covered path around the side of the house to the backyard, which ended abruptly at an almost 100-foot drop to the waters of the bay below. Evan cautiously approached the edge and peered down at the white frothy water, watching the waves crash relentlessly against the formidable rocks.

Evan found an old wooden bench covered in snow a safe distance from the cliff. He dusted off the surface with his coat sleeve and sat down. Through the dreariness of the low-hanging clouds, Evan could see Newport, Rhode Island across the bay. He made out massive castle like structures standing on top of the large cliffs. Before long, Evan lost track of time.

"Still wallowing in self-pity?"

Evan turned around to see his mom, standing behind him, her arms folded as she attempted to keep herself warm against the cold breeze. Evan didn't say anything as he looked across the bay.

After a brief pause Evan's mom changed the subject. "Did you know that our new house was built by a wealthy merchant, who was rumored to have made his fortune as a pirate?" The corners of her lips turned tentatively upward.

"Is it also rumored that our house is haunted by the merchant's terrifying ghost, who will stop at nothing to keep people from living in his house?" Evan added sarcastically.

"I think you've been watching too many horror movies," Evan's mom concluded with a smile as she sat next to him on the ice cold bench. "I know this isn't the most ideal situation, taking you out of school in the middle of your freshman year and everything, but I appreciate your willingness to give it a try. Besides, you've always been good at making friends."

Evan gave his mom a half smile. She had more confidence in his friend-making ability than he did.

"Are you nervous about the new school?" She asked. Her eyes searched his face as she waited for his response.

"It's a little odd, don't you think, that they just happen to have an open spot at the most prestigious high school in Rhode Island," Evan speculated.

"The superintendent said that the other freshman had dropped out halfway through the year. Maybe that student moved?" Evan's mom guessed.

"And there wasn't a waiting list?"

Evan's mom shrugged. "They said they allow only one student in each year on scholarship. We should feel lucky for the opportunity."

Evan rolled his eyes. He had lost this argument several times in the past couple of days.

Her expression hardened as she continued, "It's not just your future, but Jackson's as well. Since you got in, he is also allotted a spot at the school in a couple of years. He's excited. I don't know why you can't be as well."

"He's just excited about the uniforms," Evan countered.

"Jackson hates to dress up," Evan's mom said surprised. "I was sure that wearing a suit coat to school every day would be a negative to Jackson."

"It is, but the thought of not having to pick out what to wear every day is evidently very appealing to him."

"That sounds like Jackson," Evan's mom admitted.

They both laughed, the tension dissipating as fast as it had surfaced. That was one of the great things about their relationship. They never stayed angry for long. They sat on the bench in silence for a moment as the laughter died away.

"Tomorrow morning, we will head downtown to get your uniform. And if you're good, an ice cream cone, too. Okay." It was more of a statement than a question.

"I'm not six years old anymore." Evan accused, knowing his mom was joking, but hoping deep down they would still go for ice cream.

Evan's mom stood up, grabbed Evan's hand and pulled him to his feet.

"I can't wait to show you the inside," she bragged as they walked up the back porch.

"You mean it gets better?" Evan asked sarcastically.

"It has the most amazing view of the bay," she continued, ignoring his comment.

"Is that because half of the walls have holes in them?" Evan joked, as his mom led him into the back of the house.

— ·· — ·· — ·· — ··

Evan attempted to rub the sleep from his eyes. His dad yawned in the front seat as he guided the SUV down the winding road. His mom was applying eye shadow using the small mirror on the back of the visor and Jackson was slumped over, snoring in the seat next to Evan. It was early morning and the first night in their new house had been a restless one. Evan's dad had spent most of the night trying to keep the furnace chugging along to battle the frigid cold of Rhode Island. Evan's air mattress had lost all of its air around 2:30 in the morning leaving him lying uncomfortably on the hardwood floor. Their household items were supposed to be delivered in a couple of days, but until then Evan would have to make do with his leaky bed.

Evan was having trouble focusing on the trees that blurred past the SUV as they sped down the narrow coastal highway towards Jamestown, Rhode Island. He strained to see other houses or any sign of life, but the trees obstructed his view and were making him feel claustrophobic.

The trees parted as they entered a quaint-postcard-looking town. Main Street was lined with small shops and fancy restaurants on one side of the road and a rocky beach leading to the water on the other. Evan imagined the now-deserted street to be lined with people during the summer months, but in the dead of winter, other than a few cars, the street was completely empty.

"There it is!" Evan's mom declared.

Evan's dad slammed on the brakes. The SUV backfired loudly in protest announcing to the entire town that the Myers had arrived.

"There's the uniform shop," she announced a little calmer.

Evan's dad pulled the SUV over to the curb and let Evan and his mom climb out.

"Jackson and I will be down the road looking at refrigerators," Evan's dad said.

"Don't make any decisions before we get there," Evan's mom pleaded before she shut the door and waved goodbye.

"Excited to get some new duds?" Evan's mom asked as soon as the exhaust from their car had cleared.

Evan ignored his Mom's enthusiasm and sauntered toward the uniform shop.

The front window of "Wilson's Fine Suits and Uniforms" displayed several mannequins dressed in what looked to be very expensive suits and school uniforms. The uniforms were all the same shade of blue, just in different sizes. An insignia resembling a shield with an open book in the middle was sewn above the left breast pocket.

A chime at the front door announced their entrance into the small, upscale suit shop.

A short, bald man in in a three piece suit and square glasses came rushing out of the back room to greet them. One look at his customers, however, and there was a noticeable change in the man's urgency. He released his breath, as if annoyed and asked, "May I help you?"

"I need to purchase a uniform for my son," Evan's mom responded more politely than Evan would have.

"I see," the man said condescendingly. "Well, the public school uniform shop is down the road a mile or so. You will find what you are looking for there." The man turned around and glided toward the store entrance.

"No," Evan's mom held her ground. "My son will be attending Wellsford Academy next week."

"Oh, I see," the man smirked, remaining in front of the store entrance. "May I suggest you try Ranford's down the street, half a block? He normally carries second hand uniforms for the, uh, scholarship students. No need to waste a new uniform on a child who won't last the month at Wellsford, wouldn't you agree?"

"What are you implying?" Evan's mom accused in a calm, yet forceful voice.

Before the smug man could answer, a tall, thin woman walked into the shop followed by a young man around Evan's age. She wore bright red lipstick and what Evan judged to be an excessive amount of makeup for that early in the morning. Her blonde hair was tied up in a tight bun and she was wearing a very expensive looking coat and high heels.

"Mr. Wilson, we don't have a lot of time, so I want this done quickly," the woman commanded. She nonchalantly glanced at Evan and his mom as if they were merely an annoyance and then turned back to Mr. Wilson, waiting for him to respond.

"Yes, right away, Mrs. Kendell," he said without delay. Mr. Wilson took her coat and disappeared into the back room without looking at Evan or his mom.

Evan's mom looked furious at having been interrupted by the rude woman.

"New in town?" the young man asked in a thick New England accent.

Evan looked over at the boy who had just sat down in one of the fancy leather chairs and pulled out his phone. He was wearing slacks and a blazer. His dark brown hair was styled in the latest fashion, and he wore an unfriendly scowl on his face that looked oddly common place. Evan guessed he wasn't happy about shopping with his mom either.

"Um, yeah, we just moved here from Colorado," Evan answered, distracted by the impatient tapping of his mom's foot as she waited for the man to return.

"Going to Wellsford?" He asked with a smirk without even giving Evan the courtesy of looking up from his phone.

"Yes," Evan replied cautiously.

"Well, we'll see how long you last."

Evan stared at the boy in confusion. What did he mean? Evan was about to ask when he was interrupted.

"Mr. Wilson," Evan's mom said as soon as the man returned from the back room. "I hope you intend on helping us before you move on to your next customer."

Mrs. Kendell's eyes snapped up from the suit she had been inspecting. Mr. Wilson looked at Evan's mom for a moment through narrowed eyes. The tension in the room grew even more palpable. All eyes were on Mr. Wilson. Even the boy had looked up from his phone in anticipation of what Mr. Wilson was going to do.

"Mrs. Kendell, would you like anything to drink as I fit Brad?" Mr. Wilson asked with a smug look of defiance, gesturing toward the woman's son.

"Coffee for me and tea for Brad," Mrs. Kendell responded, a look of satisfaction visible on her face as she went back to inspecting the suits.

Mr. Wilson then moved in closer to Evan's mom. "Our uniform package starts at $3000.00 and by the looks of things, you don't have that kind of cash. So, I would suggest, as I did previously, that you look into another option."

"$3000.00 for a uniform?" Evan's mom repeated feeling defeated.

"Yes, plus tax. Now, if you don't mind, I have an important customer to attend to." Mr. Wilson rushed out of the room to fetch the drinks.

Beaten, Evan and his mom showed themselves out into the cold morning air.

"I have never been treated so…"Evan's mom trailed off, visibly flustered and upset. "I have half a mind to go back in there and tell that little man what I really think of him and his fancy store. And that woman! She actually thinks she's better than us! Because she has money!"

"Tell you what Mom," Evan interrupted in the hope of changing the subject. "Why don't I head to Radford's and you go make sure Dad is getting the right fridge."

"Do you have any money?" She asked as she reached for her purse.

"Yes, I'll be fine," Evan answered confidently as he started to walk down the road in the direction Mr. Wilson had pointed.

"Come and find me if you need more money," Evan's mom called after him.

"I will," Evan answered without turning around.

Evan found "Radford's Books" on a narrow one-way street off the main road. It looked very out of place, sandwiched between an upscale bagel shop and a small jewelry store. Evan peered through the unwashed, large front windows of the shop, but couldn't see inside because of the unevenly stacked books blocking his view.

As Evan opened the shop door, he felt as though he was entering an old, cluttered library and he wondered if this shop only carried books. He speculated that Mr. Wilson had told them about the used uniforms just to get rid of them. He had never seen so many books, or dust for that matter, stacked into such a tiny space before. The books looked to be organized into sections, the categories were sloppily etched onto the book shelves. Most of the sections were labeled for a period of history, but the section closest to him was labeled fiction.

Evan pulled a book off the shelf nearest to him and blew a thick layer of dust from its cover. *"The History of the Ottoman Empire,"* Evan read softly.

Obviously, the books weren't as organized as Evan had first thought. Putting the book back on the shelf, he made his way through the maze of stacked books on the floor and shelves before reaching a small desk covered with loose papers and an old cash register.

Evan rang a small bell that was sitting on the desk. No response. He waited and rang the bell again. This time, Evan heard movement in the back of the shop. An old man limped through the back doorway. He wore suspenders, a partially tucked-in white shirt and light brown, wrinkled slacks. The man's thick white hair was matted down on one side and Evan wondered if he had been sleeping.

The man yawned and made his way to the desk. After adjusting his reading glasses, he peered down at Evan with eyes that did not match his worn body. Evan's dad had told him once that you could tell everything from a person's eyes. This man's dark blue eyes were alive, not weary and defeated as his body suggested.

"Can I help you young man?" he asked in a gruff voice.

"I'm looking for a school uniform," Evan stammered. He felt strange asking for a uniform in a bookstore. "Mr. Wilson said I might find used ones here."

"He did, did he?" The old man turned and limped to the back room. "I assume, if you were at Wilson's shop, that you are going to attend Wellsford Academy," the old man called from the back room.

"Yes, Sir." Evan could hear boxes being dragged across the floor.

"Here we are," the man said as he emerged with a cardboard box full of uniform jackets in his arms.

The man set the box on the counter and pulled out one of the jackets. He shook the jacket a couple of times sending a cloud of dust towards Evan. Evan coughed.

"Sorry about that. Dust mites love these things."

The old man handed the jacket to Evan. It was the right shade of blue, maybe a little faded, but had the same insignia sewn above the pocket as the ones in Mr. Wilson's shop.

"Well, try it on. You need to make sure it fits, because I don't accept returns," the man motioned Evan towards an old mirror hanging crookedly on the wall.

Evan put the jacket on and looked into the mirror. The previous owner must have been broader in the shoulders and had longer arms than Evan because the sleeves were a couple of inches too long and the jacket looked a bit baggy on Evan's frame.

"It looks a little big, but I suppose you will grow into it," the old man observed, pushing his glasses with one crooked finger further up his nose. "You'll need to get pants and shoes from the department store, but I would say you are well on your way."

"How much do I owe you?" Evan asked as he reached into his pocket and pulled out his wallet.

"Ten dollars should do it," the old man said.

Evan pulled out a ten dollar bill, relieved because he only had twenty dollars in his wallet, and put it into the old man's outstretched hand. Pushing a couple buttons on his old cash register, the man deposited the money and then slowly turned toward the back room. The man stopped just before disappearing out of Evan's view.

"Don't let them get to you at Wellsford. Under their fancy clothes and smug expressions, they are just like you and me," the man called over his shoulder. And then without turning around, he disappeared into the back room.

Evan stood by the counter, wondering what the man had meant. The man's words marked the third time that day he had been warned about his new school; the first two times in Mr. Wilson's stuffy shop by Mr. Wilson and the rude woman's son, Brad, and now by the old man. Worried, Evan tucked the jacket under his arm and left the shop in search of his family.

Chapter Five

Wellsford Academy

It was early morning, well before Evan thought that any sane human should be awake. In the acceptance paperwork that Wellsford Academy had sent to him, he was instructed to arrive at the school promptly at 7:00 a.m., an hour before the rest of the students would show up. Evan let out an audible yawn as he tried to rub the sleep from his tired eyes.   It was still dark outside. The SUV's dim headlights danced off of the frozen landscape as he and his mom wound their way along the coastal highway heading to Evan's first day of school at Wellsford Academy only three days after arriving in Rhode Island.

Evan tugged at his collar as he sat in the passenger seat next to his mom. He wondered how he was going to get through an entire school day with his shirt tucked in and a tie around his neck. The Wellsford blue blazer purchased from Radford's had cleaned up nicely and, just as the old man had suggested, they had found everything else at the local department store for a fraction of the price they would have paid Mr. Wilson.

"You have nothing to worry about," Evan's mom assured, noticing his fidgeting. "I have no doubt that you will make friends."

Evan shrugged nervously.

"Who knows, you might even meet a cute girl at school today," Evan's mom said smiling.

Evan rolled his eyes and shook his head disapprovingly, not indulging his mom's comment in the least.

He had not slept well the past few nights, lying awake on the air mattress worrying about his new school. Mr. Wilson and Brad, the rich kid Evan had met in the uniform shop, had made it perfectly clear that Evan was not cut out for Wellsford. The warning given by the old man at Radford's didn't help matters either.

Evan's mom turned the family SUV off of the highway onto a narrow road adjacent to a small, unimpressive sign pointing in the direction of Wellsford Academy. The dense trees blocked any sign of civilization, if there was any, leaving Evan to wonder what kind of school his parents had enrolled him in.

Through the trees Evan caught a glimpse of a frozen lake, its surface twinkling in the moonlight. Evan scanned the shoreline for any sign of the school. On the far side of the lake, he spotted a boat house sitting on the shore nestled in the thick trees which surrounded the lake. Behind the boathouse, overlooking the lake, rose a steep, tree covered hill on which perched the backside of a massive building, which looked aglow from the numerous windows spewing out its interior lights. Before he could take in the impressive sight, the dense trees swallowed them up again as the road wound up and around the hill, away from the lake.

"Did you see that building on the hill?" Evan asked his mom as he strained to get another look.

"I didn't see anything," Evan's mom exclaimed as she kept her eyes glued to the road. "What did it look like?"

"It looked like," Evan struggled to find a description that matched the building he had seen. "It looked like a European castle or," Evan thought for another moment before concluding, "a palace."

"A palace in Rhode Island?" Evan's mom laughed at what could only be an exaggeration. "Maybe your new princess is awaiting your arrival."

"Seriously," Evan said. "You never give up, do you?"

"Never," his mom answered as she started to laugh.

However, when the thick trees cleared again, Evan's mom stopped laughing and the SUV slowed to a stop as they both stared at the front of the giant structure at the head of a long snow covered field.

"Okay, you weren't kidding. A palace it is," she said as she nudged the vehicle back up to speed.

The building stood at least four stories tall. The giant windows, encased in ornate stonework, were ablaze with light in the faint early morning. The steep roof was littered with dozens of chimneys, some of which were spewing out white smoke.

The small road wrapped around the field and led them to a large fountain in front of the building. In the middle of the fountain sat a white statue of a man on a war horse, but instead of wielding a sword he held books in his hand. Evan's mom stopped the car in front of the entrance.

The building towered above the SUV, the stonework even more impressive up close. Next to the giant wood doors of the main entrance stood a glass atrium. Evan could see plants of all colors and even a tree growing inside through the glass walls, providing a stark contrast to the frozen landscape on the outside.

"What I would give for a tour of that place," Evan's mom said as she strained to see the entire building through the partially fogged windows of the SUV.

"You can always join the PTA," Evan suggested with a nervous laugh.

"Do you think they have a PTA?" she asked in an excited tone.

"I was kidding, mom," Evan explained. The last thing he needed was his mom walking into the school on his first day asking if she could join the PTA. Evan doubted this was the kind of school where parents volunteered.

"That must be your welcoming committee," Evan's mom said cheerfully, as she pointed to a chubby kid wearing a blue blazer just like Evan's. The boy was rubbing his arms in an effort to stay warm by the front door.

"Yeah, I guess you're right," Evan said, still gaping up at the school.

"You'll do great," she encouraged, looking anxiously at her son.

Evan took a deep breath and reluctantly slid out of his warm seat. He was met by the unwelcoming cold, morning breeze sailing in from the ocean which caused him to inhale sharply. He was tempted to jump back into the spot he had just abandoned.

"I'll be here to pick you up at 3:30," Evan's mom reassured before pulling away.

Evan had no option but to face whatever was behind the large wooden doors of Wellsford Academy.

"I'm Phillip Johnson the third."

Evan jumped. He hadn't noticed that his welcoming committee had walked down the front steps to greet him.

After quickly regaining his composure, Evan turned to face his new classmate, "I'm Evan Myers, the first, I guess." Evan grinned.

Phillip's cheeks and nose were red from standing out in the cold wind, but he was wearing a large smile. He was a good head shorter than Evan, had large brown eyes and thick, black hair that was plastered to his head, not a hair out of place.

"You could have waited inside," Evan said noticing how badly Phillip was shaking.

"No one should have to walk into Wellsford Academy for the first time alone," Phillip answered. "This is your first time at Wellsford isn't it?"

"Yes," Evan answered. "Why do you ask?"

"You look familiar," Phillip answered. "I know I have seen you before, but I can't seem to place where I saw you."

"I just moved here three days ago from across the country. I guarantee you we have never met."

"I guess," Phillip said as he turned to walk inside, but before Evan could follow, Phillip abruptly turned around. "You're the kid from the news!" Phillip said excitedly. "That's where I saw you!"

"What?"

"The kid from the world news that I watch every night. You're the one who saved that little girl at Niagara Falls. The one they're calling a hero." Phillip continued.

Evan new exactly what Phillip was talking about, but he had hoped that only the local news stations had covered the Niagara Falls incident.

"I was just in the right spot," Evan conceded.

"At the right time, I know I saw the interview. It was all over the news. I can't believe I'm meeting a true hero. I can't wait to tell the other students."

"No!" Evan said a little louder than he had planned. "Let's just keep this between us." Evan said hoping that Phillip was the only 15 year old kid who actually watched the news.

"Got it. You want to be treated like every other student," Phillip said with a wink.

"Exactly," Evan said. "So, how did you get stuck showing the new kid around?" Evan asked, hoping he had put the hero thing to rest.

"I volunteered!" Phillip said excitedly. "I like to get to know the new kids. And besides, I'm president of the welcome committee which means it's my responsibility to welcome all new students."

"That's exciting," Evan lied. He suspected that Phillip was likely the president and only member of the committee.

"Yes, it's a very important job. I need to make sure you get your student body card and check in at the front office before school starts." Phillip paused at the top of the stairs. "Are you ready for your first day?"

"I guess," Evan said humoring his excited, solitaire welcome committee member.

"Welcome to Wellsford Academy," Phillip announced as he opened the solid wooden front door.

Phillip led Evan inside the school. Taking a deep breath, he launched into a narrative about the history of the school, which he had obviously memorized. Evan, however, was no longer listening. The butterflies in his stomach had returned, but with more intensity, as he realized just how far out of his league this school actually was. The academy looked more like a museum than a school. The large main entrance was big enough to fit Evan's entire house inside of it. The room had forty foot ceilings, marble floors and a massive stone staircase rising all the way to the fourth floor. Above the landing on the second floor, giant windows glowed from the sun that would be peaking over the horizon any moment. The walls were covered with expensive paintings that appeared to be guarded by several suits of armor. The floors gleamed from a recent polish job and looking down, Evan found himself standing on a giant W in the middle of the room.

"And that's why they don't allow students to use that fireplace anymore," Phillip said pointing to the large fireplace in the corner of the room as he laughed at his own joke.

Oh no, Evan thought to himself, he hadn't been listening to Phillip, he hoped there wasn't going to be a quiz at the end.

"What do you think?" Phillip asked.

"I can't believe this is a school," Evan answered.

Phillip smiled. "You're not the first scholarship kid to say that."

"What do you mean by that?" Evan asked confused.

"Well, what I meant to say was. I mean," Phillip stammered, shifting awkwardly. "I just meant that most of the kids who come here on scholarship have never seen anything like this before. They are pretty overwhelmed the first time they come through the doors. I guess that's probably why most of them don't stay long."

"What do you mean, don't stay long?"

"Well, the last kid who came here on scholarship lasted one week before he quit. And the kid before him lasted one month," Phillip said. "In fact, I think there are bets going on how long the next one, well you, will last."

"Why would I leave?" Evan asked, shocked that kids were betting on how long he would last.

"Everyone says they can't make it here, that they are not smart enough, or aren't the right fit, but I don't believe that. I think it's the way they are treated," Phillip explained, his tone suggesting that he didn't approve of what went on.

"What happens to them?" Evan asked confused.

"I haven't seen it first hand and don't know exactly what happens," Phillip was talking so quietly now that Evan had to lean in to hear him. A look of concern had crept across his face as he talked. "I heard they have plans for you."

"They?" Evan whispered.

"Some of the other freshmen," Phillip answered. "They think it's their responsibility to rid their class of scholarship students."

"What are they going to do?" Evan asked.

"They want to get you out on the first day, set a new record, but I don't know how they plan on doing it."

The answer was not what Evan wanted to hear. He didn't scare easily and didn't have problems standing up for himself, but there was something about the urgency in Phillip's voice that left him with an uneasy feeling.

"I'll need to be careful then," Evan said trying to convince Phillip that he wasn't worried, but his tone fell flat, and neither of them felt convinced.

Phillip looked as though he wanted to say more but reluctantly returned to the tour as he led Evan out of the entryway.

"The original building was built by a successful businessman in the late 1800s to be his personal residence, but after a couple of bad business decisions he was forced to sell. The school's founder and first Headmaster, a man who was virtually unknown at the time, purchased the estate and started Wellsford Academy. After he acquired the building and grounds, he set up several trust funds which have helped fund the school ever since. No one knows exactly how Thomas Wellsford acquired his money or why he wanted to start what has become the most prestigious private school in the world, but his legacy will live on forever."

Their footsteps echoed as they walked down a hallway, past exquisite paintings and artifacts until reaching a set of open doors.

"Here we are," Phillip announced. "Welcome to one of the greatest libraries in the world."

The air in the library was stuffy, filled with the aroma of old leather. Thousands of books were stacked on rows of shelves located on the main floor and the second and third floor balconies which towered above Evan's head. Large windows on the far wall looked out towards the frozen lake Evan had seen from the car earlier that morning and wooden tables for studying sat in rows near the windows.

Phillip led Evan towards a desk piled high with old books. Behind the mound of leather books sat an elderly woman. She wore a sweater and skirt and was bent over a small light, with a magnifying glass held inches from her eye by a homemade contraption attached to her head. She was focused on repairing an old, leather bound book. She didn't look up or acknowledge that she was no longer alone. She continued concentrating on the intricacies of her expertly crafted stitches, as if she were a surgeon performing a lifesaving procedure.

"First edition 1861, and good as new," The old lady said after several minutes. "Some people like the new-fangled electronic reading devices, but me, I like holding the old leather and turning the pages with my fingers, reading the book as the author intended." She placed the book down and looked up at the two young students. Her right eye looked four times the size of the left eye, magnified through the thick magnifying glass and Evan and Phillip snickered at the odd sight.

"What is it?" she asked, looking at her clothes, expecting to find something out of place.

Phillip pointed at the magnifying glass.

"Oh really, boys. You would think you were still in kindergarten." She removed the band around her head which held the magnifying glass in place. "Now then," she said seriously. "What brings you boys here so early in the morning? You shouldn't have homework yet, not with the new term only starting today." She reminded Evan of the grandma every kid secretly wanted. The kind that baked sugar cookies, made homemade syrup and could beat them at card games.

"Just welcoming our newest student," Phillip replied. "Evan, this is our librarian and head researcher, Ms. Flinders."

Evan reached out to shake her hand and was surprised by her firm grip and the intensity in her eyes. Something told Evan that this was not your average grandma.

"Starting halfway through the year?" she asked with a questioning look.

"Yes, we just moved here from Colorado," Evan responded.

"Colorado, huh? Well, you will need a library card."

She reached into a desk drawer and removed an electronic card with the school's insignia on it. She wrote Evan's first name and then she paused, as if remembering something and then wrote Evan's last name, Myers, on the card and handed it to him. Evan stared at the card surprised.

"Did I spell your last name correctly," she said eying Evan suspiciously.

"Yes, but how did you know my last name?"

"I know every student in this school. Keep that in mind should you ever lose one of my books," she said in a threatening tone.

"I will," Evan stammered, taking the card and stuffing it into his pants pocket.

"You had better get him up to the main office before school starts," Mrs. Flinders said, grabbing another damaged book from her pile. "*A Tale of Two Cities*, one of my favorites." She slid the contraption back down over her face and returned to the task.

"We will have to finish our tour another time Evan," Phillip said. "I don't want you to be late on your first day of school."

Phillip led Evan back the way they had come through the main entrance and up the stairs to the third floor of the school. Several students were starting to fill the halls, greeting friends that they hadn't seen since the start of winter break. None of them seemed to notice Evan. Before long, they reached the administrative offices in the east wing of the school.

"Just take a seat," Phillip told Evan. "They will call you when they are ready."

"Do we have any classes together?" Evan asked as he sunk deep into one of the leather arm chairs in the waiting area.

"Yes, all the freshmen students have the same classes. I'll save you a seat," Phillip replied as he headed out of the office.

Evan felt as if he could have been sitting in the executive offices of any high power law firm or major corporation. There were several chairs just like the one Evan was waiting in, expertly placed around the large office. A fire blazed in a large fireplace, warming the room. After his restless night, Evan closed his eyes, nodding off for several minutes.

"Evan Myers."

The high-pitched, nasal voice startled Evan, who shot up to see a stern-looking woman sitting behind a large reception desk. Her brown hair was pulled tightly into a bun, and she wore, what looked like a permanent scowl on her thin, wrinkled face.

"Yes, I'm Evan," Evan walked quickly over to the desk.

Evan read the nameplate on her desk, Ms. Pritchett.

"Here is your class schedule and locker assignment. Dr. Daniels will see you now." She turned back abruptly to her computer.

"Dr. Daniels?" Evan asked, confused about where to go and with whom he was supposed to talk.

"The school's counselor," Ms. Pritchett replied pointing down the hallway, annoyed by the question.

Evan took the papers, stuffed them into his pocket, along with his new library card, and started in the direction she had pointed. Several offices lined the hall but, at this early hour, not many were occupied. Evan stopped at the last office on the right.

"Dr. Daniels, Student Development," Evan read on the gold nameplate on the door.

Evan knocked and waited, expecting to encounter another unfriendly person, but as the door opened, he found himself staring at a woman who looked to be in her twenties. She had short, bleached blonde hair and wore several earrings in each ear. She stood about as tall as Evan, had bright, multi-colored fingernails and wore glasses. She looked nothing like what he had expected a school counselor, or anyone who worked at this school, to look like. Her blouse and skirt were professional attire, but she wore big, fuzzy, yellow slippers on her feet.

"I'm Dr. Patricia Daniels," she said introducing herself.

Evan continued to stare at her shoes.

"The most comfortable footwear I own," she said, noticing Evan's stare. "Of course, I can't wear them outside of my office. But behind my desk, they never notice," she said smiling. "You must be Evan from Colorado." She directed him into her office and shut the door. "School ski team; straight A's; younger brother, Jackson; favorite subject, math; and oh yea, you think you are way out of your league and wonder if this was a mistake. I read your profile," she said with a smirk.

"That's all in my profile?" Evan asked, amazed by the detail and accuracy.

"Well, actually, not all of it," she chuckled. "The last part I guessed by how nervous you look. It's my official job to welcome you to this fine academy and to let you know what a privilege it is for you to have this opportunity." Her tone sounded very proper, and Evan realized she was mocking something or someone. "Now that, that is done, let me say what a great opportunity it is for this school to have you as its newest student. Every year, one student is offered a scholarship to attend Wellsford Academy. This is part of the school's charter, part of its heritage. There used to be many more students on scholarship, but for the last ten years the rules have been interpreted differently. Now, only one new student per year is allowed to enroll. Currently, you are the only student in the school on this program."

"Shouldn't there be at least four of us?" Evan asked.

"Yes, but the others dropped out or were asked to leave before they even completed their first year." The smile faded from her face.

"Why did they leave?" Evan asked. Phillip had answered that question earlier, but Evan wanted to know what a member of the faculty thought.

"Officially, they couldn't meet the academic requirements. Unofficially, however, no one wanted them here." She paused for moment, taking her glasses off and rubbing the bridge of her nose where the glasses had rested. She took a deep breath, and stared at Evan with a look that made him feel very uncomfortable. "I know that this is a hard thing to ask of you Evan, but I need you to stay. I need you to be smart. The school needs people like you to break the mold and help restore this school to the great institution it once was." With that, Dr. Daniels put her glasses back on and turned to her computer screen. "It looks like you have a full and challenging schedule ahead of you and starting half way through the year won't be easy. Good luck, Evan," she said as she stood abruptly, straightened her skirt and directed him to follow her. "Your first class starts in five minutes. You do not want to be late on your first day."

Dr. Daniels led Evan out of the admin offices and to the other side of the school, where Phillip had told him all the classrooms were located. "Math class, and only a minute late," she announced as she looked at her watch. "Honestly I always forget how big this school really is," she said shaking her head. "It's your first day, I'm sure he'll forgive your tardiness." Any questions before I leave you?"

Evan had questions, but none of which he thought was appropriate for the school counselor.

"Have a great first day!" she said with a smile before turning around. "Oh, your math teacher's name is Dr. Parkinson. He's not as bad as he seems." Evan heard her say before she disappeared around the corner.

The large oak door outside the math classroom creaked loudly as Evan opened it. Everyone in the classroom turned to look at the late-arrival, including an old, gray-haired man wearing a blue three piece, breasted suit, who had been writing on the board.

So much for sneaking in unnoticed, Evan thought to himself.

"You're late," the old man growled as Evan searched for a seat.

"Yes, I'm sorry. My meeting with the counselor went long," Evan admitted sheepishly.

He looked for an open seat among his fellow freshmen. Surprisingly, Evan recognized Brad, the kid he had met in Wilson's uniform shop, staring him down with a menacing look. He said something to his friends sitting next to him and they laughed, as if Evan was the pun of the joke. Luckily, he spotted Phillip on the other side of the room, pointing excitedly to the empty seat next to him. Evan quickly moved away from the front of the room and sat down, trying to blend in and hoping the teacher would forgive his tardiness. The white-haired man didn't return to the board, but stared at Evan for a moment before speaking very deliberately.

"Excuses are for the weak Mr.?"

"Myers," Evan finished.

"Oh, yes. Mr. Myers. The new scholarship student, I presume. Let's hope this is not a sign of things to come with you." He turned back toward the board to finish the scariest looking equation Evan had ever seen. "This math problem was solved two hundred years ago. If you use your expensive electronic devices, you will be able to find the solution in a matter of minutes, but I don't care about the solution, I want you to try new methods to solve this problem. I want innovative thinkers. The person who can come up with a new way to solve this problem will get an automatic A this term." Dr. Parkinson, the math teacher, looked directly at Evan. Some of you will need a miracle such as this in order to pass my class."

Brad looked over at Evan and snickered again.

The old man then turned back to the board and started a lecture on advanced calculus. Evan stared at the board, completely lost. He had never studied calculus before, let alone advanced calculus. Feeling overwhelmed, he slumped back in his seat.

Maybe I won't be able to hack it at this school after all, he thought to himself.

Evan glanced around at his fellow classmates to see if everyone was as lost as he was. Phillip was taking notes on his laptop looking like he understood every word. Most of the other students were doing the same. Some were even nodding in agreement as the teacher made important points. The only students not fully engrossed in the lecture were Brad and his group of friends, who were all playing games on their phones and not following the lecture at all.

Were they so smart they didn't have to listen? Evan wondered.

"Phillip," Evan whispered.

"Yeah?" Phillip responded, almost too quietly for Evan to hear.

"Do you know that kid?" Evan inquired, pointing to Brad, the kid he had met in the uniform shop.

"That's Brad," Phillip whispered with disdain, quickly looking down at his notes as the teacher turned around. "Do you know him?" Phillip asked after several minutes.

"Sort of. I met him at Mr. Wilson's uniform shop."

"Stay as far away from him as you can," Phillip warned, looking up from his notes. "He is nothing but trouble."

"Mr. Johnson," Dr. Parkinson boomed in a stern, terrifying tone as he looked at Phillip. "Is there something you would like to share with the class?"

"No, sir. Sorry Dr. Parkinson," Phillip said, his face turning red.

"Let's keep it that way," Dr. Parkinson snarled.

Evan and Phillip quickly lowered their heads and didn't say anything for the rest of class.

The bell rang just in time to save Evan from brain overload. Math used to be his favorite subject, but after that lesson he wasn't sure he ever wanted to do math again.

"Wasn't that exciting?" Phillip asked, jarring Evan out of his overwhelmed state.

"I'm not sure exciting is the word I would use to describe that class," Evan admitted as he gathered his things and started to walk out of the room, still in a daze after the information overload.

"Don't worry, it will get better," Phillip reassured him.

It didn't get better though. The next two classes before lunch, English and biology, were as overwhelming as the first class had been. The teachers might as well have been speaking a foreign language. The English teacher had decided to test the public school system by asking Evan a series of questions that he failed to answer. After a full ten minutes of questions ranging from classical books to complex sentence structure, she finally drew the conclusion and announced to the entire class that our nation's public schools were indeed as bad as she had assumed, pointing in Evan's direction. He had fared slightly better in biology, where he had only answered two questions wrong.

The halls were packed when Evan finally emerged from the biology classroom. He was drained and dreaded going to the lunch room. He knew everyone was going to lunch, but he had completely lost his desire to be around his classmates, who by now, all knew that he had no business being in their school. Evan quietly looked for a place to hide for an hour.

Maybe in the library? Evan thought to himself, remembering the secluded tables tucked away among the thousands of books. Before he could make a beeline for the stairs, he was stopped by a familiar voice.

"Coming to lunch?" It was more of a statement than a question, and Phillip grinned up at Evan. "You won't believe the food they serve here," he continued, oblivious of Evan's need to be alone.

"I guess," Evan answered reluctantly, succumbing to the deep grumblings coming from his stomach.

The lunchroom was filled with the sound of students greeting their fellow classmates as they secured their spots at the tables. Evan and Phillip were the last ones to file in the back of the lunchroom.

"We have a vegan option and a gluten free option," Phillip said as he pointed to the different lines.

"I'll think I'll try this line," Evan said pointing to the only line without any allergy warnings or other restrictions listed.

"I'm going with the vegan option today," Phillip said. "Find me afterwards," Phillip picked up a tray and disappeared into the sea of blue jackets.

Evan grabbed a tray and moved past the first few options quickly, not recognizing the food, until he found something that looked vaguely like spaghetti. He dished up a full plate, grabbed a carton of milk, and turned to look for Phillip and hopefully an extra chair at the table.

Evan quickly spotted his new friend across the lunchroom grabbing a chair from another table to make a spot for Evan at his table. There were two other students moving their chairs to make room for Evan. Evan smiled and made his way through the crowded lunch room. He was about to greet the two kids with Phillip when, out of nowhere, something caught Evan's foot, sending him falling forward. He tried to catch himself, but whatever had caught hold of his foot wouldn't let go and as if in slow motion, he landed face down on the lunchroom floor with a loud crash. Evan laid there for a moment, motionless. The entire lunchroom had gone silent. He quickly assessed his situation. He was okay, but he had landed directly on top of his spaghetti dish. His newly dry-cleaned jacket was splattered in thick red sauce. His white shirt and light slacks were stained red as well. He looked back to see what he had tripped on, not accustomed to being so clumsy.

"I knew you were dumb, Hero, but I had no idea how clumsy you were." Brad slowly pulled his foot back from the aisle, making sure Evan saw what had tripped him.

How did Brad find out about Niagara Falls? Evan thought to himself.

Brad slowly stood and looked down at Evan and laughed at his own joke. The other boys at Brad's table joined in. "Phillip told us your story, a real hero at our school. I had to make sure we ran into each other."

Evan's blood started to boil. It was bad enough that this troll thought he was better than Evan, but he actually had the audacity to trip Evan and act like it was Evan's fault.

"He looks like he is going to cry," Brad announced as he scrunched up his own face, pretending to cry. The entire lunchroom broke out in laughter.

Evan rose to his feet and began brushing off the extra meatballs that still clung to his clothes. He was usually very calm, but every nerve in his body screamed to wind up and hit Brad squarely on his perfect chin.

"You don't belong here Hero," Brad hissed, moving closer and closer to Evan, daring him to make the first move.

Does he want me to hit him? Evan thought to himself, getting ready to land the first blow. Every muscle in Evan's body tensed. He had only been in one fight in his entire life, against a kid who had been picking on Jackson. He had won that fight with one punch and he was intent on winning this fight as well.

"What are you going to do? Hit me?" Brad taunted again, leaning his chin closer to Evan.

All at once, Evan knew exactly what was happening. Brad wanted Evan to hit him. He wanted to give the headmaster a reason to expel Evan. Phillip's warning came ringing back to Evan.

Evan could play this game. "Sorry, I didn't see your fat foot in the aisle," he said with a smirk.

"My fat foot? I should teach you a lesson you little, worthless, piece of trash," Brad threatened, beginning to lose his temper. "Do you know who you are talking to? My father practically owns this school, not like your father who probably empties its trash."

Evan didn't like the last comment. He could insult Evan, but not his family. He needed to end this quickly, before he lost his temper and hit the beef head.

"I'm new here, so I will let your insults against my family slide this time. Put it there friend," Evan offered as he pushed his hand forward, a juicy, sauce-covered meat ball concealed in his palm.

Evan released the ball as his hand fully extended. The ball and sauce soared from Evan's palm and collided with Brad's shirt. Sauce exploded from the meatball, covering his shirt before rolling down his pants and landing on his newly polished shoes.

Brad looked down at the damage as he watched the meatball come to rest on the ground, and then slowly he looked up at Evan, who was smiling, his hand still outstretched. Brad's eyes were filled with hatred.

"I'm sorry, I didn't see that leftover meatball there," Evan said, baiting Brad.

Brad didn't require any more baiting. He flung himself at Evan both fists flying. Evan ducked the first punch, but was caught in the eye by Brad's second punch. They both fell to the sauce- covered ground.

"Break it up! Break it up!" A voice boomed from somewhere on the other side of Brad.

A young male teacher grabbed the swinging Brad and pulled him off of Evan, who was trying very hard to suppress his smile.

"Who started this?" the teacher asked, panting slightly from the exertion of pulling Brad off of Evan.

"He did. The new kid," Brad insisted as he pointed in Evan's direction with malice.

"Actually, Brad threw the first punch as Evan went to shake his hand, and that was after Brad intentionally tripped Evan," Phillip defended Evan, as he came up behind him.

"Mind your own business runt," Brad seethed, staring at Phillip with hatred.

"Sounds like you were out of line Mr. Kendell," the teacher said as he stepped between Phillip and Brad. "Regardless, school policy states that both offenders must see the headmaster. Follow me."

The teacher led both boys out of the lunchroom and toward the headmaster's office.

Evan's excitement over having won was starting to wear off. He may have won the battle only to lose the war. The headmaster was sure to side with Brad. Brad said it himself, his dad practically owned the school. They had just reached the east wing, it would all be over soon.

"I'm Mr. Heywood," the teacher said introducing himself to Evan as Brad trailed behind. "I teach history. What's your name?"

"Evan Myers."

"Where are you from?" Mr. Heywood asked.

"Uh, Steamboat Springs, Colorado," Evan replied, shocked that a teacher would show interest in him. This teacher was not like the teachers he had met earlier in the day. He didn't seem to care that Evan was at the school on scholarship.

The teacher tried to comb back his bushy brown hair with his hand, a little disheveled from breaking up the fight. "I've been to Steamboat Springs. Best skiing I've ever experienced," he said with a smile. "Do you ski much?"

"I grew up on the slopes." Evan said excited that someone at the school had been to his home town.

"I'm probably not as good as you are, but I love the feel of fresh powder," he finished as they stopped at an office door. Evan silently read the gold plaque on the door, Dr. William Marshall Headmaster.

"Stay out here while I talk to the headmaster," Mr. Heywood said as he knocked and then entered the office, leaving Brad and Evan alone in the hallway.

"Bet you think you're pretty smart, Hero," Brad said, still looking furious.

"The name is Evan."

"You are going to be expelled for sure. There is a no fighting policy here at the academy," Brad said with a smirk.

"Lucky for you," Evan said staring directly at Brad. Brad backed up a little.

"With my dad's donations to the school," Brad continued nervously. "I'll get off with just a warning. But a poor kid like you, doesn't stand a chance," Brad abruptly stopped as Mr. Heywood exited the headmaster's office.

"Come on, Brad, let's get you back to class," the teacher directed as he shot a nod of encouragement in Evan's direction.

"Just walk on in. He's expecting you," Mr. Heywood said as he led Brad back toward the hallway.

"I can't go back like this," Brad whined as they walked away. "I need a new shirt and slacks."

Evan stood outside the headmaster's office for a moment, gathering his thoughts as he watched Mr. Heywood and Brad disappear around the corner. Evan took a deep breath and entered the office. Its interior resembled the rest of the school, expensive and extravagantly decorated complete with a grandfather clock and large oak desk. Large windows looked out on the Atlantic Ocean and expensive paintings of old fishing vessels filled the walls. Behind the desk sat the headmaster. He could have been the CEO of a Fortune 500 company by the way he commanded respect. He had a head of thick, gray hair and wore glasses that had slid down his nose. His expensive suit was adorned with a white handkerchief sticking out of his left breast pocket. He was reading something and did not look up at Evan who had stopped in the doorway waiting awkwardly. After a minute, which seemed like an eternity to Evan, the headmaster finally looked up, his eyes focusing on Evan's spaghetti-covered clothes. He held Evan's gaze for a moment before looking down at the papers on his desk.

"It states here that you were an excellent student and never got into any trouble at your last school and yet on your first day here at the finest academy in Rhode Island, you manage to get into a fight with one of our most promising students and athletes," the headmaster stated calmly. "Care to explain yourself?" he said a bit more forcefully.

"I, I tripped and fell on my lunch. Brad slipped when he tried to help me up. It looked like a fight, but really it was just a big, um, misunderstanding," Evan stammered.

"Misunderstanding you say?" the headmaster asked unconvinced, eyeing Evan. "Let me be perfectly clear, so that there are no more misunderstandings." Standing up from behind his desk, he towered above Evan, "You don't belong here. The only reason I allow scholarship students to attend my academy is for charity and the tax break. All I have to do is enroll them. Whether they stay is of no concern to me." He stared down at Evan over his thick glasses. "I don't think you will last the month, but since, technically, you did nothing wrong and Dr. Heywood collaborated your story, I can't expel you today," he said, raising his voice slightly. "I am going to put you on probation and move your locker assignment away from the other students into our overflow locker area. This way it will be harder for you to cause trouble. Also, if you are late to class more than one time, your grades will be docked a full letter grade. Let's be honest, you will have to work hard to maintain your grades and not fail out of this institution. Now, if you don't mind, I have more important matters to attend to. Your parents have been called and are on their way to pick you up. I don't want to see you in this condition in my school again! You can stop by Ms. Pritchett's desk and get your new locker number and combination," he concluded as he returned to his desk and resumed his paperwork.

Evan quickly left the office. Ms. Pritchett was sitting at the same desk where Evan had met her earlier that day, looking even more annoyed. She handed Evan his new locker assignment without a word. Evan left the office. He made his way down to the front steps of the school and waited. The weather was still bitter cold, but he didn't want to run the risk of running into Brad, again.

By the time he saw his family's SUV making its way up the winding road, he had already made up his mind. He wouldn't tell his mom about the fight or the details of the worst day of his life. He had tripped. His story was that simple.

Chapter Six

The Fourth Floor

Evan rolled over in bed and peaked through a small hole of his cave of blankets. It was still dark, but the stars outside his windows were starting to dim, promising dawn within the hour. His backpack laid on the floor next to his desk where his laptop still stood open. He had spent most of the night researching his new school. The great Wellsford Academy was the poster school for all prestigious private schools. Its students scored higher on exams, were more likely to attend Ivy League schools, and according to its own website, were superior in every way.

Evan's first day of school at Wellsford Academy had been worse than a nightmare. The memory of his walk of shame from the lunchroom, covered in red sauce, was by far the most embarrassing thing that had ever happened to him. He feared he was not likely to live down the incident anytime soon.

Evan had already pressed the snooze button on his cell phone twice, and he knew that pressing it a third time would earn him a wakeup visit from his mom. If it hadn't been for the aroma of bacon floating up to his bedroom, he might have played sick, or maybe hidden under his large quilt for the remainder of the school year. Bacon was one of his weaknesses and his mom knew it. It was only a matter of time before he lost the battle with his empty, rumbling stomach.

Even though he had been at Wellsford Academy for only one day - or half a day, technically - before being sent home, it was clear that the teachers hated him, questioning Evan's intelligence in front of the entire class. Further, he had already made an enemy, someone intent on getting him kicked out of school. Brad had even given Evan a nickname: Hero. It wasn't the word that bugged him so much, it was the way Brad had said it, as if implying that the title was self-anointed. He didn't consider himself a hero. He wished the reporter had never said it.

Evan's parents had interrogated him about his first day of school, especially after his mom had been called to pick him up. To hide the humiliation of how he had been treated, however, he stuck with his story about tripping in the lunchroom. He couldn't let them know how bad his first day had really been. Evan had just recently changed his sour attitude about the move. After listening to Jackson's amazing account of his first day of school, where he had made lots of new friends and loved his classes, Evan couldn't start complaining, not again. He wouldn't be the family downer, so as far as his parents and Jackson were concerned, Evan loved everything about his new school.

The courage he had felt after the fight, fueled by adrenaline and the satisfaction of outwitting Brad, faltered now as a wave of anxiety rushed over him. What if today was worse? What if everyone stared at the large spaghetti stain on his blazer? What if Phillip, his only new friend, didn't want anything to do with the new kid?

"What's the shame in quitting?" Evan muttered to himself under his blankets.

"If you're thinking of quitting your battle against the alarm button, I agree you should quit," Evan's dad announced, startling Evan, who thought he was alone. Evan peeked out to see his dad walk across the room and sit on the corner of his bed. "But, I don't think that is what you meant," he continued with a concerned look on his face. "Was your first day, maybe not as good as you led us to believe last night?"

"No, um, it was great Dad," Evan stammered, feeling his ears turning red. "I was thinking of quitting my subscription to my ski magazines." Unable to think of a better lie, Evan cursed himself as he continued his story. "Maybe I'll subscribe to some surfing ones instead. You know, Jackson makes it sound so exciting."

"Magazines, huh? Don't you cancel a subscription, not quit it?" he questioned.

"Yeah, but I really like skiing," Evan continued, trying to sell his bogus story.

His dad paused for a moment and then decided to let it go. He stood and started heading out of the room, but then turned back. "Anything worth doing is never easy."

Evan had heard his dad say this many times before, he just wasn't sure going to Wellsford Academy was worth doing.

"But I will tell you this, Evan. Whatever you decide to do about your, magazine subscriptions," his dramatic pause assured Evan that his dad hadn't believed the lie after all. "Your mother and I will support you." He turned and disappeared into the hallway, his footsteps echoing toward the kitchen.

Evan remained in bed for a few more precious moments and then followed the bacon smell down to the kitchen. Jackson had just finished off his first plate of pancakes and was reaching for a handful of bacon when Evan entered. He was about to head straight to the table to wrestle what crumbs he could from his kid brother when he noticed his Wellsford jacket hanging on the back of a chair at the table. It was spotless. Evan looked over at his mom in disbelief. She let out a yawn, as she flipped a pancake. Evan realized that she had stayed up all night cleaning his spaghetti-soaked jacket.

Maybe today will be better, Evan thought to himself as he smiled at his mom and filled his plate with crisp bacon.

The driveway in front of the school was lined with fancy SUVs and town cars. It was much busier than it had been on Evan's first day when his mom had dropped him off an hour early. Kids in Wellsford blue jackets were filing into the school. The rusted family SUV looked out of place as Evan's mom pulled up in front of the school. Several kids looked over as the SUV backfired loudly.

"Love you," Evan's mom called loudly as Evan got out of the car.

"Love you too, mom," Evan replied quietly as he joined the sea of blue jackets pushing through the front doors.

"I can't believe you weren't expelled," Phillip exclaimed as he rushed up to Evan through the crowd.

"Do people normally get expelled for tripping in the lunchroom?" Evan asked, with a serious look on his face.

"No, of course not. But you didn't just trip. You got into a fight with Brad. No one stands up to Brad, not even the teachers."

"I wouldn't exactly call it a fight," Evan shrugged. "It was more like a glorified shoving match."

"I guess," Phillip said. "Anyway, I took notes for you yesterday." He pulled sheets of paper out of his backpack. "You missed a lot of good information."

"Thanks for the notes," Evan said shoving the loose papers into his backpack.

"Have you picked up your books from the library yet?" Phillip reminded him as they walked through the front doors of the school.

Several minutes later, Evan left the library struggling under a stack of books that towered above his head. He looked up the stairs with despair, dreading the long climb to his new locker on the fourth floor.

Breathing heavily, Evan finally reached the top of the stairs. The fourth floor looked deserted and, judging by the thick layer of dust on the floor, Evan wondered if it hadn't been used for quite some time. The hallway was flanked by several open doors. Evan looked into one of the classrooms. The broken chairs and lopsided desks gave the floor an eerie feeling of neglect. They must use this floor as storage, Evan thought to himself as he continued to move down the hallway under the dim lights until he finally located a small row of lockers next to the last door.

Exhausted, Evan dropped the heavy books to the ground in front of the lockers with a loud bang. The noise wouldn't disturb anyone up here. He fumbled in his pocket for the small piece of paper with his locker combination.

"Locker 305," Evan mumbled to himself as he unfolded the wrinkled piece of paper.

Pulling his jacket sleeve over his hand, Evan rubbed the dusty gold plaques on the doors of the lockers, until he found locker 305. It was in the middle of the row. The locker's green paint was chipped in several spots revealing rusted metal underneath. It was larger than the lockers downstairs, taller than Evan and slightly wider too.

"Let's see... 5 - 12 - 55."

The dial resisted as Evan attempted to turn it clockwise. Finally, with added effort the dial moved, breaking loose whatever rust that had held it fixed. The other numbers were equally difficult, and Evan wondered how long it had been since this locker had been opened. He paused for a moment before opening the locker, imagining what he might find inside, but to his disappointment, the locker was empty. Evan shivered slightly as a draft of cold air escaped the locker, and for a moment, he thought he saw his breath.

I guess it's fitting to give the scholarship kid the biggest piece of junk locker in the entire school, Evan thought to himself.

Evan looked at his watch and realized that he was going to be late to his math class again. Quickly, he threw his books into the locker and rushed back down the stairs.

"You sure like to cut things close," Phillip commented as he tapped his watch anxiously. "Ten more seconds and you would have been late. Again!"

"Yeah I know, but my locker is all the way up on the fourth floor. I'm going to have to start carrying all of my books with me." Evan explained with an exasperated sigh as he settled into his seat.

"The fourth floor? Isn't that where they store all of the old school furniture? Why is your locker up there?" Phillip asked surprised.

"To keep me out of trouble." Evan winked at Phillip, who laughed a little too loudly, causing Dr. Parkinson to scowl at both of them.

Evan removed his math book from his backpack and looked up to see Brad glaring at him. He looked livid.

"Brad thought you had been expelled. Maybe it was good you came in right before the bell rang. Now he has to give back all his winnings." Phillip whispered.

"Winnings?"

"Yeah, for failing to get you kicked out on your first day," Phillip nudged Evan playfully.

Evan couldn't help but smirk at Brad, as his friends started asking for their money.

Math class went better today, Dr. Parkinson didn't single Evan out once, and he even understood the review portion of the lecture. As class ended, Phillip leaned over to Evan.

"I've been asked by Ms. Daniels to help you catch up," he said excitedly.

"You mean, be my tutor?" Evan clarified as he started packing his things in his bag.

"Yes! I was thinking we could meet at the library after school tomorrow," Philip suggested.

"Sure, sounds great. I need all the help I can get," Evan said as he followed Phillip to their next class.

Biology and English went off without a hitch, and before Evan knew it, he was back in the lunchroom trying to decide what to eat. He stayed away from red sauces and chose a fish taco and steamed vegetables. As he scanned over the crowded lunchroom, he noticed Phillip waving him over to a table in the corner. Steering clear of Brad's table, Evan wound his way over to Phillip. Several students in the lunchroom watched as Evan made his way to his seat. "Are you sure you want to be seen sitting next to me?" Evan teased. "I'm not the most popular kid at school."

"This is Cooper Bain and Janelle Hastings," Phillip introduced them as he motioned to the two other students sitting at the table. Evan recognized them from class.

"We don't care about that crap," Cooper stated. "We saw the fight yesterday and it was awesome! You're the first person to ever stand up to that jerk Brad and live to tell the story," said Cooper dramatically.

Cooper was a skinny kid with strawberry blond hair, blue eyes and a rather large nose.

"It was all just a misunderstanding," Evan assured, not wanting to admit it had been anything more.

"Is that how you got out of being expelled? Telling the headmaster it was all a misunderstanding?" Cooper asked amazed. "Genius!"

"Leave him alone," Janelle warned. "He obviously doesn't want to talk about it."

Janelle's black hair was pulled back in a tight ponytail. Her glasses made her look smarter and more sophisticated than an average freshman.

"Where are you from?" Cooper asked.

"Colorado."

"Out west, huh? Did you have a horse and cowboy hat?" Cooper asked.

Evan stared back in confusion. After an awkward pause he responded, "Why would you think I had a horse?"

"How else would you get around on dirt roads and trails?"

"Coop, have you ever been to Colorado?" Janelle asked as she shot him an annoyed look.

"No, but I've seen lots of old westerns," Cooper seemed excited to meet a cowboy.

"I didn't have a horse, but I've seen some of the old westerns, and Colorado is nothing like that," Evan explained, as Cooper's excitement drained. "I have ridden a horse before though, and Steamboat Springs does have a cowboy hat store on Main Street, which at one time was a dirt road."

Everyone at the table laughed.

"I can't believe the first swim meet of the year is this Friday!" Cooper uttered excitedly after the laughter had died down.

Janelle rolled her eyes. "Why does our conversation always have to return to swimming? Honestly I don't understand why everyone makes such a big deal about the swim meets."

Cooper started hyperventilating. "Why? Big deal?"

"Is he okay?" Evan asked as Cooper grabbed a paper bag and started breathing into it.

"You see Evan, to Cooper, swimming is everything. And Janelle, well Janelle likes to act like she doesn't care, but she does." Phillip said, as he threw one of his French fries at her.

Cooper finally gained control of his breathing. "And the dance after the swim meet, how can anyone, not be excited about that?"

"Dance?" Evan asked confused.

"Not just any dance, but the king of all dances."

Evan looked past Cooper. Brad had just stood up. Evan had never had a nemesis before, but Brad fit the description perfectly. Evan's attention was pulled away from Brad as a girl with long blonde hair stood up next to him. She was beautiful!

"Evan!" Cooper said jarring him back to reality.

"Oh, sorry, I was just..." Evan tried to explain embarrassed.

"You were just," Cooper turned around to see who Evan was looking at. "Oh! No worries. That's Madison Bates."

Janelle rolled her eyes.

"Is she Brad's girlfriend?" Evan asked.

"He wishes," Cooper said.

"He and every other guy at this school." Phillip added.

"Tell us more about Colorado, Evan," Cooper asked turning back around. "Did you have a six shooter?"

The group laughed, and for the first time since moving to Rhode Island, Evan was beginning to feel like he belonged.

■ ·· ■ ·· ■ ·· ■ ··

The ride home from school that day was quiet following the initial string of questions from Evan's mom about how his day went. Evan had answered yes or no to all of her questions, but his mind was somewhere else. As they pulled into their gravel driveway, Evan couldn't hold it in any longer and was ready to accept the consequences that were sure to follow.

"Mom?" he broke the silence.

"Yes, dear."

"Can you teach me how to dance?" Evan cringed, anticipating something he was not going to like.

Evan's mom slammed on the brakes, and the SUV skidded to a sudden stop. Instantly, Evan regretted his question as a large smile formed on his mom's face.

"Why do you want to learn how to dance?" she asked, barely holding back her excitement.

"There's just this dance at school on Friday night."

"Is someone special going to be at the dance?" She asked, trying to keep it cool.

She wasn't fooling Evan. He knew that she craved these one-on-one conversations that normally transpired between a mom and daughter. Since she only had sons, these types of conversations were very rare.

"No girl. Just a dance," Evan fibbed, hoping his red face would not be a dead give-away.

Her smile grew. She knew he was lying, but not wanting to spoil the moment, she tried to keep her excitement to a minimum.

"Sure, I can teach you."

Evan found himself thinking of Madison. If he mustered up enough courage to ask her to dance, would she say yes?

Chapter Seven

The Swim Meet

It was Friday before Evan knew it, the day of the swim meet and the dance. He caught himself humming one of the tunes from the crash course of dance lessons he had received the past three nights from his mom and dad. He had no idea how hard following a beat could actually be until the music started. He did alright just moving his legs to the beat, but adding his arms into the mix was something his brain just couldn't handle. By the end of the night he had mastered only two basic moves, unlike his brother Jackson, who was annoyingly a natural at dancing.

The day dragged on, as Fridays normally did, but this Friday seemed different. The excitement in the air couldn't be ignored as the students counted down the minutes for the swim meet to start. Even the teachers were giving less homework, adding to the excitement. Everyone had brought a change of clothing for the dance, which were hanging in their lockers. Some were even in fancy garment bags to keep them in mint condition. After witnessing one student try to shove her expensive, formal dress into her locker, Evan wondered if the slacks and shirt Phillip told him to bring were going to be formal enough.

The entire school filed into the hallways after the last class of the day, talking excitedly about the meet and the upcoming dance.

"Save me a seat," Evan told Phillip as he rushed up the stairs to drop off his books.

The only sign that anyone ever visited this floor of the school was his own footprints in the thick layer of dust. Evan turned the old rusty dial on the locker to the sequence of numbers he had recently memorized. The locker door squeaked in protest as the cold draft Evan had grown accustomed to hit him in the face causing him to shiver. Quickly, he threw his books on the floor of the locker and slammed the door shut, rushing back the way he had come.

The school's giant indoor swim arena was named Atlantis after the ancient, mythical city that was swallowed up by the sea. A giant mural towered above the pool depicting the sea as it would be seen if you were submerged in its depths. The bottom of several ships covered in barnacles could be seen floating on the ceiling. The sky and clouds appeared beyond the opaque surface of the water as if the people in the arena were fish swimming in the ocean. Triton, King of the Mermaids, was depicted on the wall next to an electronic score board, reigning over all creatures with power and grace.

Evan scanned the energetic crowd hoping to find his friends before the meet started. The large bleachers were divided into sections. Closest to him was a section that read "Reserved for Faculty and Parents." Evan instantly recognized Brad's mother from the unpleasant encounter at Mr. Wilson's uniform shop a week ago. She was speaking to the headmaster, who was glaring at Evan with disgust, most likely for being late. Evan was tempted to remind him that he was the one who had assigned Evan a locker in Siberia, but decided against it.

In the next section sat about 50 students from the opposing high school wearing red jackets. A banner that stretched between some of them read, "GO RADFORD!" They looked a bit uncomfortable in the intimidating surroundings.

Evan rushed passed them, desperately trying to find a seat before the swimmers emerged.

The student section was not hard to find. In front of a sea of blue blazers, the cheerleaders danced to music provided by the school's pep band. Unlike Evan's old high school band, this band was actually pretty good. Evan spotted Janelle, Phillip and Cooper on the top row and quickly moved toward the group feeling relieved to finally blend in.

"It took you long enough to get here. The meet is about to start," Janelle said as Evan sat down next to Cooper.

"It takes time to get to the fourth floor and back," Evan whined, still a little out of breath.

"Fourth floor? Why were you on the fourth floor?" Cooper asked.

"The headmaster changed Evan's locker to one on the fourth floor to keep him away from the other students. You know, so he can't cause any more trouble," Phillip answered, winking at Evan.

"But not the fourth floor. It's, it's haunted," Cooper gasped, a terrified look on his face.

"Really Cooper?" Janelle gawked. "You don't believe in that nonsense, do you?"

"What? Do I believe in ghosts or the story about Karen?" Cooper answered his own questions without hesitation. "YES, and yes." Cooper took a deep breath and then started into one of the schools darkest secrets. "Several years ago, a student had to be institutionalized after she was found on the fourth floor muttering to herself." Cooper explained, as he stared transfixed at something beyond the pool that only he could see. "She kept saying the word Karen over and over again."

"Did a senior tell you that story to, uh, protect you?" Janelle snorted, obviously not believing a word of what Cooper was saying.

"Yes. He said it was his duty to pass along the truth so that Karen's story would never be lost."

"Okay, I know I'm going to regret asking this, but what happened to Karen?" Janelle asked, skepticism written all over her face.

"She had a locker on the fourth floor, just like Evan." He looked in Evan's direction, his eyes opened wide. "It was a night just like tonight. Karen, a pretty sophomore had gone to her locker on the fourth floor to get something that she had forgotten. Her friends waited for her at the bottom of the stairs, expecting that it would take her only a couple of minutes. When she didn't return, her best friend Amy decided to see what was keeping her. While the others waited at the bottom of the stairs for Amy and Karen, excitedly discussing their plans for that evening, the peaceful night was shattered by a blood curdling scream. When the group looked up the staircase, they saw a man rushing down from the fourth floor. He didn't stop but burst out of the school into the cold night. Karen's friends rushed up the stairs to the fourth floor to see what had happened, but the only person they found was Amy curled up in a ball covering her face. The police searched the school and the grounds, but neither Karen nor the mysterious man were ever seen again. Several years after Karen's disappearance, students reported hearing odd sounds on the fourth floor and other strange occurrences."

"What kind of strange occurrences?" Phillip asked with concern, hanging on every word.

"One day they found muddy footprints leading down the stairs from Karen's old locker and out of the school."

"What's so weird about that?" Evan asked skeptically.

"There were no muddy footprints leading up to the fourth floor, and as far as I know, there is no mud on the fourth floor."

Phillip took a deep breath as he realized what Cooper was saying. "Karen's ghost made the footprints," he whispered, slowly turning to look at Evan.

"Ha! There could be several explanations for the footprints," Janelle challenged, not believing a word of the story.

"Like what?" Cooper spat. If it wasn't for Janelle, Phillip would be wetting his pants right now.

"Someone could have brought muddy shoes into the school, put them on and walked down from the fourth floor," Janelle suggested with a smug look on her face.

"Fine, don't believe it then, Janelle, but Evan, I would be careful. They never found Karen's body, and no one saw her leave. Her body could still be up there, rotting away." Cooper looked serious. "Karen is still up there all right, just waiting for the right moment to exact her revenge."

"I'll take my chances," Evan shrugged, sounding a lot calmer then he was feeling.

Swimmers in red warm-up suits started filing out from a doorway labeled "Visitors." They looked nervous as they scanned the impressive surroundings. One boy, distracted by the mural on the ceiling, tripped over a starting block.

"Boo! Boo!" students around Evan started to chant.

"Is this team supposed to be any good?" Evan asked Cooper as the last of the visiting athletes made their way onto the deck.

"The tall kid, over there in Radford red," Cooper said, pointing to a leggy boy, stretching on the side of the pool. "Is one of the best in the state. He has already been offered scholarships to several Ivy League schools. He will swim anchor in all the relays tonight."

"Anchor?" Evan asked, not familiar with the use of the term.

"Seriously?" Cooper asked.

"I've never been to a swim meet before," Evan admitted.

"What?" Cooper shouted. "Seriously, you've never been to a swim meet before? Where are you from, Mars?"

"Here we go again," Janelle apologized. "He is a little too obsessed with swimming and forgets that there are a few of us who just don't care about the sport."

"Don't care? Why am I sitting here with you? I can't believe this!" Cooper placed his head dramatically between his hands.

"Calm down, Cooper. Just because Evan doesn't know anything about the sport doesn't mean he's not going to be a fan. Give him a chance," Phillip encouraged, trying to make peace. "Think of this as a great opportunity to mold his opinion, before it is spoiled by Janelle's sour attitude."

Before Janelle could comment, the lights dimmed and beams of light shot around the room randomly until coming together to illuminate the entrance to the home team's locker room. The band started playing. The heavy beat of the drums challenged anyone in the arena to remain still.

The announcer's voice came over the speakers. "From the depths of the Atlantic Ocean. In a city buried in myth and mystery. Beneath the large ocean vessels and mighty sailors come a species of swimmers who defy all odds. Wellsford put your hands together to welcome your swimmers!"

The crowd erupted with cheers and whistles as the swimmers emerged from the dark tunnel. They were dressed in Wellsford blue warm-ups, walking out in a single-file line. Every athlete wore an expression of complete concentration and determination. Evan felt intimidated, and he wasn't swimming for the opposing team.

The boys team emerged first, led by two large kids who must have been seniors. They were followed by Brad and a line of other swimmers Evan had never met.

"They are coming out in order of greatness," Cooper explained.

"I'm surprised to see Brad so close to the front," Evan muttered, surprised that a freshman was so far up on the totem pole.

"Our team lost most of its good swimmers a couple of years ago. We won nationals that year and now our team is starting to rebuild. Brad is one of the best swimmers this school has seen in a long time. He is a natural."

Evan was about to ask another question when he saw Madison emerging from the dark. He froze, his mouth gaped open. She was in the number one slot. Even with a swim cap on, she still took Evan's breath away.

After all the swimmers had made their entrance, the music faded and the lights came back on.

"The men's 200 medley relay will begin in five minutes," the announcer stated.

Four boys in Wellsford blue removed their warm-up gear, revealing what looked like blue bicycle shorts.

"What's a 200 medley relay?" Evan asked, completely lost.

"Four different strokes, 50 meters each. Each stroke is performed by a different swimmer; backstroke, breaststroke, butterfly, and freestyle. The anchor and best swimmer will swim the freestyle. Evan noticed that Brad was one of the four swimmers getting ready.

"Is Brad the anchor?" Evan asked, hoping that he wasn't.

"No, John Weston is," Cooper motioned toward one of the tall swimmers Evan had seen exit first from the locker room. "He's the best we have this year, but Brad is closing in on him fast, even though he's a freshman."

The first swimmers from the two teams jumped into the water, turned and faced the pool wall grabbing hold of the handles on the bottom of the starting blocks. The crowd grew silent.

"Take your mark," came the voice of the announcer over the loud speakers.

The two swimmers lifted themselves out of the water and waited for the start. It felt like time stood still. The air was heavy with anticipation. A loud beep sounded, startling Evan, and the swimmers launched themselves with backward arching dives into the water.

The crowd erupted with cheers and Evan found himself on his feet with the rest of the school, cheering at the top of his lungs. Even Janelle was caught up in the moment cheering on the swimmers flying through the water. The crowd cheered louder as the swimmers made their first turn and sprinted to their waiting teammates at the opposite end of the pool.

A moan went out from the crowd as their Wellsford swimmer touched the wall seconds behind the Radford swimmer. The cheers for the next leg of the race were subdued as the Radford swimmer distanced himself even further ahead of the Wellsford swimmer.

Brad launched himself into the water a full three seconds after his Radford opponent, a tall muscular upper classman. Brad attacked the water, gaining on his opponent. The Wellsford student section went wild as Brad pulled himself seconds ahead of his opponent by the time he punched the wall releasing John, Wellsford's final swimmer. Evan continued to cheer, momentarily forgetting his grudge with Brad.

The freestyle of the last leg looked frenzied, legs and arms thrashing through the water. The Radford Ivy League bound swimmer was gaining on Wellsford's top swimmer and at the turn, John's lead had diminished. The spectators were going crazy as the two swimmers strained down the final stretch to get to the wall first, but in the end, Radford's swimmer moved ahead of John. Wellsford had lost the first race of the night.

"This is a major blow to Wellsford's chances," Cooper mumbled as he slumped down in his chair, looking depressed.

"The night is still young," Evan encouraged his sullen friend.

Cooper pulled a crumpled paper from his pocket and laid it out for Evan to see. It was his list of races and projected winners. He had a big question mark next to the 200 medley relay, which Evan guessed meant it was too close to call.

"Relays are worth twice the points. Losing that first race puts us at a big disadvantage," Cooper explained as he filled in points in the box next to Radford's name. "Dual meets are especially challenging. Normally, you have several schools competing at the meet, and the points are divided among them all. For the relays, however, you either get the points or you don't." He put the paper back in his pocket. "Hopefully the girls will do better."

Evan spotted Madison getting ready for the women's 200 medley relay.

"What about the girls relay team?" Evan asked, trying to hide his true interest.

"They don't have a lot of experience, but they are fast and should blow this race out of the water."

"Do they have any freshmen on the team?" Evan asked wanting to hear more, but not wanting to ask specifically about Madison.

"Madison Bates, the girl you saw in the lunchroom yesterday," Cooper pointed in her direction.

"Oh, Evan knows Madison," Phillip teased with a huge smile on his face, nudging Evan playfully with his elbow.

"You like Madison Bates?" Janelle asked, noticing Phillip's tone.

"I never said I like her," Evan huffed, disliking Phillip at the moment.

"You didn't have to," Phillip responded.

"I don't understand what guys see in her," Janelle sighed, unsuccessfully masking her jealousy.

"She's beautiful, smart, and is our school's best female swimmer," Cooper replied. "What's not to like?"

"Swimmers take your mark," the authoritative voice of the announcer interrupted the group's conversation, much to Evan's relief.

Two swimmers jumped into the water and pulled themselves into the ready position. Silence again fell over the crowd. Evan didn't understand why he felt butterflies in his stomach. He was sitting in the nose-bleed section, far above the action below.

The beep sounded. The two swimmers launched themselves backwards off of the wall.

The crowd cheered as the swimmers pounded the water. The Wellsford swimmer pulled ahead of the Radford swimmer by the first turn inspiring the crowd to cheer even louder. Everyone, except for the Radford fans were now on their feet willing their school's swimmer to the wall.

A huge cheer went up from the crowd as the Wellsford swimmer touched the wall a full two seconds before the Radford swimmer, launching the next Wellsford swimmer into the water with a sizable lead.

Even though the cheering continued, Evan could see that the Wellsford lead was diminishing with each subsequent leg. By the time Madison flew into the water from the starting block, her team was a full three seconds behind the Radford swimmer. The entire school was cheering not wanting to lose the second relay of the night. With every stroke, Madison cut the lead of the Radford swimmer. Evan had never yelled as loud as he was at that moment. With 25 meters left, Madison pulled even with the Radford swimmer. Evan thought the top of Atlantis was going to be blown off as the volume increased. Every person was cheering, all eyes glued to the two swimmers sprinting for the wall.

Time stood still as both swimmers reached for the wall. Evan looked at the judges for confirmation. It was too close to call. The suspense had silenced the crowd. Then the points were awarded to Wellsford and the student section went wild as Madison's teammates pulled her from the water, hugging her with excitement.

Cooper quickly took the score card from his pocket and awarded Wellsford their first points of the meet. Interest in the individual events that followed didn't match the excitement of the relays, but as the daylight faded from the sky above the peaceful Atlantic Ocean, the swimmers started prepping for the last races of the night. It was evident from Cooper's score card that the final two team freestyle relays would determine which school earned the victory.

The boys teams lined up first, and to everyone's surprise, especially Cooper's, Brad was in the anchor position and John had been moved to the third leg of the relay.

"A freshman in the anchor position? This is a first for the boys team!" Cooper exclaimed, surprised by the sudden change in lineup.

"The coach must have been unhappy about losing the earlier relay. It looks like John has been demoted," Phillip added, also surprised by the change of events.

The starting swimmers lined up on the blocks. The anticipation was killing the spectators. Evan was on the edge of his seat, taking in every moment. Win or lose, the coach was making a statement about the future of his swim team.

"Swimmers take your mark."

The buzzer sounded and the swimmers dove into the water. The teams were separated by only fractions of a second until John finished the third leg an entire two seconds ahead of the Radford swimmer. He was obviously trying to prove a point.

Brad launched himself into the water while the Ivy League boy from Radford watched in the ready position. At last, he too released from the starting blocks and began the chase. Slowly, he gained on Brad. The two swimmers pounded the water with everything they had.

As Brad made his last turn and headed for the wall, the Radford swimmer pulled even. Both schools were on their feet cheering loudly. The Radford swimmer started to fall behind, unable to keep up the pace and Brad beat him to the wall. Atlantis went crazy as the band struck up a version of "Another One Bites the Dust." Students jumped up and down yelling their congratulations to their team. The girls team still had their relay to swim, but the boys had pulled off the upset of the night.

The girls team won easily after an impressive swim, beating Radford by three seconds. The excitement of the meet was still fresh in the air as the students began filing out of Atlantis. Evan and his gang waited until the students had left before heading to their lockers.

"What a meet!" Cooper repeated over and over again.

"Are you all going to the dance?" Evan asked, as they left Atlantis.

"Attendance is mandatory!" Janelle reminded him with a look of disgust.

"You don't like dances?" Evan asked, innocently.

"You mean, do I like standing around waiting for a boy to get up enough courage to ask me to dance, while I sip punch and watch all the other girls compliment each other on how nice they look?" Janelle admitted, getting red in the face.

"Um, I didn't mean it that way." Evan stumbled over his words. "I guess I never thought of it like that."

"Janelle doesn't like not being in control of a situation," Phillip offered as the group exited Atlantis.

Evan left his friends at the lockers on the main floor and headed up the stairs to his own locker. By the time he reached the fourth floor, he was slightly out of breath and his thoughts were preoccupied with the dance.

Will I have enough courage to ask Madison to dance? Evan thought to himself.

The fourth floor was darker than usual without daylight filtering through the windows and only half of the fluorescent lights functioning. He could hear students on the floors below, but on his own floor, his footsteps echoed eerily as he walked briskly to his locker. Suddenly, he heard something scramble across the floor behind him and into one of the empty classrooms. Evan flipped around but didn't see anything except for the partially opened classroom door.

"The story about Karen was obviously made up," Evan reassured himself. "How could a girl simply vanish? It doesn't make any sense." He hesitantly moved toward the open classroom door to see what had made the sound. "It's definitely a story told to scare new freshmen students." He said to himself becoming less certain the closer he got to the classroom.

94

The door made a horrible screeching noise as he pushed it fully open. The partial light from the hallway illuminated the dark corners of the room. Besides some old desks and an upended chair, the room was empty. Evan looked around for what might have made the noise. Perhaps it was a mouse, or maybe a rat, but he saw nothing.

He quickly retreated from the room and headed back to his locker. He didn't want to be on the fourth floor any longer than he needed to. Fiction or not, the thought of a dead girl wandering the halls at night creeped him out. Evan fumbled clumsily in the darkness with his lock, his trembling hands trying to dial all three numbers.

"Why are my hands shaking?" Evan asked himself out loud, staring at his outstretched hands with disgust.

All he wanted to do was to grab his clothes for the dance and go. Evan prematurely stopped at 50 instead of 55 for the last digit and lifted the handle before he realized what he had done. To his surprise, the locker opened.

Not only is my locker on the haunted floor, but it doesn't even lock properly, he thought to himself as he threw his jacket into the locker, grabbed his clothes for the dance and headed to the restroom to change.

— ·· — ·· — ·· — ··

The familiar beat of one of Evan's favorite songs welcomed him as he descended down the last flight of stairs to the bottom floor wearing his light colored slacks and dark blue button up shirt.

At least good music is universal among teenagers, he thought as he walked into an extravagantly decorated ballroom. Why do I ever think anything is going to be normal at this school?

95

The already elegant ballroom, with its giant chandelier, masterful molding and giant fireplace with crackling fire left nothing more to be desired. There were tables and chairs set around the perimeter of the expansive room. Laid out on long tables next to the giant frost covered windows was a buffet decorated with several ice sculptures, a giant chocolate fountain, and an assortment of decadent foods and desserts.

At the front of the room on the stage surrounded by teenagers jumping up and down to the beat of the music was one of his favorite bands, not a cover band, but the real band!

"Didn't expect a live band?" Phillip asked as he walked up to Evan at the entrance of the ballroom dressed in a smart looking, grey suit

"No, I just didn't expect this particular band," Evan gawked. "How did they even get them to play at a school dance?"

"We have a great PTA, one with connections," Phillip answered as he nudged Evan with his elbow.

Evan hadn't eaten since lunch and the aroma from the food made his mouth water and his stomach rumble. Phillip led Evan to a table close to the succulent temptations where Cooper and Janelle were already seated. Cooper was sporting all the latest styles which put him somewhat over the top. He wore purple pants and a red sport coat. He was still talking to a disinterested Janelle about the more exciting points of the swim meet, as if Janelle hadn't been there.

Janelle didn't succumb to the social pressures of Wellsford by wearing a fancy dress. She wore a simple skirt and sweater and looked uncomfortable. Her hair was still tied up in a ponytail, but the ends had been curled slightly.

"The food looks great! Why isn't anyone eating?" Evan wondered out loud as he sat down next to Janelle.

"We can't eat until the swimmers arrive," Phillip explained as he rubbed his stomach.

As if on cue, the band stopped playing and the entire swim team emerged from the main entrance. Each swimmer from the boys team escorted a member of the girls team. The other students stood and applauded the victors.

No wonder Brad has a big head, Evan thought to himself as he saw Brad enter the room looking more pompous than usual, "The swimmers in this school are regarded as royalty."

Evan's hatred for the freshly-anointed best swimmer at Wellsford quickly transformed into jealousy as he noticed who Brad was escorting. At that moment, Evan wanted to be the boy he disliked more than anything. Madison's curled hair hung loosely around her shoulders. She wore a beautiful black formal dress, but it wasn't what she wore or how her hair was styled that attracted Evan. It was her smile, the way she lit up the room.

"You're drooling," Phillip teased as he slapped Evan on the back to bring him back to reality.

"Are you going to ask her to dance?" Cooper asked. "You only live once and you can bet that after Brad sees you dance with his girl you won't have much longer to live."

But it would be worth it, Evan thought to himself.

The band began playing one of their current hits. The room came alive with activity: kids dancing, while others heaped piles of food on their plates.

The night was almost over by the time the group finished what felt like a five course meal. Although most of the students had been out on the dance floor at least once, the four misfits stayed in their seats discussing school and making every attempt to keep Cooper away from the topic of swimming.

"One more thing about the meet..." Cooper started.

"Janelle, do you want to dance?" Evan asked out of desperation, not wanting to listen to one more swimming statistic.

Everyone at the table stared at Evan with shock, especially Janelle.

"Do you even know how to dance?" Phillip asked.

"Yes, I think so. My mom taught me," Evan said as he got out of his seat and walked toward Janelle.

Evan offered Janelle his arm, just like his mom had taught him, and he led her away from Cooper and Phillip who were still sitting at the table in total disbelief.

"I'm not a very good dancer," Janelle admitted, as they moved to the center of the dance floor.

"I'm not either. I just learned last night, but I don't think anyone is watching us." The music had slowed to a tempo that matched some of the steps he had learned the night before.

Janelle put her hands on Evan's shoulders and Evan put his hands on Janelle's waist. Awkwardly they started to move to the beat of the song.

"What do you think of Wellsford?" Janelle asked, trying to break the silence.

Evan realized how little conversation he had previously had with Janelle. They were always listening to dialogue between Phillip and Cooper.

"It's different than Colorado," Evan replied not wanting to go into the details.

"My family goes skiing in Colorado every winter," Janelle said.

Evan was dumbfounded. He had no idea Janelle skied. This girl was getting cooler by the minute.

"Did you ever go skiing in Colorado?" Janelle asked, as they started moving to the beat.

"Skiing was my life in Colorado! I skied on the school team and basically lived at the resort. My family had a house at the bottom of the main ski resort in Steamboat Springs."

"I've been skiing in Steamboat Springs. What a beautiful place! Did you know they have a cliff that skiers go down called Devil's Slide? Or maybe it was Devil's Chute? Crazy right?" Janelle smiled.

Evan had rarely seen Janelle smile. He didn't know if it was her smile or the fact that she had been to Steamboat Springs, but Evan hoped the song wouldn't end. They spent the rest of the dance talking about Evan's trip down Devil's Chute. The song ended too quickly and before he could ask Janelle for a second dance, she had already politely thanked him and walked back to the table. Evan, feeling awkward, walked in the opposite direction to get some punch. Halfway through pouring his drink he realized that he should have walked Janelle back to her seat. He turned abruptly, almost bumping into Madison.

Evan stood there silently, unable to move his mouth.

Madison started to move away. With considerable effort Evan regained control of his voice, "Amazing swimming today. That was my first swim meet."

"Thanks. Really? You've never been to a swim meet before?" she asked stunned.

"No, I grew up skiing. I can swim, but it's more like a dog paddle compared to what you did today," Evan admitted.

Madison laughed, and she blushed.

"This will be the last dance of the night," the leader of the band announced as the first chords of their current number one hit song commenced.

Madison and Evan stood there for a moment, until Evan spotted Brad heading in their direction. He didn't seem pleased that Evan was talking to his girlfriend. Without thinking, Evan blurted out, "Do you want to dance?"

Madison paused briefly, surprised by the sudden request, and then with a smile she agreed.

Evan quickly led her onto the crowded dance floor and away from the menacing Brad. As they disappeared into the crowd, Evan's heart pounded. He couldn't tell if it was from being with Madison or from knowing that he was going to have to answer to Brad as soon as the dance ended. When Evan turned to face Madison, he no longer cared about Brad. As they danced, Evan completely forgot about the other students and the band. He was only thinking about the most beautiful girl he had ever seen, and he hoped this moment would never end.

— ·· — ·· — ·· — ··

"You danced with Madison Bates?" Phillip repeated his question for the second time.

Evan had just thanked Madison for the dance and walked off the dance floor or maybe he floated back to the table where his friends were sitting. At that moment, his head was spinning and he couldn't remember.

"You do know that Brad believes she's his girlfriend?" Phillip asked with a look of terror in his eyes.

"Yes, I know," Evan shrugged, still thinking about the dance.

Evan looked at the clock on the wall and realized that his mom was probably waiting for him outside. "I've got to go. I'll talk to you later," Evan called over his shoulder to Phillip, Cooper and Janelle as he raced out of the ballroom and up the stairs to the fourth floor to get his school clothes.

Remembering that the lock was broken, Evan opened his locker door not bothering to put in the combination. He was about to grab his Wellsford jacket from the hook inside of his locker when he stopped. For the second time that night, Evan heard shuffling noises behind him. Slowly, he pulled himself out of his locker and turned around. Brad and two of his friends must have been hiding in the open classroom Evan had looked in earlier.

"Evening," Evan greeted, his voice much calmer than he felt. "Can I help you with something?"

Evan recognized Brad's friends. They swam on the swim team with Brad and were all freshmen. They were both bigger than Brad and therefore bigger than Evan. Caleb had black hair and dark eyes. With his size he could have passed for an adult except for his poor attempt to grow facial hair. A few long hairs grew on his chin and below his nose. Josh was a bit smaller than Caleb, but broader in the shoulders. He had blond hair and his ears and nose were large. When he smiled, which wasn't often, his lack of hygiene was evident by the food stuck in between his teeth.

They didn't answer Evan's question.

"Did you have fun at the dance?" Evan asked politely.

Brad looked menacing as the veins on his forehead pulsed. Instead of answering Evan's question he smiled slightly and then nodded his head. Josh and Caleb rushed Evan. Evan ducked Caleb's punch to his head but couldn't avoid Josh's punch to his stomach. Evan fell to the ground gasping for air. Brad's friends picked Evan up by his arms and held him as Brad walked closer.

"You think you are good enough to dance with Madison, Hero?" Brad hissed through his clenched teeth as he backhanded Evan across his face.

Evan had never been hit in the face before, and the blow was paralyzing. For several seconds Evan didn't say anything or look at his attackers.

"Answer me!" Brad yelled at Evan.

Evan raised his head and looked directly at Brad, his face only inches from Evan's. "I thought anyone with a boyfriend like you, might like a break from dull conversation," Evan countered as he spit blood at Brad.

Brad took a handkerchief from his pocket and wiped Evan's blood from his face. "Hold him tight," Brad told Josh and Caleb.

Evan was slammed up against his locker so that he couldn't move.

"Let me go," Evan shouted trying to free himself. It wasn't any use, Brad's friends were stronger than he was. He was not going to escape.

Brad hit Evan in the stomach. The pain was fierce and he couldn't breathe. Before he could recover Brad hit him again in the stomach. Evan wondered if he would ever be able to breathe again. As Evan's head fell forward, and he struggled to take a breath Brad hit him in the face and the back of Evan's head smashed into his locker. Evan fell to the ground as Josh and Caleb released him.

"I think you knocked him out," Evan heard Josh say.

"He's moving a little," Brad said in reply.

"Should we just leave him here?" Caleb asked.

Evan struggled with consciousness. Their voices sounded like they were coming from deep within a tunnel.

"Throw him into the locker," Brad ordered. "Someone will find him eventually,"

Evan felt Josh and Caleb grab his arms and push him into his locker. After Evan's back was shoved against the back wall of the locker, Josh and Caleb pushed his legs into the locker so that his knees were touching his slumped head. When they slammed the locker door shut Evan was trapped and very uncomfortable. His head ached and he felt dizzy. He tried to position his legs so that he could stand, but he was wedge into the locker so tightly that he could scarcely move.

The lights from the hallway filtered into the locker through the vents on the door, dimly lighting his surroundings. Evan looked for something to grab to help pull himself to a standing position so he could open the locker door, but his vision started to blur. Before long he felt as though he was engulfed in a thick fog and could barely see his knees inches in front of his face.

Evan closed his eyes.

"Relax," he said to himself. "I can figure this out."

Breathing became harder and his legs began to ache from his awkward position. Evan wanted to cry out for help, hoping someone, anyone would hear him and come to his rescue. A strange feeling overcame Evan. He couldn't explain what was happening, one moment he was pinned in his locker and the next he felt as though the locker walls, which had constrained him, had disappeared and he found himself lying on the ground. Evan felt a warm breeze on his face and the stale locker air had been replaced with the scent of pine trees. Evan tried to hold on to consciousness so that he could process what was happening to him, but his world began to spin out of control. As Evan lost consciousness he wondered if this is what it felt like to die.

Chapter Eight

A Bad Dream

Evan didn't know how long he had been lying on the ground, but he felt as though he were waking up from a deep sleep and he was struggling to remember where he was and how he had gotten there. Evan opened his eyes and had to squint as the bright sun shined down on him through the thick pine branches high above his head. He could hear birds singing in the distance and a stream babbling over rocks nearby. A squirrel squeaked a warning at an unknown danger in the distance. These were all familiar sounds to Evan since he had grown up in the mountains of Colorado. But why was he hearing them now, in the middle of winter?

Evan's eyes adjusted to the sun and he sat up. His head pounded. He touched the back of his head and found a small gash where his head had hit his locker. His head was covered in blood.

Evan's mind began to clear and he remembered the dance after the swim meet and the ambush by Brad and his goons at his locker. What wasn't returning, however, was the memory of how he had gotten here.

Evan looked at the forest around him, trying to see anything that might be familiar. Anything that might make sense. He was surrounded by pine trees as tall as any he had ever seen. The forest floor was covered with thick underbrush and green moss which grew on the rocks and tree trunks. He could only hear the sounds of the forest, no cars driving by on a nearby road or planes soaring above his head.

Evan stood up, and all he could see was forest in all directions.

"Is anyone there?" Evan yelled. His voice echoed through the forest scaring a few birds which flew from their branches.

"Anyone?" Evan repeated a little softer the second time.

Evan could only think of three possibilities for what he was experiencing. One, there was a very real possibility that he was dead. This thought terrified him so Evan quickly moved on to possibility number two. Hitting his head on the locker must have knocked something loose in his head. In short he had gone crazy. The thing was he didn't feel crazy, but maybe people who went crazy thought they were perfectly normal. Realizing that there was little he could do about options one or two, he moved on to option three. Maybe he was dreaming. This option was the most pleasing one to him, because if he were dreaming then he would eventually wake up and everything would be normal. Touching the gash on the back of his head once more he started to doubt that this was a dream. He had never felt pain in a dream before.

Panic hit him full force. Nothing was making sense.

Evan recklessly stumbled through the bushes toward the nearby stream. He fell to his knees on the soft sandy bank and splashed ice cold water onto his face, trying to wake himself from this nightmare. The water shocked him back to reality and helped clear his foggy mind, but he didn't wake up. He was still lost in a forest.

Defeated, Evan sat by the stream and watched a small fish fight the relentless current. Evan was dazed and confused. At one point, he looked for cameras, thinking this was a big joke. Maybe Brad and his friends were filming his breakdown to show the entire school at the next pep rally. But there were no cameras.

After several minutes of watching the fish Evan decided that he needed to do something. Sitting on the bank was not going to help matters. First thing first he needed to clean the blood from his hair. He removed his shirt, shoes and socks that he had worn to the dance. He hung his shirt from a pine branch and placed his shoes and socks next to a sun bleached log and waded into the stream. The small pebbles on the bottom of the stream bed felt nice between his toes as his shirtless back absorbed the sun's rays. Evan dunked his head into the water and began scrubbing the blood from his matted hair. He winced as he touched a large goose egg and the long gash on the back of his head, but the bleeding had stopped and the pain was diminishing.

As Evan pulled his numbed head out of the cold, clear water, he heard a twig snap. He froze. Evan strained to hear from which direction the noise had come. The snap echoed through the empty forest, and Evan guessed its origin was some distance away. Just as soon as the sound faded, another twig snapped and then another.

The forest was coming alive with new sounds. Something was moving fast through the forest. Evan stumbled out of the stream and jumped onto the sun bleached log to get a better view. He scanned the forest, but the underbrush was so thick that he had a hard time seeing anything. His eyes followed the sounds as it moved through the forest to a break in the underbrush. Evan saw a flash of what he thought was a rider on a horse, but before he could decipher more the underbrush swallowed them up again. There was another break, another flash and then nothing.

"Help! I need help!" Evan yelled.

The rider didn't stop. Panicked, Evan jumped from the log into the underbrush and sprinted to intercept the rider. The bushes tore at his flesh as he ran through the bushes without his shirt and shoes. Evan ignored the pain as he increased his speed. He had to get the riders attention. The rider was only twenty feet away now and still hadn't noticed Evan.

Evan abruptly broke through the underbrush and landed on a small trail just in front of the rider. Evan waved his hands high in the air in an attempt to get the horse to stop. Evan's sudden appearance on the trail and desperate waving spooked the horse. The giant animal skidded to a stop feet away from Evan. The rider almost fell over the horse's head. The horse then reared up on its hind legs. Evan fell on his butt to avoid being kicked. The rider lost his grip on the reins and fell hard on the ground as his horse ran away. The rider lay motionless in the center of the trail.

Shaking, Evan stood and moved slowly towards the fallen rider. He was lying on the ground face down. A jacket covered his head and Evan couldn't tell if the rider was young or old. He was smaller than Evan and wore dark pants and leather boots.

"Are you okay?" Evan asked.

The rider didn't answer.

Evan moved next to him and knelt. He then grabbed the rider by the shoulders and carefully rolled him over onto his back.

As Evan rolled the fallen rider over, he was surprised to see that he was actually a she and that she was staring at him with alert, blue eyes. What surprised Evan even more was that she held a knife which she pointed directly at Evan's stomach.

"Get your hands off of me or I will slice you wide open!" She ordered in a threatening tone.

Evan slowly moved his hands from her shoulders and held them defensively in front of him as he moved backwards.

"I'm sorry, I didn't mean to frighten your horse," Evan explained.

She stood and straightened her jacket, which looked more like medieval cloak. The girl's long brown hair was disheveled from the fall. Even though she was smaller than Evan, there wasn't fear in her eyes as she held the knife steady.

"Who are you?" the girl demanded.

Evan contemplated the question for a moment. He wasn't sure he wanted to give up any information before some of his questions were answered.

"Who are you?" Evan countered.

"I asked you first," the girl answered. "And besides I'm holding the knife."

Evan looked at the knife and then back at the girl. The dark pants and light shirt under her cloak, were not a style Evan expected to see in Rhode Island or this century for that matter.

"Where am I? And why are you dressed like that?" Evan asked ignoring her question.

"For someone without a weapon you ask a lot of questions," the girl said ignoring Evan's questions.

Evan stared at the girl amazed by her defiance even though he was bigger than she was. "My name is Evan," Evan conceded keeping his hands in front of him. "I'm sorry I didn't mean to..."

"Frighten my horse? You already said that," the girl finished. "Why would you jump in front of my horse, if your intention was not to frighten it?"

"I needed help," Evan said giving up on getting his questions answered. "I saw you riding past me and ran to catch you."

"Ran from where?" the girl asked.

"Through there," Evan answered as he pointed back towards the stream.

"What are you doing in the forest?"

Evan paused before answering. He had no idea why he was in the forest.

"Answer me! Why are you in the forest?" the girl insisted as she stepped forward, her knife still pointed dangerously at Evan.

"I don't know," Evan quickly answered as he took another step back.

"You expect me to believe that you don't know why you are in the forest," the girl said.

"It's the truth," Evan spat.

"All right," the girl answered cautiously. "How did you get in the forest?"

Evan lowered his head as if ashamed by his answer. "I don't know."

"How do you not know?" the girl asked.

"I don't know," Evan answered, once again feeling lost and confused.

The girl lowered her knife slightly. "Why should I believe you?"

"Because I'm telling you the truth," Evan stared at the girl. Even with the knife pointed at him, Evan couldn't help but notice how beautiful she was.

They stood there for a moment without saying a word, each daring the other to blink first. After what seemed like an hour, but was more like a minute, the girl slowly lowered the knife and put it back in the sheath under her cloak.

"I'm Emma," the girl offered.

Before Evan could respond, he was interrupted by two riders approaching quickly down the trail.

"Don't say anything!" Emma ordered as she turned to face the riders.

The horses skidded to a stop in a cloud of dust. Before the dust had settled the two riders dismounted, drew swords and moved towards Evan.

Evan began to back away.

"Who are you and what are you doing in the forest?" the larger of the two riders yelled as he approached Evan. He was taller than Evan and looked a few years older. He too wore a cloak. His hair was brown and his eyes dark. He moved with confidence.

Emma stepped in front of him, stopping him and the other rider abruptly. "Peter," Emma said. "His name is Evan. I think he's lost and needs our help."

The one Emma had called Peter looked at Evan for a moment and then back at Emma and then to Emma's horse some distance off of the trail grazing in the forest.

"How do you know this, sister, after spending only five minutes with him?" Peter countered.

Emma remained silent.

"Your cloak is dirty and your horse is in the forest over there. It looks like you were thrown from Smokey." Peter observed. "Did the boy have something to do with that?"

"Yes, but he was just trying to get my attention. He didn't mean to startle Smokey." she explained.

"Did he tell you that?" the younger boy asked.

The younger boy had jet black hair that hung loosely around his shoulders. He was about the same size as Evan, wore a cloak just like the other two and didn't seem to believe Emma's assessment of Evan.

"I can tell when someone is lying to me Alec," Emma answered as she stared at the smaller rider.

"You are naïve, little sister," Alec spat. "Do you think it is a coincidence that you found him in the forest on the night after someone broke into the castle?"

"I didn't find him, he found me." Emma countered. "If he truly was part of that, why would he find me?"

"Enough," Peter ordered.

"But," Emma started to say.

"Emma," Peter said as he held up his hand to silence her. "Alec get some rope."

Evan looked back in the direction he had come. If he ran, could he lose them in the forest?

Perceiving Evan's intent Peter stepped forward past Emma and pointed his sword at Evan. "Do what we tell you and you may live. Attempt to run and you have no chance."

Evan looked at Emma.

"It will be okay," she mouthed.

Alec brought forward a long piece of rope. "Your hands." Alec ordered.

Evan didn't move.

"Show me your hands," Alec ordered a second time.

"I didn't do anything wrong," Evan said, speaking for the first time.

"We will be the judge of that," Peter said. He stepped forward and roughly pulled Evan's hands in front of him.

Alec tied Evan's hands together and then gripping the other end of the rope, he got back onto his large black horse.

Peter put his sword back under his cloak and jumped onto a spirited white horse.

"I'm sorry," Emma whispered to Evan. She then called to her horse. Smokey trotted to Emma's side and nudged Emma with her nose. Emma jumped onto the grey horse. "Can't we at least let him ride back to the castle?" Emma asked Peter and Alec.

"The walk will be good for him," Alec said as he kicked his horse in the ribs. The black horse lunged forward and the rope leading Evan tightened before he had a chance to react. Evan was pulled off of his feet. For a moment he flew through the air. As gravity took control Evan's face smashed into the dirt. The stallion continued forward dragging Evan painfully over the rough trail for a few feet, before Alec pulled the animal to a stop.

"Sorry about that," Alec offered sarcastically.

"Alec!" Peter yelled in anger. "Do that again and you will walk and the stranger will ride."

Alec's grin quickly disappeared.

"Let's get moving," Peter called out as he nudged his horse forward.

Still looking back at Evan, Emma allowed her horse to follow Peter.

Evan slowly stood and spit dirt out of his mouth. He glared at Alec in anger.

Alec nudged his horse behind Emma's horse and Evan was forced to follow like a leashed dog.

Who were these people? Where were they taking him? Evan's confusion grew as he followed the horses down the dusty trail.

Evan's bare feet developed blisters within the first mile which made every step painful. His mouth was dry and still caked in dirt. He craved water. They crossed several streams of clear blue water as they traveled through the forest, but Alec never stopped to allow Evan to drink. Relentlessly he was dragged forward not knowing when they would stop or where they were going.

Evan breathed heavy as they climbed a grassy hill up and out of the dense forest. As far as Evan could tell the forest had been deserted. There were no buildings, no sounds signifying civilization and no people.

"Keep up," Alec yelled behind him as the rope leading Evan tightened again when Evan started to lag behind.

"Maybe if you slowed down," Emma pleaded. "He's been walking for miles."

"He'll survive," Peter called back. "Emma, ride ahead and tell Captain Curtis we are bringing a visitor."

Emma looked at Evan with pity and then kicked her horse into a full gallop up the hill and out of site.

Evan struggled to put one foot in front of the other. He needed a break, but knowing that Alec and Peter would never allow such a request he kept his mouth shut. As they moved up the hill, more of Evan's surroundings became visible. Evan hoped that he would recognize something, anything, but as his view improved, a feeling of hopelessness overcame him. The forest was surrounded by giant cliffs which rose from the forest floor like a natural, impenetrable wall blocking out the outside world. Directly ahead of them the cliffs disappeared and Evan could see water as far as the eye could see. He breathed in salty air and realized that they were close to the ocean.

Evan looked out in the direction of the ocean and saw a giant valley filled with pine trees and farmland. In the center of the valley, surrounded by the cliffs on one side, was a deep blue lake which sparkled in the sun. In the center of the lake a solid rock island jutted up abruptly out of the water. Perched on top of the rock island, as if molded out of the hard rock, was a majestic castle whose stone walls and towers reached towards the clouds. The castle's dark rock glistened and reflected off of the motionless water below. A bridge towering above the water connected the castle to the pine covered shoreline. Nestled in the pine trees was a quaint village. The buildings of the village were painted various colors and stood close together lining a street which wound along the shoreline. Smoke rose peacefully into the sky from their steep roofs. Evan could hear people in the village below. The sight of the medieval castle and village were the last things Evan would have imagined to see as he emerged from the forest.

Evan's panic continued to grow again. He had to get away from Alec and Peter. He had to figure this out on his own.

The rope tightened again and Evan was jerked forward.

"Keep up," Alec called back annoyed as he readjusted himself back on his saddle. Evan's weight had pulled Alec back on his horse.

Alec was growing tired and Evan noticed that he was holding the rope loosely in one hand. If Evan could provide enough force, he was sure Alec would drop the end of the rope or be pulled off his horse. Once free, Evan could run back into the forest. He wondered if he could outrun the horses through the thick underbrush. He wasn't sure, but he needed to try.

As Alec's horse passed a large pine tree on the side of the trail they started their descent from the top of the hill. Evan quickened his pace towards Alec's horse to allow the rope between himself and Alec to slacken just enough for Evan to run around the pine tree. Evan hoped that the rough bark of the tree on the rope would help him hold his ground. If not he would be whipped around the pine tree and fall back onto his face in the dirt.

"Giddy up," Evan yelled at the top of his lungs in an attempt to startle Alec's large black stallion.

The yelling worked. The stallion leaped forward. Evan dug his feet into the soft pine needles. The rope snapped tight. Evan held his position with all his strength. Alec was caught completely off guard and thrown backwards off of his horse. He hit the ground with a loud smash, and the force knocked the rope from Alec's grip and in an instant Evan was free.

Evan turned and ran. Peter reacted quicker than Evan thought possible and urged his horse in Evan's direction as Evan bolted back towards the forest dragging the rope behind him. He could feel Peter's horse racing after him. He wasn't sure how close Peter was, but he knew he couldn't stop. He had to reach the trees.

"Stop," Peter ordered.

Evan did not stop. The trees were close. He was certain that if he could reach the trees he would lose Peter in the underbrush. Just as the trees were within reach, Evan was struck from behind with such force that he was thrown forward. For a moment he believed he was flying down the steep hill but then he crash landed face down on the trail. It took several seconds for the dust to settle around him. He heard Peter dismount behind him. Evan tried to roll onto his back to defend himself, but before he could move he was struck again. The pain was excruciating and Evan blacked out.

Chapter Nine

Amnesia

The stone ground on which Evan sat was cold and hard. He adjusted his position slightly to ease the pain from sitting on the unforgiving surface and noticed that the small room seemed to be chiseled out of a rock face. It was empty except for a small wooden bucket in the corner. Evan determined from the awful smell that is must be a latrine. His only connection now with the outside world was through a small barred opening in the solid wooden door blocking the exit out of his new prison. Evan had no idea how long he had been out or where Peter and Alec had gone. He was even more confused now than he had been in the forest. None of this made sense.

The room was dark and musty. Very little light filtered through the opening in the door. He was sure he had suffered a concussion. Evan stood and looked out through the barred opening in the door.

The outer room was lit by a flickering torch. A man sat outside of his door. He wore some sort of armor and a sword in a leather scabbard strapped around his waist.

Evan shivered as he rubbed his bare feet trying to encourage circulation.

The stagnant air of his room, penetrated to his core, and with no blanket or shirt, he felt more vulnerable than ever before. Evan was not sure how long he had been unconscious and since the dungeon had no windows, he had no idea what time of day it was. He was thirsty and hungry and wondered if this rock prison was to be his tomb.

Evan sat back down in the unfamiliar darkness and thought about his family and the worry that they must be feeling. He imagined his mom's panic when he didn't show up after the dance. Had she called the police or tried to search for him on her own? He imagined Brad and his friends laughing to themselves as the police searched.

The door to the outer room burst open surprising Evan. The man guarding Evan's room must have been surprised as well because Evan heard him fall out of his chair and quickly get to his feet.

"Where did you find him?" a low raspy voice inquired that Evan did not recognize.

"By the falls," Peter, the young man Evan had met earlier, answered.

"And you said the boy told Emma that he didn't know why he was in the forest," the man asked in the low raspy voiced.

"That's what Emma said, but I don't believe him," Alec said. "How can he not know why he is in the forest?"

"I agree," the man said. "He is obviously hiding something."

Evan stood and moved to the door as quietly as he could and peered past the iron bars into the small exterior, dimly lit room. The man with Peter and Alec was huge. He had arms bigger than Evan's legs and almost no neck. His bushy beard hid most of his face and he had a large, jagged scar near his right eye. His brown unruly hair was long and curly.

Although significantly larger than Peter, he listened intently, nodding every so often. Evan wondered if this was the man Peter had sent Emma to fetch, the one Peter had called Captain Curtis.

117

Without warning Alec turned around quickly, as if sensing Evan staring at him through the bars and looked directly at Evan. Evan ducked below the iron bars, feeling stupid for having done so. They obviously knew he was in the room. After all, they were the ones who had tossed him in there.

Slowly, he backed away from the door and waited in the corner of the cell. Evan had to find some way to protect himself. He didn't want to be caught off guard again.

The only object in the room was the bucket. Evan rushed to the opposite corner of the room and picked up the soaked wooden latrine. He almost as quickly threw it back to the ground. An awful smell emerged from its depths. Turning his head away from the stench, Evan held firmly to his only weapon and waited.

The whispers stopped, and Evan heard movement in the direction of his cell. He stood ready for the attack. He knew he couldn't take on the entire lot with the bucket, but if he could just take down one of them, he would fulfill some of his vengeance.

They were at the door. Evan heard a key turning in the rusted lock. There was a click and then nothing. His arms ached as he held the bucket cocked ready to throw.

The door flew open and light from the torches flooded the cell. Evan was blinded by the light. His eyes struggled to adjust. He couldn't make out a single target, only blurred figures moving through the opened door. Evan launched the bucket in the direction of the door as hard as he could, hoping to find a mark. The shadows in front of him cursed and darted to the side of the small room to avoid the flying object. Evan missed. The bucket smashed to pieces as it hit the far wall with a loud crash.

Evan ran for the door.

The blurred figures rushed towards Evan, he was only inches from freedom. He was going to make it. Just as he reached the doorway he was hit across his chest by someone's extended arm, the contact stopped the movement of his upper body, while his legs continued forward. Evan left the ground momentarily, as his body flipped in the air. He didn't know which way was up and which way was down, until his back smashed into the hard ground, knocking the wind from his body.

The bearded man grabbed Evan by the hair and pulled him to his feet.

"Try anything like that again, boy, and I will make sure you never see the light of day again," the man said in a deep, threatening voice as Evan struggled to free his hair.

"Alec, bring us a rope. I don't believe Evan is going to come willingly," Peter ordered, as he picked himself off the floor, brushing off his cloak.

Evan's eyes slowly adjusted to the light of the outer room. The man removed his arm from Evan's chest but still held his sword threateningly at his side, daring Evan to try anything. Peter walked towards Evan. When only a few feet away Peter stopped and looked Evan up and down, as if sizing up his prisoner. "Put this on," he commanded, thrusting a dirty shirt in Evan's direction.

Evan stared at the shirt. He did not want to take anything from his captors, but still shivering from the cold of the rock room, he quickly swallowed his pride and put on the shirt which was at least two sizes too big.

"Turn around," Curtis ordered as soon as Evan had finished dressing. When Evan didn't respond, the man roughly turned Evan around and then yanked Evan's arms behind his back.

Alec walked into the cell carrying a rope. He glared at Evan with dark menacing eyes. Evan stared back, anger burning inside. Alec threw the rope to Curtis, his eyes never leaving Evan.

Evan would have continued the foolish staring contest, had Curtis not cinched the rope tightly. Evan closed his eyes against the discomfort at having his arms yanked behind his back.

"Time to go," Curtis announced as he pulled Evan to his feet. "Move!" Curtis shoved Evan forward signally to Evan that he should follow Peter and Alec.

They climbed a steep circular staircase out of the depths of the rock prison.

The fear of not knowing where he was being led terrified Evan, but at least he was no longer in his cell. The air around him warmed as they wound up the staircase. They passed a guarded, thick wooden door and entered a long hallway built of stone. Evan wondered if they were in the castle he had seen from the hill top, but with no windows he couldn't tell for sure.

The group walked in silence for several minutes down dark passageways and through stone archways, their footsteps echoing off of the stone walls. Peter and Alec led them into a cathedral style room. The ceiling towered above their heads and was held up by giant stone pillars. The room had small windows and was lit by several torches which hung from the wall. At the head of the room was a large stain glass window which depicted God sitting in heaven, handing a brightly lit object to a king on earth. Evan assumed the object was symbolic of something, but had no idea what.

Evan's gaze was drawn from the glass to Emma who was speaking with a man and woman sitting on thrones at the head of the room. Emma had changed out of her pants and cloak, and was wearing a beautiful blue dress. Adding to Evan's confusion Emma was wearing a small gold crown on top of her braided, long brown hair. She looked up from the man and woman and managed a slight smile at Evan as the group approached.

The man and woman stood and Emma moved to the woman's side. Evan assumed the man was a king by the gold crown on his head. Evan had never seen a king before but had always pictured kings to be lazy, fat slobs who fed their appetites on the back of the peasants. At least that is how kings were always portrayed in movies. This man however was none of those things. He wasn't wearing a robe and was not fat. The king before Evan wore a simple shirt and pants. He was tall and strong. His long brown hair was streaked with gray and hung down to his shoulders. His eyes were a bright blue just like Emma's. At his side the man wore a sword with a gold hilt which reflected the light from the torches. The woman at his side was beautiful. She looked a few years younger than the man. She wore a silver crown and a dress much like Emma's with a black cloak around her shoulders. Evan noticed that she had the same brown hair as Emma, braided in the same fashion. It was then that Evan realized that Emma must be the man and woman's daughter. This meant that Peter and Alec were their sons.

Curtis pulled Evan to a stop. No one spoke.

"On your knees," Curtis whispered forcefully. Evan didn't understand. "Knees, now," Curtis said a second time. Evan still didn't respond. Curtis kicked the back of Evan's knees and Evan fell to the ground in pain.

Curtis, Peter and Alec kneeled as well before the king and queen. When they stood as the king motioned for them to stand, Curtis put his hand on Evan's shoulder and forced him to remain kneeling.

"Is this the boy?" the King asked in a calm tone.

"Yes. Your sons and daughter found him in the forest yesterday," Curtis answered.

"Alone?" the man asked.

"We didn't see anyone else," Peter responded.

Evan was growing frustrated, but after his experience with Curtis in the dungeon, he decided it was better if he didn't speak.

"You believe he was part of the attack last night?" the King asked.

"What other explanation do we have?" Peter answered. "He was in the forest the morning after the attack. That can't be a coincidence."

"Did he say why he was in the forest?" the Queen asked.

The captors went silent for a moment before Emma spoke, "He told me that he was lost and that he didn't know where he was or why he was in the forest."

"Why try and escape if you are innocent?" Alec asked. "Innocent people do not run."

"Maybe it is because you were dragging him to an unknown place for a reason you didn't think to explain," the King said. "Did it occur to you that he might be frightened?"

"Frightened or not we still don't understand why he was in the forest. No one has ever got to The Ledge without being detected. There is no way down the cliffs and the gates are guarded." Peter explained.

"Emma told us that he made himself known to her in the forest. That he was not trying to hide," the Queen said. "If he were the person we are looking for, why would he do this?"

Alec and Peter remained silent.

"Boy, what were you doing in the forest?" the Queen asked in a soft, but forceful voice.

Evan didn't know what to say. He couldn't tell them about Wellsford Academy or that the last thing he remembered was being thrown into his locker by Brad and his friends. He couldn't tell them that he thought he was losing his mind and that none of this made sense.

"Well?" Curtis said as he smacked Evan on the back of his head. "You were asked a question."

The Queen raised her hand, "Captain Curtis give the boy a moment. He has obviously been though an ordeal."

Finally, Evan decided to answer truthfully, "I don't know where I am or how I came here. I don't know why I was in the forest." Evan paused, wondering what to say next. "Waking up on the ground in the forest is the first memory I have." Evan intentionally left out some important details.

Evan sensed she was not completely satisfied with his answer, but she didn't push further.

I'll let them draw their own conclusions, Evan thought to himself as he fidgeted, the pain in his knees starting to intensify.

"Does he have other injuries not inflicted by us?" the Queen asked, looking sympathetically at Evan.

"He had a large knot and gash on the back of his head when we found him," Peter stated.

"I wonder if he's lost his memory," the Queen speculated, as she looked up at the King standing by her side.

"It wouldn't be the first time we have had this happen in our kingdom," the King agreed.

"What is your name?" the King asked, as he looked back at Evan.

"My name is Evan Myers."

"He had no weapons and was not hiding his presence in the forest when he called for your help," the King said. "I don't believe he is part of the group we are looking for." The King then turned toward Curtis. "Take Evan to the dorm. He can stay with the other orphans, until we can figure out who he is and from where he came."

Curtis grabbed Evan's arm and without saying a word pulled him to his feet and away from the others, towards the back of the room.

The dorm? Orphans? Where was Curtis taking him? Evan's head was spinning out of control, he wanted to scream out. He wanted to ask them where he was, or where his family was, but he stopped himself. An outburst like that might land him back in the dungeon. He needed time to figure out what was happening. He just hoped he hadn't gone completely crazy.

Chapter Ten

See What He Knows

As soon as the large doors slammed shut, the King sat down on his wooden throne. "Peter, where in the forest did you find the boy?" the King asked.

"Near the falls, father" Peter responded.

"Did you notice anything else when you found him?" the Queen quickly asked.

"No, just the boy," Alec answered.

"Remember, we didn't find him, he found us," Emma said looking annoyed.

"By startling your horse and knocking you to the ground if I recall," the King finished.

"You could have been seriously hurt," the Queen said with concern.

"But I wasn't," Emma shot back. "He said he was trying to get my attention and I believe him" Emma finished.

"You would believe a traveling sword salesman selling wooden swords claiming they were made from fine steel," Alec said mockingly.

"Enough," the Queen scolded. "Emma, it could be that he is telling the truth, but it could also be that he is lying. Until we know for certain we must be careful where we place our trust."

"I don't trust him," Alec said. "No one has made it onto The Ledge without being detected for over 20 years. And now two appear in one night! I find it difficult to believe that they aren't the same person.

"I don't trust him either, Alec," the King said. "I believe there is something he isn't telling us. But until we know what that is, we must see what he knows."

"How do we do that?" Alec said in a huff. "If he's lost his memory, he won't know anything."

"Perhaps," the Queen said as she too sat down on her throne. "He did know his name. Maybe with time he will remember more."

"I don't like it," Peter said. "We should throw him back in the dungeon until his memory returns. That way we can be sure he won't cause any trouble."

"Not everyone is trying to cause trouble Peter," Emma said. "Have you considered that he is simply lost?"

"Maybe," Peter conceded.

"How do we find out what he knows?" Alec asked.

"Take him to warrior training with you this afternoon. I would like to know what he is capable of," the King said.

"We can't just let him wander the village unsupervised," Peter said.

"I can look after him," Emma said.

"No!" the King ordered. "You are still too young, besides Rosalina will look after him."

"I am almost of age," Emma argued getting angry. "I am more capable than you think."

The King looked at Emma for a moment. She had turned into a beautiful young woman and would be performing the Crossover next year, but she still had a lot to learn.

"It is not about capability Emma," the King said calmly. "It is about responsibility. It is not your responsibility to look after the boy. You have your own responsibilities to attend to," the King responded.

"Besides I think it would be good for Alec to help out with Evan as needed," the Queen added.

"I don't have time to babysit!" Alec complained. "The Crossover is only a few months away. I need to prepare."

"You weren't that busy preparing yesterday when I caught you sleeping in the stable," the King reprimanded. "You can spare a few days. If he doesn't amount to anything when you test him then you can leave him with the other orphans."

"What if he does show himself capable of what happened last night in the castle?" Peter asked.

"Then we'll throw him back in the dungeon," the King stated as he dismissed his sons and daughter.

— ·· — ·· — ·· — ··

The King and Queen sat in silence until the outer door slammed shut.

"Alec needs to learn tolerance," the King said to the Queen as soon as they were alone.

"He will," the Queen replied as she placed her hand on the king's. "Give him time."

"How is it that you have more patience with my sons than I do?" the King asked.

"I've helped raise them for the past 16 years. In some ways, I feel like their mother," the Queen responded. The Queen paused for a moment and then asked. "Do we know yet if Damian was behind the attack last night?"

"We may never know. The man disappeared before we could ask questions," the King admitted.

"Do we know what he was after?" the Queen asked.

"Captain Curtis spotted him before he could advance far enough into the castle to take whatever he might have been after, but we can assume he knows the kingdom's secret," the King said as he let out an exhausted sigh slouching back into his throne.

"But the only people who know are the ones who have completed the Crossover and they are sworn to secrecy? How could he have found out?"

"I don't know," the King responded. "But we have to assume that someone else knows our secret."

Chapter Eleven

The Dorm

Captain Curtis led Evan out of the grand hall and into the courtyard of the castle. The warmth of the sun felt nice on his shivering body. Evan's arms were numb from being bound behind his back and his mouth was bone dry from the lack of water. What he wouldn't give for a cold glass of water.

Giant oak trees stood in the courtyard of the castle blocking most of Evan's view, but through the thick branches he caught glimpses of giant, stone walls and towers high above his head. Evan's suspicions had been right. They were in the castle he had seen from the hilltop. Two soldiers walked passed, dressed in armor, swords hanging at their sides. They addressed Curtis as "sir" before continuing down the path.

Captain Curtis led Evan through thick wooden doors and a giant stone archway and onto a bridge which led to the village Evan had seen on the shore of the lake. Evan looked down at the dark blue water of the lake a hundred feet below the bridge and then back in the direction they had just come. The castle was even more impressive up close. The walls of the stone fortress were at least 15 feet thick at their base and rose 80 feet above his head. Evan doubted an invading army would ever penetrate its walls. Evan peered beyond the castle to the giant cliffs towering above the lake and the castle, acting as a natural barrier to protect the people who lived here. It was no wonder they were suspicious of Evan. There was no possible way that he had gotten past the cliffs and into the forest. There had to be an explanation making this nightmare possible, he just couldn't fathom what that might be.

Evan stepped off of the bridge and into a bustling medieval like village. The town should have been a tourist haven with its small shops and narrow cobble stone streets, but Evan couldn't see any tourists snapping shots of the picture perfect views. People dressed in simple clothes walked down the street with purchased goods in their arms. Small children played a game in front of a candle shop which was nestled between a shoe shop and a stable. The scene in front of Evan reminded him of a postcard he had once seen of an old town untouched by time in the European mountains. The breathtaking view of the quaint village on the pine covered hillside and the castle perched on its rock island in the middle of the lake almost caused Evan to collapse from information overload. He staggered a little as he searched for something familiar.

"Keep moving," Curtis ordered. "I don't have all day."

Dazed, Evan continued forward.

"Who do you think he is?" whispered a plump woman to the man beside her.

"I don't know," the man answered.

"Did you see how he is dressed?" another woman asked her friend.

"Is he the boy they found in the forest?" a third person asked.

A group was forming as people stopped to watch Evan being led down the road. Captain Curtis didn't seem to notice or care.

"Why is that boy tied up?" a small child with a dirty face inquired.

"Just keep walking," the mom answered, as Evan passed her.

Captain Curtis slowed his pace as they neared a three story white building with dark wood trim. Colorful flowers grew in garden boxes below the windows of the building adding to its rustic beauty.

"This will be your new home for the time being," Captain Curtis said as he pushed Evan into the front door of the building. He then pulled out a knife.

"No! What are you doing?" Evan shouted as he spotted the knife and backed up against the wall.

Curtis quickly moved forward and grabbed one of Evan's arms. "Hold still," Curtis ordered as he spun Evan around. In a single motion he cut the rope binding Evan's hands together.

Evan winced as he rubbed his wrists, trying to induce circulation back into his numb hands. He felt foolish for having thought Captain Curtis was going to stab him. Evan avoided eye contact with Curtis, who was shaking his head in disapproval.

Evan looked around the room in which they were standing as Curtis picked up the pieces of rope. There was a small fireplace and a large rug covered the wood floor. A single window looked out in the direction from which they had just arrived. Evan heard footsteps and muffled voices coming from the floor above them.

"Where are we?" Evan asked.

"The Dorm," Curtis answered. "Personally, I think you should be thrown back into the dungeon or sold you to the first fishing vessel leaving The Ledge, but the King and Queen believe otherwise."

Before Evan could ask another question a plump, smiling woman entered the room. "Who do we have here?" she asked. The woman was shorter than Evan, wore a simple dress and had long brown hair that almost reached the floor.

Captain Curtis turned to the woman and smiled, which Evan thought looked very unnatural. "Good morning Rosalina," Curtis said.

Rosalina blushed and Curtis seemed to have forgotten about Evan completely as they stood awkwardly for several seconds. Then Rosalina smiled at Captain Curtis slowly bringing him out of his trance.

"Oh, yes, this is the boy Alec and Peter found this morning in the forest. The King and Queen think he has lost his memory."

"Oh, my!" she gasped, staring at Evan. "Why, he is a complete mess! Only skin and bones!" she observed. "Wherever he comes from, they obviously didn't feed him well." At this point she had walked in a circle around Evan, assessing his condition. "He will need new clothes, his are," she paused for a moment, as if searching for words that wouldn't offend Evan, "very dirty, yes we must burn, I mean wash these at once."

"Evan, this is Rosalina. She looks after the orphans. It is one of her many duties and you must follow every instruction she gives you."

"Is he to stay here?" Rosalina asked.

"Yes, until we know for certain from where he came," Curtis answered.

"Well then, Evan climb the stairs and turn to the right," she said pointing to a narrow staircase. "You'll find a trunk up there with clothes. Change and come right back down."

Evan didn't move, he was still very confused.

"We can't have you walking around the kingdom in those clothes, now can we. Up the stairs with you now," Rosalina encouraged him with a broad smile as she pushed Evan in the direction of the stairs.

Evan heard hurried footsteps leading away from the top of the stairs. Someone was upstairs. Evan wondered if others had been brought to this place as well. Maybe there would be someone upstairs who he knew.

"You have no idea where he comes from?" Rosalina whispered to Captain Curtis as Evan moved up the stairs.

Evan stopped for a moment to hear Captain Curtis's reply, but he had taken Rosalina's arm and moved her to the other side of the room, so they could talk without being heard.

— ·· — ·· — ·· — ··

The top of the stairs intersected a long hallway lined with doors on either side of the stairs. Following Rosalina's instructions, Evan turned to the right and instantly spotted the large trunk at the end of the hall. He walked to the trunk and opened the heavy lid, revealing clothes of different sizes and colors. He had just removed a pair of light colored pants when movement in a neighboring room caught his eye. Evan looked beyond a partially opened door next to the trunk and saw nothing but heard whispering again. Another door down the hallway opened, startling Evan and causing him to drop the lid. The loud bang echoed down the hallway. Several boys younger than Evan came running out of the rooms, talking excitedly with one another and then disappearing down the stairs, not paying Evan any attention.

"A little bit jumpy, aren't you?" someone asked from inside the room next to the trunk.

Evan didn't answer. Were they talking to him?

"Yes, we are talking to you. We saw you come in with Captain Curtis a few minutes ago." the person inside the room said.

Evan peered into the room.

"See, I told you Ansel. The criminal was outside of our room," said a boy lounging on one of the three beds inside the room, his arms behind his head. The boy looked to be about Evan's age, but he was taller and skinnier than Evan. His hair was bright red and freckles covered his face.

The other kid in the room, the one the freckled kid had called Ansel, chuckled and pointed at the pants Evan held in his hands. Ansel was a stocky kid with short brown hair.

"Why are you laughing?" Evan asked the big kid.

"You like to wear small pants," Ansel asked with a thick accent as his chuckles turned into a booming laugh that filled the room.

Evan looked down at the pants he had taken out of the trunk. They were at least three sizes too small and would have worked better as shorts.

Evan tossed the pants back into the hallway. "Why do you think I'm a criminal?" Evan asked, ignoring Ansel.

"You had your hands tied behind your back when Curtis brought you in here," the boy with freckles answered. "It doesn't take a genius to know what that means. You have to tell us what you did to get your hands tied behind your back."

"It was all a misunderstanding," Evan replied.

"A misunderstanding?" the freckled kid asked skeptically. "Must have been some misunderstanding."

"You could say that," Evan replied not wanting to try and explain something that he didn't understand to someone he had just met.

"By the way I'm Francis," the red haired boy offered. "And the chubby kid over there, that's Ansel. He likes to laugh, but he doesn't mean any harm."

"I'm Evan," pausing for a moment he remembered what Captain Curtis had mentioned downstairs about Rosalina looking after the orphans. "Are you orphans?"

"They like to call us that," Francis answered with an annoyed look.

Ansel started laughing again. "Orphans? We are not orphans," Ansel said.

"Always laughing." Francis sounded irritated. "They like to call us orphans because our families aren't here with us. I'm from a kingdom up the river."

"And you?" Evan asked, looking over at Ansel.

"I'm from the North where men are large," Ansel flexed his muscles.

Evan turned to face Francis, "Why did you come here?"

"To learn," Francis said simply.

"To learn what?" Evan asked, confused.

"My father sent me here to learn how to grow food, so that we have enough food to eat and more to trade. Ansel is here to learn how to fish. All of the orphans come to The Ledge to learn something to help their kingdoms."

"The Ledge?"

"That's what they call this kingdom," Francis answered.

"But why come here?"

"The Ledge is different than other kingdoms. Great minds come here to share ideas and learn."

"But, what makes The Ledge different?" Evan asked.

"It is protected by the cliffs that surround it, so they don't have to worry about being attacked. And there are the docks in the bay, two hundred feet below the village."

"The docks?"

"That's what they call the busiest port in the region. It resembles a village with ships tied to the floating dock." Francis answered. "If you haven't seen it, I'll show it to you tomorrow. A giant wheel, that turns by the force of water as it falls from the cliff down to the bay, carries goods up the cliffs, and to barges waiting at the top to transport goods inland."

Evan pictured a wooden Ferris wheel powered by water but couldn't imagine something so sophisticated in his current surroundings.

"That's why they have time to learn and share their ideas, they don't have to spend their time and resources worrying about being attacked," Ansel added.

Evan sat down on one of the empty beds, a sick feeling forming in his stomach. The Ledge didn't sound like any place he had ever heard of before. Where was he? And more importantly, how was he going to get home?

"Don't worry," Francis said, noticing Evan's panic. "This place overwhelmed me as well when I first got here. You'll get used to it."

"Time to go boys, you don't want to be late," Rosalina interrupted as she came into the room holding a small loaf of bread and glass of water.

"How did you know I was hungry?" Francis said, eyeing the bread.

"This is for Evan," Rosalina turned towards Evan. "Who hasn't changed yet," she added as she waved the loaf of bread disapprovingly at Evan.

"Sorry, I forgot," Evan apologized.

"All is forgiven," Rosalina said. "It's your first day. Just don't go learning bad habits from these two. Of all my orphans, these two need the most help, eat the most food and get into the most trouble."

"Our kingdoms aren't as civilized as yours, we just don't know how to act," Francis commented, sarcastically.

"Get dressed and get to class," Rosalina directed as she handed the loaf of bread and glass of water to Evan and then quickly exited the room.

"Class?" Evan asked.

"Yes. All orphans have to attend classes. For most of us, that is the sole purpose for us being on The Ledge. Get dressed, we'll wait for you downstairs," Francis and Ansel disappeared out the door.

"Are you going to eat all of the bread?" Ansel asked, sticking his head back into the room.

"Ansel," Francis called after him.

"What, I don't want it to go to waste if Evan can't finish it."

Evan broke off a piece of the bread and threw it to Ansel.

"I knew we were going to get along," Ansel mumbled, filling his mouth with the bread.

Chapter Twelve

Warrior Training

Evan's new pants were tight, his shirt large and apparently only royalty wore shoes on The Ledge at this time of year; not that there were any to choose from in the trunk anyway. Evan's bare feet were killing him, but regardless of the pain, he followed Francis and Ansel down the narrow streets of the village to a large, stone building. The building was larger than the other buildings in the village and, instead of being built of wood like some of the other buildings, this building had thick stone walls and stood four stories tall with several large windows overlooking the large lake. Evan paused for a moment before following Francis and Ansel. This building was on the outskirts of the village, next to the thick forest. Evan noticed a trail which disappeared into the forest beyond the village.

Should I follow them inside, or make a run for it, Evan thought to himself. He looked into the forest and wondered if anyone would notice him slip into the trees. But where would he go? He had no idea where he was, where home was, or how he was supposed to get back there. He needed more information before he left. He would have to stay with the other orphans for now. Abandoning his escape plans, Evan followed Francis and Ansel into the building.

"I'll see you later," Ansel called as he headed to a far corner of the room, where a group of kids were tying what looked like a fishing net.

Evan stayed with Francis. The building was one large room with towering ceilings, like the room where Evan had been questioned earlier that morning. Children and adults sat in small groups scattered around the room. As Evan moved deeper into the room, he passed bookshelves filled with old books and scrolls. He saw some tables covered with vegetable plants and others on which sat glass vases full of dead snakes and frogs soaking in colorful substances Evan didn't recognize.

"Why does an apple fall from a tree but float when you throw it into water?" a short, chubby bald man asked a small group of children who were sitting on a rug by the entrance of the building.

"I have no idea why an apple floats. Do you?" Francis whispered to Evan.

Evan thought about this for a moment and believed he did know the answer, but before he could reply Francis grabbed his arm and pulled him deeper into the room.

They passed another group of children who were learning how to speak a language that Evan had never heard before. Other children were being taught sewing and others ship design. But in the center of the room Evan's eyes fell on a large rock the size of a car, perfectly round, sitting on a large stone pedestal. Evan pulled away from Francis.

"Where are you going? Class is this way." Francis called after Evan.

"I'll catch up in a minute, I have to see something," Evan answered as he moved closer to the rock. He could see intricate carvings on its surface. It looked like the globe Evan's family had in their home library, but it was much, much larger.

139

Evan searched the rock for some understanding as to where he was. The carvings on the surface of the rock resembled Europe. He expectedly followed the contour of the rock to the other side, where North America should have been, but the surface was smooth, as if nothing existed there.

"Amazing, isn't it? You know, most people still believe the world is flat."

Evan turned around and found himself staring at the Queen.

Never having been around royalty before Evan wasn't sure if he should bow or maybe kiss her hand. Scenes from movies he had seen about the dark ages flashed through his head, but nothing helped so he simply stood there staring at her.

"Did you locate your home on our rock?" She asked, walking back toward the completed portion of the globe.

"Um, no," Evan admitted.

"No matter," the Queen assured him. "Not many people have seen a map, let alone a map like this one."

"Why aren't there any carvings on the other side of the rock?" Evan blurted out.

The Queen paused for a moment contemplating Evan's question. "Our explorers haven't sailed beyond that point," she replied, pointing to an island, some distance from the mainland. "I suppose, eventually, we will find out what's on the other side." She eyed Evan curiously. The Queen then walked closer to the rock and pointed to a small kingdom on the coast of a large island.

Evan looked closely at the kingdom. "The Ledge," he read out loud.

"Yes," she confirmed. "That's where we are."

Evan felt light headed again as he looked at the island the Queen was pointing at. He placed his hand on the rock to steady himself. How could that be possible? There was no way he was on the other side of the world! This had to be a dream. A very bad dream.

"Are you okay?" the Queen asked with concern as she watched Evan's skin take on a greenish tint.

Evan couldn't breathe, it felt like the room was shrinking.

"Sit down," the Queen instructed.

Evan felt the Queen help him to the floor. Moments later she was handing him a wooden mug full of water. The water helped to clear Evan's head, but the confusion lingered.

"Head injuries are hard to understand," she reassured soothingly, pausing for a moment as if wanting to say more. She reached up and touched the rock tenderly, lost in her own thoughts, and then finally, she continued, "You need to give your head a chance to heal, perhaps then you will remember your purpose for being here."

"Purpose?" Evan repeated, confused.

"I believe everything happens for a purpose, even if we don't know yet what that purpose is." The Queen quickly withdrew her hand from the surface of the rock and helped Evan back to his feet. "Your class is the last group at the end of the room. Take it slowly, join the class when you are ready." The Queen then disappeared leaving Evan confused and still a little shaky.

Evan found his class at the end of the room. There were ten kids sitting on a rug in a half circle facing an elderly man with a long, white beard.

"Ah, yes, our new student," the old, hunched man, greeted Evan as he approached the group of students. "Alec told us your," the man paused, stroking his long beard, "peculiar story," he finished with a smile.

"Please take a seat. Our discussion was just getting interesting."

Evan sat down in the only open seat on the carpet between the orphan Francis and Emma. Emma managed a slight smile in Evans direction, but then focused her attention back to the old man in front of the class before Evan could smile back. Francis leaned over to Evan.

"I had no idea, you had lost your memory and that they found you yesterday in the forest. That's very mysterious," Francis whispered.

"The problem stated on the wall behind me is one of the great mathematical mysteries of our day," the teacher instructed, motioning to a large parchment hanging on the stone wall in front of the class. "You see, problems that at first seem extremely difficult, can be dissected into basic mathematical problems which can be solved by someone with simple training. The skill of simplifying difficult, sometimes impossible looking problems into something most anyone can solve, is what separates the great mathematicians from everyone else." The old man chuckled to himself at something only he thought was funny as he removed the parchment, revealing several simplified equations. "Who would like to solve the first equation?" he asked excitedly.

Evan looked down, hoping the teacher wouldn't call on him. To his relief, almost every hand in the class went up. The teacher pointed at Emma. She jumped to her feet excitedly and ran to the paper hanging on the wall. Within a few minutes, the problem had been solved, and Emma returned to her seat looking very pleased with herself. Each following equation was solved by a different student until only one equation remained.

"Why don't we let our newest student solve the last equation?" Alec said with a smirk.

"Excellent idea," the old man agreed, as he leaned on a crooked cane.

A pit formed in Evan's stomach. The entire class was looking at him.

"You can do it," Emma whispered encouragingly.

"I hope she's right," Francis said as he scratched his head in confusion. "Because I'm completely lost."

Evan stood up and walked hesitantly to the parchment. The old man handed Evan something that resembled a pencil and smiled. Using all of his mathematical skills, Evan tried to rearrange the symbols to solve for the unknown. He struggled for the longest five minutes of his life, unsuccessfully trying several different methods he had learned in school.

"Can anyone help Evan solve the problem?" the old man finally asked the class.

Alec stood up and walked to the front of the class before the teacher could call on another student.

"Well, at least we know that wherever you came from they didn't believe in teaching their children how to think," he hissed in Evan's ear.

Scratching out Evan's work, Alec solved the equation in a matter of seconds using a method so simple that Evan felt foolish for not having thought of it himself. Alec returned to his seat with a triumphant look on his face.

The old man moved in close to Evan so that the other students couldn't hear. "You have learned how to memorize, that much is clear. Now all we need to do is teach you how to think," the old man said, pointing to Evan's head.

The old man reposted the parchment with the original equation on the wall next to all the equations the class had just solved as Evan took his seat.

Some students gasped, while others chuckled at the man's cleverness.

"Interesting isn't it, that all the equations had the same solution." The teacher remarked, chuckling again as he revealed the punchline to his earlier joke.

Evan's classmates talked excitedly with one another as the simplifications were revealed.

"I think that is quite enough for one day. Our discussion will resume tomorrow," the man concluded as he removed the parchment from the wall and rolled it up, placing it on a nearby shelf.

"Don't feel bad. It was definitely one of the hardest equations," Emma tried to reassure him.

"I'm glad they didn't call on me I had no idea how to solve the equation," Francis admitted.

"Alec didn't have any problem solving the equation," Evan said.

"Well, he is one of the smartest kids on The Ledge," Emma replied.

"And he's not shy about showing it is he?" Evan said in frustration.

"He's not as bad as he seems," Emma said trying to downplay Alec's behavior.

"You need to choose your company better Emma," Alec said as he walked up to his sister.

"You need to mind your own business," Emma shot back to her brother.

"Not as bad as he seems?" Francis said in a mocking tone.

Emma smiled weakly, but didn't try to defend Alec again.

"Let's go orphan," Alec ordered.

"Go where?" Evan asked, wanting to stay with Francis and Emma.

"Our next stop in trying to figure out which backwards kingdom you come from. Warrior training."

"Are you coming?" Evan asked Francis.

"Orphans are not welcome at warrior training," Alec rudely remarked before Francis could answer.

"Aren't I an orphan?" Evan asked.

"You sure are," Alec said. "But today we are making an exception for you, not for him," Alec said pointing at Francis.

"Don't worry about it, Evan," Francis said. "I need to head to the fields for my next class. I'll see you later back at the dorm."

"Let's go, orphan," Alec said to Evan as he walked away.

"I'll meet you there," Emma said. "Good luck."

"Why do I need luck?" Evan asked, but Emma had already turned and walked away.

—— · —— · —— · ··

Alec was silent as he led Evan down the main road of the village and then onto a trail leading into the forest. The pine covered trail reminded Evan of Colorado. The longer this hallucination lasted, the more real it became. All he wanted to do now was to return to the dorm, fall asleep and hopefully wake up in his warm bed back in Rhode Island.

"Come on! Keep up with me!" Alec yelled back to Evan, who was starting to lag.

Walking without shoes through the forest, was painful and slow. Evan tried to pick up the speed, but it just hurt worse.

"Go ahead, I'll catch up in a minute," Evan said as he plopped down on a large log on the side of the trail.

"Don't be long. Captain Curtis doesn't like to be kept waiting." Alec shouted as he disappeared around a bend in the trail with little concern for Evan.

Evan raised his foot to examine the painful blisters that had formed on its bottom. He wasn't sure how much farther he could walk. For several minutes he sat wallowing in self-pity, listening to the sounds of the forest and trying to make sense of his situation when he heard someone whistling a happy tune. The whistling grew louder until Evan noticed an old, skinny man with unruly, long white hair hobbling down the trail towards him, a large sack slung over his shoulder. The man stopped whistling when he saw Evan rubbing his foot.

"What brings you so far into the forest? Aren't orphans supposed to stay in the village?" the old man commented as he neared Evan.

"How do you know I'm an orphan?" Evan asked.

The old man sighed and dropped the heavy sack to the ground as he stopped in front of Evan. "I know everyone on The Ledge," the old man stated matter of fact. "And, since I've never met you before, I'm guessing you're the boy they found yesterday, the one who has lost his memory."

"Who are you?" Evan asked.

"Just an old shoemaker," the man answered as he took out a handkerchief and wiped sweat from his brow. "But most of the orphans call me Gramps."

"Why do they call you Gramps?" Evan asked.

"Oh, I suppose it's because I'm old," Gramps chuckled to himself. "But, you didn't answer my question," Gramps said as he eyed Evan suspiciously.

"I'm going to warrior training?" Evan answered.

"That's interesting," Gramps commented.

"What's interesting?" Evan asked.

"Nothing really, except that orphans aren't usually allowed to attend warrior training. I wonder why they invited you?"

That comment worried Evan. Why was he being allowed to attend warrior training when all other orphans weren't?

"No matter. What was your name again?"

"It's Evan."

"Well, don't worry Evan. Things will work out for you," Gramps said as he reached into his bag and pulled out a pair of old leather shoes.

"How do you know things will work out for me?" Evan asked, feeling more and more overwhelmed.

"Because they worked out just fine for the last person who showed up on The Ledge without their memory or their shoes," Gramps explained as he threw the old pair of shoes to Evan. "These should fit you."

Evan stared at the shoes for a moment, not saying a word, as he thought about what Gramps had just said.

"They are not much but my homemade sap mixture in the bottom of the shoes will mold to your feet and should help ease the pain from the blisters." Gramps said as he heaved the heavy bag back onto his shoulder.

"Thank you," Evan said as he watched the old man take a few steps down the trail. "Did you say that someone else was found on The Ledge without their memory?" Evan asked.

"And their shoes," Gramps added with a hint of laughter in his voice. "But that was a long time ago Evan and it's not my story to tell."

Evan watched Gramps hobble away for a few moments before blurting out, "Can we talk again, sometime?"

Evan had to know more. For the first time that day, he felt a glimmer of hope. The question stopped the shoemaker. For a moment Gramps said nothing. Whatever he wasn't willing to tell

Evan now, might later help Evan figure out how he had arrived in the forest.

"If you wish, you may visit me for tea in the evening. It does get lonely in the forest from time to time," Gramps admitted as he continued to hobble down the trail.

"You live in the forest?" Evan asked, surprised.

"My home is just past that clearing," Gramps pointed around the next bend in the trail. "By the way, your warrior training is just over that hill. Just follow the creek, you can't miss it."

"Thanks again for the shoes," Evan yelled as Gramps disappeared around a bend in the trail while Evan tried on his new shoes.

— ·· — ·· — ·· — ··

Evan recognized several students from class, but no one would return his gaze as he entered a large clearing which was mostly dirt with a bit of long green grass around the edge. Thirty kids of various ages stood in small groups around the clearing talking among themselves.

At least I'm not late, Evan thought to himself.

He was about to move to the far edge of the clearing, where he hoped not to be noticed, when a giant figure blocked his path.

"It's nice of you to finally join us," Captain Curtis boomed, staring at Evan with a cold, emotionless expression. "You will fight first," he ordered. "Anyone want to volunteer to fight our guest?"

Alec stepped forward before the other students could process the question. Evan wondered if this had been planned.

"I volunteer," Alec responded with a wicked smile.

"Excellent," Curtis said. "It's time we find out what you are capable of, orphan."

Curtis wanted Evan to fight Alec, to demonstrate what Evan knew. The problem was, he didn't know anything. He had only been in a couple of fights in his entire life, once in middle school and another one more recently with Brad in the lunch room. One of the other students in the class stepped forward and handed Evan and Alec wooden staffs about five feet long. Evan stared at the piece of wood, panicking, as he tried to remember every Kung Fu movie he had ever seen, for any hint of what to do with the weapon he now held in his hand.

"Right then, are you both ready?"

Evan looked past Curtis at Peter who had just entered the clearing. Had he come to see the fight? Evan wondered as Alec slowly nodded his head confirming that he was ready for the fight to start. Evan didn't nod or blink for that matter. He hoped that if he didn't acknowledge Curtis, the fight wouldn't start.

"Go!" Captain Curtis shouted as he backed away.

The sudden command caught Evan by surprise. He hadn't even raised his staff when Alec attacked. In one fluid motion, Alec jabbed the staff up under Evan's ribs, knocking the wind from his lungs. Evan doubled over in pain. Alec turned his body in a circle, gaining momentum with his staff outstretched, until it connected with the back of Evan's knees. The blow crumpled Evan's legs, and he yelled out in pain as he fell to the ground. Alec backed away from his victim, basking in the cheers from his fellow classmates. Evan lay on the ground gasping for air, his entire body trembling with pain. Evan eyed the crowd of onlookers. Most of them were encouraging Alec to finish Evan, others were looking away from Evan, not wanting to watch the beating he was receiving. Then Evan noticed Emma who had just walked into the clearing. Their eyes locked for a moment. It seemed that she was trying to offer support to Evan with her large blue eyes. Evan didn't want to look away from her, but Captain Curtis appeared over him.

"Had enough?"

Evan glared up at the smug man in anger, "NO!"

With a smile Curtis moved back from Evan.

Using the staff to help balance himself on his wounded legs, Evan stood and faced Alec again.

"You don't know when to give up, do you?" Alec taunted as he turned from his cheering friends to face Evan again.

Evan felt the blood rush to his head as he stared at Alec's cocky grin. He had no idea how he had ended up here in the dark ages. But he did know one thing for certain, he was going to knock Alec's head off!

Evan charged Alec, without thought or strategy. He raised his staff over his shoulder, like he had been taught to do with a bat in little league baseball, and then he swung the piece of wood as hard as he could at Alec, who was still standing in the same spot, obviously not expecting Evan's sudden attack. But Alec hadn't been fooled. He judged Evan's swing perfectly, simply side-stepping beyond Evan's reach and avoiding the blow. Evan's mighty swing missed, throwing his body slightly off balance and leaving his right side completely unguarded. Alec took full advantage of the situation and attacked viciously. Evan lost track of how many times Alec struck him, but within seconds, Evan was lying on the ground again, blood gushing from a cut above his eye and what felt like a cracked rib.

"Very good, Alec," Captain Curtis complimented, clapping his hands together slowly. He then bent down next to Evan, resting his hands on his knees. "First lesson, never attack out of anger." Curtis then stood up and walked towards the class, who were staring at

Evan with looks of pity on their faces. "That's what happens when you don't train properly."

Evan started to stand, but the awful pain from his cracked rib forced him to sit back down.

Captain Curtis turned back toward Evan and noticing his condition, ordered in a frustrated tone, "I need a volunteer to take Evan back to the village. We all know orphans aren't allowed at warrior training and Evan should not be here anyway."

There was silence from the class, as they all stared down at the beaten stranger, avoiding eye contact with Captain Curtis. Whether they felt pity or disgust, Evan couldn't tell.

"I will," Emma volunteered.

The kids in the clearing were silent as Emma walked over to Evan and handed him a piece of cloth from her pocket.

"But only if it's okay with you, Peter," she offered, looking past Curtis to the older prince.

Peter simply nodded his consent.

"You don't have to. Really, I'm fine," Evan said, trying to salvage what little dignity he had left.

"I know, but I want an excuse to get out of my lessons early," she whispered to Evan.

Emma reached her hand towards Evan. He wanted to tell her he didn't need help again, but the simple act of raising his hand up to meet hers required more effort than he thought possible.

"Press the cloth to the cut above your eye, and the bleeding will eventually stop," she instructed as she took hold of his arm and slowly led him away from the clearing.

They made their way toward the village following the same pine covered trail Evan had traveled earlier. The shadows were getting longer as the sun moved lower in the sky. Evan let out a deep sigh of relief as they reached the top of a small hill. They both paused for a moment looking out over the large lake next to the village, the tallest tower of the castle perched on the rock island in the middle of the lake was bathed in the sunlight. The scene might have been peaceful had Evan not been in so much pain.

"Do you need to rest?" Emma asked, as she helped Evan over to a large log.

"Thanks," Evan mumbled sheepishly as he sat upon the log, thankful for the rest. He removed the blood soaked cloth from his head. The bleeding had indeed stopped. Pain shot through his body every time he moved, but eventually he was able to find a somewhat comfortable position on the log.

"You weren't part of the attack on the castle two nights ago were you?" Emma asked, sitting next to Evan on the log and looking out over the lake.

"Is that what this was all about? They wanted to see if I could fight? They wanted to know if I was telling the truth?" Evan questioned, his anger starting to build again.

"Well, yes," Emma responded a little defensively. "But they believe you now. No one with any training would have taken that kind of a beating. Why else do you think they let me walk you back to the village? You are obviously not a threat to our kingdom."

Evan's pride deflated. She was right. His anger was quickly replaced by hopelessness. He didn't belong in the kingdom. He missed his family more than he ever had before. He had no friends, no way to get home and none of the skills that would help him survive. Confused about how he had ended up in this place and exhausted by the day's events, Evan looked out towards the lake in silence.

"Why are you helping me?" he asked, seeking clarity as to why she would go out of her way to befriend him.

Emma stood up and took a couple of steps away from the log, rubbing her hands nervously together. "Years ago I found myself in a situation where I felt alone just as you do right now. Someone helped me when I thought all was lost and that's why I want to help you."

"And I suppose you are going to teach me how to fight?" Evan asked with a smirk, looking at the petite girl in front of him.

"That and so much more," she responded with determination in her eyes.

Chapter Thirteen

Emma's Book

Evan stirred in his bed, his blanket pushed down by his feet as a result of the hot, humid night. It was late summer, almost five months since Evan had found himself on The Ledge, and Evan couldn't wait for cooler weather to arrive. He looked out of the window of his room, which he shared with Francis and the northerner Ansel. The stars were already starting to fade as the early morning sun began its ascent into the light grey sky. Reluctantly, he slid his feet onto the hard ground as he stretched his stiff body. Evan quickly dressed and walked over to Francis. The skinny red haired boy was still fast asleep on the opposite side of the room.

"Wake up," Evan whispered, not wanting to disturb Ansel.

Francis simply turned over and mumbled something about needing more sleep. Evan and Francis had been roommates since the beating Alec had given Evan over four months ago. Since Evan's poor performance in warrior training, he was no longer considered a threat to the kingdom and had been living with the other orphans ever since. Life as an orphan was not that bad. Evan attended class every morning and evening where he learned everything from mathematics to how to grow crops. After class he worked in the fields to earn his keep. He came home tired every night, but Rosalina always kept him and the other orphans well fed. Emma had remained true to her word and trained Evan every morning before class. He had learned how to fight, shoot and ride. Everything a boy his age needed to know to survive on The Ledge.

Evan shook his friend more forcefully. "Come on, get up! You don't want to keep Emma waiting," Evan smirked.

Although they had never discussed it, Evan knew Francis liked Emma. Whenever she spoke to him, his face reddened, matching the color of his hair.

"I'm up. I'm up," Francis moaned, slowly sliding his skinny frame out of bed. His long red hair, covered half his face. He rubbed the sleep from his eyes, as he glanced annoyingly at Evan. His freckled-covered face peered out the window as he sighed. "Okay, I'm ready. I'm ready," Francis finally announced with a huge yawn.

Ansel stirred, snorted and then fell back asleep.

Evan looked sternly at his friend, reminding him to be quiet. They didn't want the other kids in the dorm knowing where they went every morning.

"The building could be falling over and Ansel wouldn't wake up," Francis snorted, disappearing out of the doorway.

Evan followed his friend through the darkness towards the kitchen.

"My two favorite orphans," Rosalina greeted, not looking up from the pot she was stirring.

The kitchen had a fireplace with a large black pot suspended over a meager fire, an oven made of thick brick where Rosalina cooked delicious bread and cakes and a large table where the orphans ate all of their meals.

"Have you been cooking all morning?" Evan asked, noticing all of the dirty pots lying around the kitchen.

Rosalina looked up with a big smile, flour covered her face. "It's what I live for."

"And we are grateful for it," Francis commented, as he grabbed a piece of bread from the table and stuffed it into his mouth.

For a skinny kid, Francis could eat more than any of the other orphans, including Ansel, who must have weighed twice as much as Francis.

"You just missed Emma," Rosalina announced.

Evan and Francis exchanged concerned looks. "Emma who?" Evan asked.

Rosalina looked up from her pot with a smile. Evan wasn't fooling anyone, especially not Rosalina. She had become a second mom to Evan in the absence of his real mom.

"Big plans today?" Rosalina asked, grabbing a piece of bread for herself as she sat down at the table.

"We're heading out to the forest for some more training," Evan replied.

"I thought orphans weren't supposed to train," Rosalina stated. "Or go into the forest."

"I haven't seen any rules against teaching ourselves," Francis responded.

"And not going into the forest is more of a guideline then an actual rule," Evan added.

"Training on your own then?" Rosalina inquired, raising one of her eyebrows questionably.

Evan coughed hard, a large piece of bread had lodged in his throat as he inhaled quickly. Rosalina knew exactly who was providing their training.

"Don't worry, my dears. Your secret is safe with me," Rosalina assured with a wink as she got to her feet and returned to the pot of boiling water suspended in one of the large fireplaces.

With full stomachs, the two boys ran through the darkness of the dense forest on a familiar trail that they both knew by heart, having traveled it many times throughout the summer. Evan smiled to himself as he raced along through the forest. It was no longer painful to run long distances, and in fact, Evan looked forward to racing down the pine-covered trails early each morning. Whatever body fat Evan once had was long gone and had been replaced with muscle, and he could feel himself getting stronger every day. His hair had grown as well over the summer months and soon would reach his shoulders. He still often thought of his family and his last day at Wellsford Academy. But his situation didn't make any more sense now than on the first day he had arrived on The Ledge, so instead of dwelling on what he couldn't explain, he tried to make a life for himself on The Ledge.

The sun finally peeked over the tall cliffs, and the early morning forest greeted them with sounds of birds singing and babbling water of the creek. Evan increased his speed, wanting to beat Francis for the first time. Ever since Emma had promised to help Evan they had been meeting every morning in the forest before classes. Emma taught him everything from how to ride a horse to how to shoot a bow. She taught him how to think and solve problems, the customs of The Ledge, and anything else she decided to prepare for their lessons. Evan looked forward to his time with Emma and found himself thinking about her during the day. Two months into the training Evan was asked to bring Francis as a sparring partner to give Evan someone else to fight besides Emma. Evan liked Francis, but he missed his time alone with Emma.

Evan increased his speed with the clearing in view, Francis' long legs kicked into gear, out striding Evan and leaving him behind again.

"Beat you again!" Francis huffed, falling to the green moss blanketing the forest floor.

"Yeah but just because you have freakishly long legs," Evan teased, as he bent forward, his hands resting on his knees.

The small clearing stood at the edge of a deep pool of water fed by a small waterfall tumbling down the large cliff. Grazing at the edge of the forest was Smokey, Emma's beautiful, smoke-colored horse with a long dark mane and tail that almost reached the ground. The horse snorted loudly, signaling to Emma, who was sitting on a log reading a book, that they had company

"About time you got here. What took you so long?" Emma asked as she closed the book.

"We don't have a horse, remember?" Evan joked.

"What are you reading?" Francis asked as they neared Emma.

"Just a book," Emma responded, avoiding the question, as she laid the book down on the log.

"It must not be a very good book," Evan toyed, eyeing Emma suspiciously.

"Why do you say that?" Emma asked defensively.

"Usually when you're reading a book, you can't wait to tell us about it, but with this book you say, 'Ah, it's just a book.'" Francis answered, doing his best Emma interpretation. "What's the big secret?"

"It's nothing really. It's just a book that's been in my family for years, sort of like a journal."

"Everything is in there? Your family's entire history?" Francis inquired, excitedly.

"Well, not everything," Emma shrugged, looking a bit disappointed.

"What do you mean?" Evan asked. "What's missing?"

"Does it talk about the Crossover?" Francis asked, before Emma could answer Evan.

Emma looked up at Francis, startled. "What do you know about the Crossover?"

Francis, looked away from the book. "Oh nothing I, I just heard some of the other kids talking about it."

"What's the Crossover?" Evan asked, confused.

Emma gave Francis a suspicious look and then looked back at Evan. "Every year, children, who are of age, are given the opportunity to perform the Crossover."

"Like a test?" Evan asked.

"More like a rite of passage into an elite group," Francis responded. He obviously knew more about the Crossover than he was letting on.

"There's no elite group or rite of passage," Emma shot back defensively. Completing the Crossover charges that person with a great responsibility to The Ledge and our people."

"Responsibility and secrets known only to the chosen," Francis added. "Does it talk about the secrets in your book?" Francis moved towards the book, which Emma picked up and held protectively in her arms.

"It's not for you to know," Emma snapped defensively.

"Why? Because I'm an orphan? Because I wasn't born on your precious Ledge?" Francis asked, raising his voice.

Evan quickly stepped between Emma and Francis, "You're out of line, Francis."

Francis and Evan stood inches apart, tension building. Evan tightened his fists. He had never seen this side of Francis before, and he didn't like it.

"You're all the same," Francis hissed at Emma.

"What's that supposed to mean?" Emma asked.

"You know exactly what that means! You think you're more righteous than the other kingdoms. Better because you know more. Well, I have news for you! You're just as messed up as the rest of us!

"Francis that's enough!" Evan repeated.

"And you," Francis pointed at Evan. "You defend them, but you're like me. They will always treat you as an outsider. Don't fool yourself Evan, you will never be one of them." And with that Francis turned and disappeared into the forest.

"What was that all about?" Evan asked, scratching his head.

"He's just echoing the hatred of his father's kingdom," Emma admitted, as she placed the book back on the log.

"His father's kingdom?"

"Yes, and every other kingdom, who believe we are hiding secrets from them."

"Why would they think that?"

"I don't know," Emma answered honestly. "Maybe it's because we don't usually allow anyone to participate in the Crossover who wasn't born on The Ledge."

Disappointment spread across Evan's face, which he quickly hid from Emma's view by turning towards the forest. Evan wasn't born on The Ledge. Maybe Francis was right. He would always be an outsider.

"Well, regardless, I've lost my training partner," he murmured, turning back towards Emma.

"No matter." Emma picked up the book and walked over to Smokey. She carefully placed the book in a satchel which hung from the saddle.

"How will I get better?" Evan asked, not understanding her lack of empathy.

Emma walked back to Evan and standing close to him, she looked up into his eyes. "You've learned faster than anyone I know. It's not just your skill, but your instincts."

"My instincts?"

"Yes, you're ready."

"Ready for what?"

"Just promise to meet me at warrior training this afternoon."

"Warrior training? You know they don't let orphans near warrior training because they don't want us to learn how to fight the way you do."

"Today is different. It's not normal warrior training. Everyone is invited." Emma took Evan's hand in hers. "Please, you have to promise."

Evan would have agreed to anything with Emma holding his hand. "Okay, I'll be there."

Emma lingered for a moment, neither wanting to move. Feeling neglected, Smokey moved her large head between Evan and Emma, forcing them apart. They both laughed.

"I want to tell you thanks," Evan said. "Without your help, I'm not sure where I would be right now."

"It's something I needed to do." Emma answered.

"But why? You told me someone helped you when we first met, but you never told me the story."

Emma walked over to the log and sat down.

"I haven't told anyone that story. Sometimes I think the person who helped me didn't exist at all since I have never seen him since."

"What do you mean?"

"When I was a little girl, my mother took me down to the docks on a summer day to get material for a dress. She instructed me to sit down on a bench as she talked with the shop owner. After a few minutes of looking out of the shop windows at the ships, the temptation became too strong for an adventurous little girl and I slipped out of the shop to bask in the sunlight. There were new and interesting sights and smells and before long I had completely forgotten about the shop, my mother and her instructions. I wandered out onto one of the smaller piers leading into the city of docked ships. The pier was busy with men loading heavy bundles of goods onto the giant ships. Being young, I quickly became engulfed in the crowd, moving further and further out into the bay on the small docks which looked like floating streets.

After some time, I remembered the instructions my mother had given me and decided to return to the shop, but the giant ships towering above my head blocked my view, and I couldn't decide which direction would lead me to the shops and which direction would lead me further into the bay and further away from my mother. Finding a pile of bags out of the way of the busy sailors, I sat down and began to cry.

I don't know how long I was there, but I remember a woman touching my trembling hands and asking me if I was all right. She was kind and told me she wanted to help. I was young and scared, and I believed her. She led me onto the deck of a nearby ship, with the promise that it would improve our view to help find my mother, once on the ship she grabbed my arm tightly. I told her she was hurting me. She tightened her grip. By the time I realized what was going on, the woman had pulled me down into the hull of the ship. I screamed and struggled, but it was no use. The thick wooden hull of the ship masked my screams from the sailors on the floating dock and any hope of rescue. She locked me in a dark room in the depths of the ship and left me alone. I remember hearing men moving on the deck, preparing the ship for departure. I looked for a way to escape, but it was useless. I finally resolved to sit in the corner, and I began to cry."

Emma stopped for a moment, wiping tears from her eyes. Evan wanted to say something comforting, but nothing seemed appropriate, so he waited for her to continue.

"I was terrified that I would never see my family again, but then when I thought all was lost, the lock on the door turned and an old man entered the small room. I don't remember much about the man, but I do remember how old and frail he looked. He spoke to me as if he knew me, calling me by name, but I had never met him before. He told me to come with him and that he would return me to my mother. I quickly agreed, not wanting to stay in the depths of the ship a minute longer.

My hand in his, he led me to the deck of the ship, where a burly sailor and the woman met us. The woman started to yell at the old man. He said nothing in return. The old man looked tiny in comparison to the burly sailor, but with determination in his eyes, he ordered the two to step aside. The sailor stood firmly for a moment, testing the man's determination. The woman continued to yell at us. The old man simply continued forward, forcing the sailor to step aside. I don't know if the woman and sailor didn't want to attract unwanted attention from the sailors on the docks but the sailor stepped aside and the old man led me back onto the docks."

"I saw guards searching the pier and my mother yelling my name. The old man let go of my hand, and I ran to my mother's outstretched arms. After explaining the ordeal to my mother, I turned to introduce her to the old man, but he was gone. The dock was empty. I never saw the man again."

Emma paused for a moment. She looked at Evan with the glint of tears still in her eyes. "The fear that I felt that day, that I will never forget, I saw in your eyes your first day on The Ledge. I knew that day that I needed to help you." Emma jumped up from the log and wiping the tears from her eyes, she jumped on Smokey.

"I helped you, now I need you to do something for me," Emma said. "Be at warrior training this afternoon. That is all I want in return."

"Alec isn't going to like this," Evan said.

"I'm counting on that," Emma said as she kicked Smokey into a full gallop, leaving Evan alone in the clearing.

Chapter Fourteen

Francis

Francis remained hidden on the edge of the clearing just out of sight from Evan and Emma.

"The people of The Ledge believe they are so much better than everyone else!" Francis muttered.

Francis was angry at Emma for defending The Ledge. Emma had never left The Ledge and she didn't understand how the other kingdoms struggled to survive. She didn't understand that her kingdom prospered at the expense of the other kingdoms. He was also angry at Evan for protecting her. Evan didn't understand that he had no status on The Ledge, just like Francis. Evan was blinded by his friendship with Emma. He couldn't see The Ledge for what it truly was.

"While my people starve, the people of The Ledge enjoy food enough to feed five kingdoms!" Francis whispered. "My father is right. The Ledge must be destroyed so that the other kingdoms can share in the wealth that The Ledge keeps to themselves. But what about Evan?" Francis asked himself. "Evan has done nothing. He is an outsider just like me. There is no reason why he must be enslaved with the people of The Ledge. I will save him," Francis declared. "He can come with me and live in my father's kingdom after I have finished what I was sent to do."

Francis slipped behind a tree so Emma wouldn't see him as she rode Smoky down the trail. Francis looked back towards Evan who was still standing in the clearing.

"I can't help Emma, but there is no reason Evan should suffer the same fate." Francis thought as he turned and disappeared into the forest.

Chapter Fifteen

The Challenge

Evan's last class of the day took him to the outskirts of town, to the farmlands, where he usually spent most of his time farming to earn his keep. His teacher was a portly, loud man, who liked to hear himself talk. The class had already gone over an hour and Evan hoped it would end soon so that he could get to warrior training. Evan wanted to ask how much longer he planned to talk, but he knew better than to ask that question. Every time a student asked that question the man would drag on for a least another half hour.

"Irrigation systems allow us to control which plants get how much water and when. This is how we are able to grow several different species of plants in such a small area," he instructed in a slightly monotone voice.

This was Evan's least favorite class of the day.

"But how do you keep bugs from destroying your crops?" Francis asked.

Evan and Francis hadn't spoken a word since the incident with Emma earlier that morning.

"Good question, Francis. The answer is a secret that has helped us grow crops for generations."

Evan wished the teacher had worded that differently as he watched Francis cringe.

"The secret is to maintain just the right balance between the good insects and the bad insects."

"Aren't all insects bad?" a boy in the back of the class asked.

"No, no, no," the teacher responded. He always repeated no three times when he wanted to correct a great misunderstanding. "Some insects are good. They kill insects that eat plants. Other insects pollinate plants. As long as you keep the right ratios, the good insects will keep the bad insects in line. If you don't have enough bad insects, then the good insects will not have anything to eat." The teacher paused, allowing his words to sink in. "My, my, I believe it is getting late. Class dismissed."

"Where are you going?" Francis yelled after Evan, who had already started walking away from the edge of the field.

"Emma wants me to go to warrior training today," Evan replied without stopping

"Why?"

"I don't know. She wouldn't tell me."

"More secrets?" Francis smirked, as he spat on the ground.

Evan stopped on the trail. "This stops right now, Francis. Emma has been nothing but kind and gracious to both of us. I will not let you treat her the way you did this morning."

"You're right. You're right," Francis mumbled sheepishly. "I'm sorry."

"I'm not the one you need to apologize to."

"You're right."

"She'll be at warrior training. Maybe you should come along," Evan offered, not wanting to be the only orphan to show up.

— ·· — ·· — ·· — ··

The clearing was packed with people standing shoulder to shoulder. Evan grew nervous as he and Francis looked for a familiar face in the growing crowd. Standing on a log on the opposite side of the clearing, waving excitedly, was Emma, looking relieved to see them. Evan guessed she had been wondering if he was going to show up.

"What's going on? Why are so many people here?" Evan asked, as they reached Emma.

"It's the challenge," Emma answered. "The first day of the Crossover season."

"What are you talking about?" Evan asked confused.

"You remember what I told you about the Crossover this morning and how kids who are of age have the chance to perform the Crossover?" Emma explained.

"Yes, but what does that have to do with me being at warrior training."

"The King only chooses kids who are of age, who he believes are ready to participate in the Crossover." Emma pointed to the five boys standing next to Captain Curtis.

Evan recognized all of the boys from class. Alec looked as cocky as ever as he talked with his friend Barrett. Barrett was the size of a full grown man and was the only boy standing by Captain Curtis who had started to grow a beard. Unlike Captain Curtis's thick beard, Barrett's beard was patchy and thin, but it was a beard none the less. Simon, a tall skinny kid with bushy black hair, was talking with Gale, an especially loud kid who was always cracking jokes. Gale had broad shoulders and long brown hair that almost reached the middle of his back. Thomas, a short kid with blond hair and a round face, was the last kid standing next to Captain Curtis. He wasn't talking to anyone, had his hands in his pockets and was kicking the dirt in front of him nervously as he waited.

"What if you aren't chosen by the King?" Evan asked as he noticed several kids of age around the clearing who were not standing next to Captain Curtis.

"That's why the challenge exists," Emma said enthusiastically. "Today is the chance for anyone of age or younger to show that they should be considered for the Crossover."

Evan still didn't know what this had to do with him and why he needed to be here.

"Great to see you all here for the kickoff of the Crossover season," Captain Curtis announced in a loud booming voice. "I would like you to give a special welcome to Peter, our future king and the leader of this year's Crossover," Captain Curtis announced enthusiastically. The crowd went wild.

"Thank you, Curtis," Peter responded after the cheers had calmed down. "Today, we take part in the annual challenge!" Cheers went up from the crowd in anticipation. "Anyone not chosen to participate in the Crossover this year, all those who are under age, or those not born on The Ledge have the opportunity to prove themselves worthy to perform the Crossover."

The crowd cheered again and Evan began to realize why Emma had invited him.

Peter waited for the cheering to calm down and then in a loud voice yelled. "Do we have a challenger?"

"That's why you wanted me here today?" Evan asked Emma amazed by what he believed she was asking of him. "To prove that I'm worthy to perform the Crossover?"

Emma looked back at Evan, saying nothing. She raised her hand high in the air and called in a loud voice, "I challenge!"

The crowd went silent as all eyes fixated on Emma.

"Evan, you are ready for this," Emma whispered to Evan. "And I'm going to prove to you that you are. You just need a bit of confidence." Emma left Evan's side to approach her brother and Captain Curtis.

"What is she doing?" Evan hissed to Francis, who, by the expression on his pale face, was just as shocked as he was.

"Emma, does mom know what you are doing?" Peter asked in a loud voice for all to hear as she reached the center of the clearing.

The crowd laughed.

"I didn't know that I needed permission?" Emma responded.

Peter then turned to Curtis, and reluctantly nodded.

Curtis hesitantly walked over to the group of older kids who were all of age.

"Who will answer the challenge from the Princess?"

Silence followed his question. Whether it was the fear of hurting the Princess and being dragged before the King or of actually losing the fight, no one would step forward to answer the challenge.

"If no one will accept my challenge, then I shall choose," Emma announced, irritated that no one would face her. "I choose Barrett." She selected a staff and marched to the middle of the clearing, ready for the fight to begin.

To Evan's surprise, Alec's large friend Barrett stepped forward.

"He must be three times Emma's size!" Francis gauged as the large boy walked to the center of the clearing and tentatively picked up a staff. He dwarfed Emma in every way, except maybe for determination.

Peter stepped between them and then, addressing both fighters but glaring only at Emma's opponent, he warned in a stern voice. "You can win the fight in one of two ways: disarm your opponent, which is preferred, or get your opponent to cede the fight. Are you both ready?"

Emma took a fighting stance, the one she had made Evan practice for hours in the clearing by the waterfall. Barrett stood in his spot, staring down at the small girl in front of him, amusement apparent on his face.

"He doesn't even look like he is going to try," Francis muttered out loud, as he jumped up on a log for a better view.

Francis was right. Barrett didn't seem threatened in the least by his competition.

"Go!" Peter yelled, moving quickly to the edge of the crowd.

Even before Peter had moved completely out of range, Barrett charged swiftly towards Emma, catching everyone by surprise. Everyone, except Emma. As he reached Emma at a full charge, she moved quickly to the side to avoid Barrett, wedged her staff between his legs, and tripped Barrett, causing him to dive, face first, into the soft, dry dirt. The crowd erupted into cheers as the dust settled around the downed elephant.

Emma stepped back and resumed her fighting stance, allowing her opponent to rise and brush himself off.

Everyone continued to cheer except for Evan who was a nervous wreck. She was going to get herself hurt and all to prove a point to him.

Embarrassed and dirty, Barrett moved cautiously toward Emma, looking more determined than before. He had underestimated Emma, and he was not going to make that mistake again.

Emma stepped backwards as Barrett moved cautiously toward her. Evan had learned from Emma that an opponent's weaknesses were revealed as they attacked. She was waiting for him to attack.

Once within range, Barrett struck again, moving faster than Evan thought possible, jabbing his staff towards Emma, hoping to catch her off guard with a stunning blow. Emma quickly sidestepped and deflected his blow with her staff. Barrett switched direction and came at her again. This time their staffs collided in the air above Emma's head. Using brute force Barrett forced his staff closer to Emma. Emma strained under the weight of Barrett's staff. Just as Emma's strength gave out and Barrett's staff came crashing down Emma moved to the side and with the other end of her staff smacked Barrett on his unguarded ribs.

This time Evan cheered with the rest of the people in the clearing.

In pain, Barrett swung his staff recklessly at Emma's head which she ducked. Barrett swung again and their staffs collided. He swung again and their staffs collided again, Emma still waiting to attack.

As Barrett attacked again a slight smile appeared on Emma's face. Evan knew Barrett was in trouble. Emma always smiled when she figured out Francis's weakness when they fought in the clearing during training. The smile might as well have been a death sentence for Barrett. The problem was Barrett didn't know it.

In one fluid motion, as Emma moved out of the way of Barrett's latest attempt, she forced her staff upwards with all her strength, striking him right between his unguarded legs. Barrett crashed to his knees in pain and with a groan, dropped his staff to the ground.

The small forest clearing, which only moments ago had been silent except for the clanking staffs, erupted into cheers as Emma helped Barrett to his feet. Peter strutted, like a proud brother, over to Emma declaring her the winner of the challenge. Smiling from ear to ear, the triumphant Emma returned to Evan as Peter addressed the group once more.

"Do we have another challenger?" he yelled over the cheers of the still hysterical crowd.

"I had no idea you could fight like that," Francis admitted, looking very impressed.

"It's your turn now," Emma turned to Evan.

"I can't fight like that," Evan said.

"You're right, you can't. You can fight better," Emma assured him as she took Evan's hand in hers. "When we fight, I can't find your weaknesses. You are a natural." She gazed up at Evan with big, convincing eyes.

"So is Alec, who hates every orphan and never wastes an opportunity to prove we are inferior," Evan added, as he slowly raised his hand high in the air. "I challenge!" Evan called out, sounding more confident than he felt.

The crowd stood stunned. No one said a word. Apparently, everyone had heard about Evan's first battle, and his reputation was not good in the warrior world. As he walked past the bewildered spectators, he could hear the whispers.

"What is he thinking?"

"Only the best try the challenge."

"I heard he didn't even know how to hold a staff last time he fought."

Finally, Evan reached the stoic Peter.

"Well then, I didn't expect this," Peter chuckled, playing the crowd. Peter leaned in close to Evan so that no one else could hear. "Are you sure you want to do this, Evan?"

"Yes," Evan responded. Evan walked into the center of the clearing and picked up a staff.

Peter turned to Curtis, shrugged and then nodded.

Before Curtis could extend the challenge to the small group of kids who were of age, Alec stepped forward, picked up a staff, and walked to the center of the clearing to face Evan. He glared at Evan with hatred as he took his fighting stance. Evan gripped his staff tightly and taking his own fighting position, glared back at Alec, waiting for Peter's signal.

"Go!"

Alec charged Evan with his staff pulled back preparing for a powerful jab, which had rendered itself successful last time. However, this time was different. Evan was ready. Alec jabbed at Evan's stomach but missed as Evan sidestepped the powerful move. Alec quickly switched directions and attacked again. The hours of practice Emma had put Evan through were paying off.

Evan didn't have to think about how to move. His body naturally reacted to Alec's advances as if he had been training his entire life. He needed to concentrate; he needed to find Alec's weaknesses. They moved from one side of the clearing to the other, Evan trying desperately to avoid Alec's blows and Alec trying to knock Evan's head off with every attack. And then Evan saw it, the weakness he had been looking for. With every block Evan made, Alec became angrier. Before long Alec's emotions were controlling his attack and causing him to forget his training. As Alec attacked he started to over-rotate leaving a small opening. Evan knew that if his attack wasn't timed perfectly, Alec would flatten him, but he had to try. With Alec's next attack, Evan countered for the first time.

He blocked Alec's staff and then delivered a solid jab to Alec's unguarded ribs. Evan heard a crack and knew that his staff had found its mark. Alec staggered backwards and grabbed his rib, his face distorted with pain. The crowd was silent. This was not what they had expected. Evan hoped Alec would yield, but he simply gritted his teeth and attacked again with more vigor and determination.

Evan was pushed backwards as he attempted to repel a flurry of blows. Evan didn't know how much more he could take and decided to try a desperate move. Alec was going to find a weakness in Evan's defense soon. He needed to act now.

As Alec shot forward again, Evan purposely left his right side unguarded. Alec saw the opening and decided to end this fight once and for all. Blinded by his anger, Alec didn't notice that Evan was baiting him. Evan twisted his body away from the brunt of the blow, but allowed some contact, to make it look real. As Evan twisted, he raised his staff above his head, finished a complete rotation and with his strength, he brought his staff down on Alec's exposed wrists. Alec cried out in pain as he released his staff, letting it fall to the ground.

Alec had lost the battle. He stared in silence at his staff lying on the ground. The crowd was silent. Evan maintained his fighting stance, not believing that the fight had ended. Peter walked towards Evan with Captain Curtis.

"Well done, Evan," Peter offered solemnly, still amazed at the outcome. "Who taught you how to fight like that?"

"Your sister," Evan responded gratefully, as he handed Peter the staff and started to walk back towards Francis and Emma.

Alec left his staff on the ground and retreated from the clearing in the opposite direction, without saying a word.

"Wait," Curtis called to Evan as the crowd parted, giving way to the champion.

Evan slowly turned toward Curtis who was looking at Peter.

"Evan deserves a chance to run the Gauntlet," Curtis said.

Peter watched Alec disappear into the forest and then looked at Evan. "But he is an orphan!"

"It has been done before," Curtis responded.

Peter shook his head from side to side, "I hope I don't regret this."

Captain Curtis laughed and turned back toward Evan. "Looks like you're in kid."

— ·· — ·· — ·· — ··

"Wahoo!" Francis shouted as Evan made his way back to the log through the dispersing crowd.

Evan sat down, exhausted and confused.

"What's wrong Evan?" Francis asked as he plopped down next to his friend, his excitement dampened. "You just slaughtered Alec, you should be excited."

"Did they let you in?" Emma asked, her eyes wide with excitement.

Evan looked at Emma, "You were expecting this."

"I was planning on it." Emma simply replied.

"Planning on what Emma?" Francis asked.

Emma's smile grew.

"Emma, what did you get me into?" Evan asked.

"You're the first orphan to be allowed to run it, in years. You are going to be the talk of the kingdom!"

"Emma, what have you done?"

"Technically you're the one who beat Alec."

"Emma!"

"You get to run the Gauntlet!" Emma shouted.

"What's the Gauntlet?" Evan asked.

"It's how the kids chosen by the King and those who prove themselves during the challenge show they are worthy to perform the Crossover."

"I didn't think orphans could perform the Crossover?" Francis spat.

"Not normally, but if they win a challenge, especially against the best fighter in the group like Alec, then they can be invited to run the Gauntlet. It's not guaranteed, but you did it! And if you complete the Gauntlet then you can perform the Crossover."

"What's the Gauntlet like?" Evan asked.

"Oh it's grueling! Almost worse than the Crossover itself," Emma said as she jumped off the log and started to walk back to the village."

"Worse than the Crossover?" Evan repeated.

"I would assume. I've never performed the Crossover or run the Gauntlet, but I've heard the stories. Last year two kids ended up breaking bones and one kid, well he hasn't been the same since." Emma said. "I'm so excited for you, this is amazing!"

Evan and Francis stared at each other. Emma had an abnormal idea of excitement.

Chapter Sixteen

The Outsider Must Fail

Deeper in the forest, away from the clearing, it was quiet, almost peaceful. Alec sat next to a small stream wallowing in self-pity.

"That orphan made you look like a fool," Curtis said as he walked up to Alec.

"He got lucky!"

"Lucky or not, he will have a chance to run the Gauntlet."

"What?" Alec screamed as he jumped up from the log where he had been sitting. "You can't let an outsider run the Gauntlet!"

"We have to. I made sure of it."

"But why?" Alec asked.

"If we excluded him after he beat you, it would make you look weak, not worthy to participate in the competition yourself. We had to let him into the competition for your sake."

Alec shook his head in disbelief. "I don't trust him."

"I don't trust him either, but now that he has a chance to run the Gauntlet he also has a chance to find out about," Curtis stopped.

"About what?" Alec prompted.

Curtis had said too much. There were things that he couldn't yet tell Alec, not until Alec completed the Crossover. "It's nothing, we just need to ensure he doesn't finish the Gauntlet."

"How do we do that?"

"Leave that to me, just make sure that you manage to finish."

Chapter Seventeen

The Cottage

Evan followed a deer trail deep into the dense woods, his footsteps almost silent on the pine-covered trail. He looked up at the sun, through the thick pine branches. He still had time, but maybe only an hour or so before he needed to meet the rest of the kids to run the Gauntlet. It had been three days since he had beaten Alec in the clearing on Challenge day and he still didn't have any more information about what the Gauntlet was. Emma was very little help in preparing Evan for the unknown, since she had never run the Gauntlet herself. Evan had asked Rosalina, but she had just smiled and said that he would do great. It was times like this that Evan truly missed the support of his family.

Evan wasn't any closer to finding answers as to how he had ended up on The Ledge, than he had been the first day he was dragged before the King and Queen. He had searched the forest for the bank of the stream he remembered from his first day on The Ledge, to see if there were any clues as to how he had gotten to The Ledge, but he hadn't found it. Searching was also made more difficult by the rule that orphans were not to wonder off into the forest. Evan did break this rule everyday by meeting with the Emma and occasionally when he went to meet Gramps, but he figured that since Emma was royalty and Gramps a respected member of the kingdom, he somehow had permission at those times. He still had questions, but with every passing day he wondered if the life he had left behind was simply a figment of his imagination. Some nights he would lie awake thinking about his family and friends, but as time went on he wondered if they were real or part of a dream.

The vegetation on the forest floor grew sparser as Evan neared the harvesting grounds. By the time he reached the oldest section of the forest on The Ledge, the temperature had dropped several degrees and Evan could no longer see the sun through the canopy of pine branches that towered above his head. It was no wonder they referred to this part of the forest as the shadows. Gramps, the old shoemaker Evan had met his first day on The Ledge, had told Evan during one of their visits that this part of the forest had the oldest, largest trees on the entire Ledge and was the best place to gather the perfect sap for the soles of his shoes. It was easy to spot Gramps among the large pine trunks kneeling down next to one of his taps, humming to himself as he always did. Positioning his already heavy leather bag, he caught the thick sap as it dripped from the tree.

"Gramps," Evan called out as he waved.

Gramps waved back before turning back to his tap to stop the flow. He unscrewed the tap from the pine tree, dumped it into his old leather satchel, and cinched it tightly closed. Gramps took a piece of cloth from his pocket and wiped large drops of perspiration from his forehead.

"Glad to see you," he greeted, as he handed Evan the heavy leather bag.

"I thought as much," Evan chuckled, putting the strap around his shoulder.

"Are you ready to run the Gauntlet tonight?" Gramps asked with a smile.

"How did you know?"

"It's been quite some time since an orphan has been allowed to participate, so naturally everyone is talking about it."

"What are they saying?" Evan asked. He suspected most people didn't approve of his invitation to participate.

"It doesn't matter what people think," Gramps said disapprovingly. "The only person who can really affect the outcome tonight is yourself."

"That's reassuring," Evan said sarcastically.

"It should be," Gramps corrected. "If you believe you can do this then you will be successful, but if there is even an ounce of doubt, if you hesitate even slightly, then you will likely fail."

"Is that supposed to make me feel better?" Evan asked.

"No, the Gauntlet is grueling. I am glad you're running it and not me." Gramps picked up his walking stick and started limping down the trail to his cottage.

Gramps' cottage looked like something out of a fairy tale book. The walls were built of stone similar to the castle but they were rough and jagged. The steep thatched roof rose between two large pine trees, making it look like the cottage was part of the forest. The two windows and door stood open. Gramps had told Evan many times that he loved the smells and sounds of the pine forest and couldn't imagine shutting them out.

Evan placed the heavy sap bag on the stone step in the front of the cottage and sat down in what had become his usual spot. Most of the orphans called the shoemaker Gramps, but with Evan, it meant something more. Gramps had become the closest person Evan had to family in this strange place. Gramps went into the cottage, emerging a moment later with two mugs of his famous flower juice, which he made from extracting juices from a pink flower found in the forest. Evan took a long drink, leaned back on the steps, and shut his eyes. This was the only place where he truly felt at home on The Ledge.

Gramps had taken a liking to Evan over all the other orphans. He told Evan once that Evan reminded him of the son whom he had lost many years ago. Evan, whose grandpa had passed away when he was young, had adopted the old man as his own.

"How does Emma feel about you getting into the competition?" Gramps asked, sitting down on the steps.

"I don't know," Evan shrugged.

Gramps looked at Evan with a raised eyebrow. "You don't know?"

"I guess she was excited. She did teach me everything I know about fighting."

Gramps laughed. He, like Rosalina, knew Evan had feelings for Emma, even though Evan had never expressed them.

Gramps paused for a moment before asking Evan the next question. "Do you know why Emma wants you to perform the Crossover?"

"After hearing about how grueling it is I figure she wants me dead," Evan answered.

Gramps managed a slight smile before continuing, "Evan, what do you know about the Crossover?"

Evan had just recently learned about the Crossover and realized that he knew nothing about it.

"Not much," Evan responded.

"You already know that the King decides who gets to participate in the Gauntlet and that the challenge is a way for others to prove they are worthy to participate as well." Gramps explained. "What you may not know is that only two or three will make it through the Gauntlet and be allowed to perform the

Crossover. For those who complete the Crossover their lives are changed forever."

"Emma told me that when someone completes the Crossover they are given great responsibility to the people of The Ledge."

"That's true Evan. The day they return, they become leaders on The Ledge and as leaders they are entrusted with the wellbeing and the safety of the people. It is their choice what they do with this leadership. Some choose to be warriors, other choose to be captains of mighty ships. Some choose to spend their lives learning and teaching others and then there are some who choose to perfect a trade. Whatever they choose they are to put the people first as they lead."

"Francis said that the people who complete the Crossover keep secrets."

"Francis doesn't know what he is talking about!" Gramps responded. "The other kingdoms want to believe we are keeping secrets from them. It gives them something to hate us for and to justify why they have nothing and we prosper."

Evan took another long drink before blurting out a question that had been on his mind since earlier that morning. "Did you ever perform the Crossover?"

Gramps leaned forward for a few moments, seeming to contemplate the question. "That was many years ago," Gramps replied with a distant look on his face.

"Is it dangerous?" Evan asked.

"Yes. There are some who never return."

"What happens to those who don't return?" Evan pressed.

Gramps cleared his throat and then slowly continued. "Most of the time, we never find out. They were either killed while performing the Crossover, or simply decided not to return, choosing a life away from The Ledge."

Evan watched Gramps closely as the old man gazed into the forest lost in thought "Is that what happened to your son?" Evan inquired in a hushed tone.

Gramps looked back at Evan, his eyes filled with tears. "Isn't it time for you to get back to the village?" He slowly got to his feet and turned towards the cottage.

"Yes, I guess so," Evan responded.

Without saying another word, Gramps walked into his cottage and shut the door which normally stood wide open. Feeling confused, and suddenly aware of the lateness of the hour, Evan got to his feet and started toward the village at a brisk jog, not wanting to be late to the Gauntlet.

Chapter Eighteen

Memory

Gramps watched through the window as Evan disappeared into the forest before leaning his back against the closed door of his cottage, his weathered hand wiping away the flood of tears that cascaded down his cheeks. Gramps looked around the cottage. The room was sparsely furnished, but tidy, everything in its place. He walked over to an old, battered nightstand next to his bed and opened the top drawer revealing his most prized possession carefully wrapped in a white cloth. Using both hands, he carefully unwrapped the object from the cloth. To anyone else the object would have looked like an ordinary stone, but to Gramps it was so much more. The stone was small, no larger than the palm of his hand and dark grey with a small vein of purple which ran down its center. Holding the stone tightly he closed his eyes and concentrated on a specific memory, one he would never allow himself to forget.

Gramps' mind instantly returned to an early morning many years ago. A boy, about Evan's age, with sandy blond hair and blue eyes, stood outside the cottage just as Evan had a few minutes earlier. He held a bow in his hand and arrows and supplies slung on his back. The boy looked excited.

"Goodbye father, I will return triumphant in a couple of days," the boy declared.

A much younger Gramps stood on the stone steps leading up to the cottage. "Remember everything I taught you," he implored.

"I don't think I will have time to make rabbit stew," the boy said with a smile.

"You know what I mean," the younger Gramps said as he shook his head disapprovingly. "Be smart and be careful. The outside world is a barbaric place."

"You've told me all of this before," the boy said.

"I love you," the younger Gramps declared as a single tear slid down his cheek.

"I love you too."

The two looked at each other for a moment, wanting to say more, but not knowing what more could be said. The boy then turned and jogged down the same trail which Evan had just traveled. As the memory of his son vanished, Gramps dropped the stone onto the bed and a violent shiver shot through his body. Gramps exhaled deeply, his breath visible, as if he were standing outside on a chilly, winter day. Gramps carefully re-wrapped the stone and returned it to its resting place. He then grabbed a blanket from his bed and wrapped it around his old, feeble body, feeling chilled and very tired. Gramps hoped that Evan would never perform the Crossover. He couldn't lose him as well.

Chapter Nineteen

The Gauntlet

Evan sat on his bed in the dorm looking out the window at the spires of the castle gleaming in the afternoon sun. If he didn't want to be late, he would have to leave soon.

"I brought you something," Emma said as she entered Evan's room with a bundle in her arms.

"What is it?"

"It's going to be cold out there tonight and I thought you might need a heavier cloak to keep you warm," Emma said as she held out the dark cloak for Evan to see.

"Thanks," Evan said as he reached for the cloak. His stomach was tied in knots because he was nervous and he felt like he was going to throw up at any moment. Evan removed his old cloak and wrapped the new one around his shoulders. "How do I look?"

"Like a champion."

Evan smiled. Emma had more confidence in him than he did, but her support meant everything.

"Are you ready?" Emma said with a smile.

"I'm not sure what to expect," Evan admitted with a nervous sigh. "Other than where and when to meet, I have no idea what's going to happen."

Emma moved in closer to Evan and touched his hand. "I know you can do this, you just need to believe in yourself."

As Emma stared up at Evan with her beautiful blue eyes. Evan was no longer thinking about the Gauntlet. He was only thinking about Emma. He wanted to thank Emma for training him all summer. He wanted to express how much their friendship meant to him. He wanted to tell her that he had never felt this way about anyone before, but the words wouldn't come. Even if he did manage to say something, there was little chance that she felt the same way. After all, she was the princess and he was only an orphan.

"It's time," Emma said after a moment.

Evan stepped away from Emma. "Thanks, I don't want to keep Captain Curtis waiting." Evan slowly walked towards the door.

"Evan," Emma called.

Evan stopped and looked back.

"Remember to use everything around you to your advantage, especially when all feels lost, don't ever give up."

— · — · · — · · — · · — · ·

The clearing where Evan had beaten Alec only a day earlier was completely empty. The sun had set an hour ago and the first stars began to appear in the clear night sky. Evan wondered if he had gotten the time or perhaps the location wrong. He reviewed his discussion with Captain Curtis and was sure he had not misunderstood. The Gauntlet would start in this clearing at dark.

Evan walked over to a pile of staffs on the ground and picked up one. "Will I be allowed to use weapons tonight?" He asked himself, dropping the worn staff back on the pile.

Evan heard movement and saw a dim light dancing through the trees. Captain Curtis emerged a moment later carrying a torch which cast shadows on the serious faces of the boys following him.

Alec was in the lead followed by Alec's large friend Barret, Simon, Thomas and lastly Gale. Evan guessed that having them show up together was meant to be a message to Evan that he didn't belong.

"Listen up!" Captain Curtis shouted when he reached the center of the clearing. "I'm only going to explain this once. Each one of you has a single goal tonight. It is to retrieve a rock from the other side of The Ledge and return it here before sunrise. If you complete this task, you may qualify to participate in the Crossover.

"That's it?" Barret asked, looking more confident than he had a moment earlier. "We just need to bring back a stupid rock?"

Captain Curtis scoffed, but didn't respond to Barret's comment. Evan guessed there was more to it than what Barret assumed.

"The rocks lie at the Reflection Pool."

"Where is the Reflection Pool?" Evan asked.

Captain Curtis looked at Evan for a moment and then back at the group, ignoring Evan's question. "Remember you only have until sunrise." Captain Curtis stepped away from the middle of the clearing. "Let the Gauntlet begin!" He yelled as though announcing it to the entire forest.

Suddenly the forest surrounding the clearing came alive. Soldiers carrying clubs and staffs rushed at the boys. Alec and Barret saw a gap between the charging men and rushed for the forest, disappearing into the underbrush. Evan tried to follow, but was immediately blocked by a small soldier with missing front teeth. Evan ducked as the man wielded a staff at Evan's head. The man forced Evan back to the center of the clearing with the other boys, who were now surrounded. Thomas and Gale had picked up staffs and were engaging the soldiers in a fight. Gale was knocked hard to the ground and Thomas's staff snapped into two pieces as a soldier smashed his club through it. Evan knew he wouldn't stand a chance against the soldiers in combat, his only hope was to escape to the forest.

The soldiers were now advancing slowly toward the remaining four boys. Captain Curtis stood on a log at the edge of the clearing with his arms folded as he watched his students. Emma's words returned to Evan, just as two men singled Evan out from the rest of the group.

"Use anything you can. Never give up."

Evan frantically searched his surroundings, his eyes moved towards the small mound of dirt where the staffs remained. Instead of picking up a staff, Evan grabbed a handful of dirt and turned to face the men.

The soldier with missing teeth smiled at Evan and Evan smiled back in return. The man looked back at the other, larger soldier.

"What are you waiting for, he's just a small boy," the larger soldier shot back.

"Yeah, but he smiled at me."

"I don't care if he gives you a hug. Let's finish this."

The soldier with missing teeth charged at Evan, swinging his club at Evan's stomach. Evan waited until the soldier had fully committed to his swing before he took a step backwards. The man's giant swing missed Evan by an inch and caused him to over rotate leaving his body unguarded. Evan stepped forward and kicked the soldier right between his legs. The soldier's face turned white from pain and, moaning, he dropped to his knees. The second soldier stepped forward.

"Try and do that to me and I will make sure you have a permanent limp when I'm done with you."

To the soldier's surprise, Evan charged at him. The soldier prepared to give Evan a punishing blow, but just as Evan moved within range, Evan threw his handful of dirt directly into the soldier's face. The soldier screamed as the dirt made contact, momentarily blinding him. Evan sprinted past the soldier and into the forest. Thomas, Simon and Gale saw the opening too and followed behind Evan.

Evan continued running until his lungs begged him to stop. The boys who had followed Evan stopped as well.

"Nice thinking orphan," Thomas said.

The boys ducked down into the underbrush as several soldiers rushed past.

"Orphan," Simon whispered. "Reflection Pool is that way," the boy pointed towards the cliffs in the distance. "Move that way until you find a stream. The stream will lead you to the pool, which is right next to the cliffs."

"Good luck orphan," Gale said. "Make sure you don't get your head knocked off."

The boys then disappeared, one at a time, into the underbrush.

— ·· — ·· — ·· — ··

A couple hours later Evan knelt to drink from the cool water in the small stream. Reflection Pool must be at the head of this stream, Evan thought to himself, recalling the instructions Simon had given him. Evan was about to take another drink, when he heard a twig snap not far away. Evan froze and stared into the darkness. He heard another twig snap and then another. They were moving in his direction. Evan stood and looked for cover, he was twenty feet away from the nearest tree and would never make it. Quickly he dove into a bush just as two soldiers emerged from the trees. These were the two soldiers from the clearing. If they caught him he didn't want to imagine what would happen.

"Where do you think he is?" The smaller of the two soldiers asked as he walked into the clearing.

Evan held his breath and hoped they couldn't see him in the darkness.

"I don't know," the larger soldier complained. "But if we don't find the orphan soon the Captain is going to kill you."

"Why me?" the soldier with missing teeth asked with concern.

"Because you're the one who let him escape the clearing."

"You were there too," the soldier with missing teeth answered.

"Yeah, but you had the best opportunity to take him out of the competition and you missed. Now we are stuck chasing a small boy in a huge forest," the large soldier answered

"Even if we can't find him, there's no way he will be able to retrieve a rock from the pool, not with what the Captain has prepared for the boys."

"Did you hear that?" the larger soldier whispered as he motioned for the smaller soldier to be quiet. The soldiers moved towards Evan.

Evan held every muscle painfully still. He hoped they couldn't see him, but the bush was small. The men crept past the bush and disappeared into the trees at the edge of the clearing. Gale emerged out of the forest a few seconds later. He moved along the bank of the stream just as Evan had done moments earlier. Evan wanted to warn Gale about the soldiers, but he knew that by so doing he would give his position away. Evan held perfectly still hoping the soldiers wouldn't see Gale.

As soon as Gale reached the center of the clearing the soldiers ran from the trees. Gale tried to escape, but their attack was timed perfectly. Cornered, Gale kicked the soldier with the missing teeth in the stomach and for a moment Evan thought he might escape as the soldier fell backwards, but the large soldier knocked him to the ground with a single blow before he could make a run for it. Once on the ground, the large soldier quickly pinned him and tied his hands behind his back.

"Let me go you overweight pig!" Gale yelled as he struggled to free himself.

"This one's still got a little bit of fight in him," the soldier with missing teeth said as he got up holding his stomach. "Why don't you break his arm? That should remove whatever fight he has left."

Gale shut his mouth and held perfectly still.

"Smart boy," the larger soldier said.

"One down," the soldier with missing teeth said as the larger soldier pulled Gale to his feet.

"Yeah, but now we have to get rid of the baggage," the larger soldier said.

The soldiers left the clearing as quickly as they had come, dragging Gale behind them.

Evan stayed hidden for a moment longer before pulling himself out from the bush. He should have helped Gale. That could have been his fate just as easily. Evan made a decision that if given the opportunity again he would help, not just hide in a bush and do nothing. Instead of following the stream as Gale had done. Evan disappeared into the forest, moving in the direction of the pool.

— · · — · · — · · — · ·

Reflection Pool held true to its name. The cliffs dropped into the pool on one side. The waterfall entering the pool was nothing more than a trickle of water that snaked its way down the cliff to the water's surface. The flow hardly disturbed the water at all, allowing the water to mirror the night sky flawlessly. The large pool sparkled with the light from the thousands of stars shining above.

There was no beach surrounding the edge of the pond. The forest had swallowed the bank of the pond completely, tree branches hung over the bank and vines reached down towards the water's surface.

Evan stayed hidden in the forest. He didn't see any soldiers or fellow competitors, but more importantly, he didn't see any rocks. Evan moved slowly along the edge of the pool looking for anything out of place until he came to a narrow trail leading into the pool. Two cloaks were lying in the brush off to the side of the trail. I must be in the right spot, Evan thought to himself. But where are the others and why did they leave their cloaks here? Cautiously, Evan continued moving along the bank, aware of everything around him and being careful to stay hidden in the brush until he reached the cliff.

Evan looked up at the giant cliff which separated The Ledge from the other Kingdoms. It was almost 150 feet tall at this spot and rose straight up out of the pool. There was no way the boys had scaled the cliff. Evan continued to search the pool, he had to be missing something. Evan's attention was drawn back towards the pool. The water near the cliff wasn't reflecting the stars nearly as brightly as it had on the other side of the pool. Evan was about to continue his search when he noticed that the water in the pond was faintly glowing. Evan searched for the source of the light, but the pond was too deep. "Were the rocks at the bottom of the pool?" Evan looked back at the cloaks he had found on the bank. "Had the others swam to the bottom of the pool? Were they still down there? If they were, could they still be alive?" Evan swallowed hard.

Slowly Evan removed his own cloak and stepped into the water. It was freezing cold, but Evan was out of options. He had to see what was on the bottom of the pool. Taking a deep breath Evan dove into the water and swam towards the glowing light at the bottom. He swam deeper and deeper into the pool using the cliff to guide his descent until he reached the bottom of the pool. Whatever was emitting the light wasn't coming from the bottom of the pool, as Evan had initially thought, but from a small cave at the base of the cliff. Pushing himself forward, Evan swam into the cave, which angled upward. Evan's lungs were on fire as he swam, his body screamed for air and he began to feel light headed. With every kick of his legs the light grew brighter. His head finally breached the surface of the water and Evan drank in gulps of stale air.

Treading water, Evan looked around the small cave. A burning torch dimly cast shadows on the walls. A soldier could be concealed anywhere. And, where were the others? On the floor beneath the torch sat a pile of rocks. Each rock looked to be about the size of a silver dollar, flat and perfectly round. Evan counted them quickly, six stones. That meant that none of them had been taken from the pile. Had the others been captured before jumping into the water? Evan thought to himself.

Evan silently swam over to the bank of the cave. He climbed out of the water and moved into the shadows next to the wall. Something wasn't right. The soldier had mentioned that the boys would never be able to retrieve a rock from the pool, but here they sat unguarded on the cave floor. It seemed too simple. He decided to wait in the shadows for a few minutes and watch.

Dripping and shivering from the cold Evan still hadn't heard anything after fifteen minutes of waiting. Evan decided to move forward, but just as he took a step out of the darkness he heard the water move against the rocks in the cave. Someone was swimming through the cave. Evan quickly moved back into the shadows just as two boys surfaced out of the water.

"I told you we would be the first ones here," Alec announced triumphantly as he looked at the rocks under the torch.

"Do you think we were the only ones to make it out of the clearing?" Barret asked as he followed Alec out of the water.

"I know one who definitely didn't make it out of the clearing," Alec answered.

"It's pathetic that they even let him run the Gauntlet," Barret said as he walked over to the rocks. "Everyone knows he got lucky when he beat you."

"Barret be quiet!" Alec whispered as he took a defensive position, staring at the back of the cave.

Evan had sensed movement as well. The noise Alec and Barret had made after surfacing had alerted whoever was waiting for them.

Two soldiers rushed out from an opening at the back of the cave. Alec dodged the first soldier's swing and shoved him in Barret's direction as he dashed for a rock. The first soldier slammed Barret against the cave wall while the second soldier rushed after Alec. Alec was so focused on the rocks that he didn't see the second soldier until it was too late. The soldier hit Alec with his shoulder, sending him forcefully into the rock wall. The impact knocked Alec to the ground, where he laid motionless.

"Tie their hands," The second soldier ordered. He was visibly older than the other, skinnier soldier.

"Look who we have here," the skinny soldier exclaimed as he finished tying Barret's hands together and moved to Alec. "I don't believe I have ever caught a royal before. What did you do to him?"

"I barely touched him. I swear these kids get weaker every year," the older soldier said

"Let's take this one and put him with the rest." The older soldier said as he gagged Barret and, with the younger soldier's help, dragged him into the shadows.

As soon as the soldiers were out of sight, Evan ran to the pile of rocks. With any luck he would be gone before the soldiers even knew he was there. Evan was about to reach for a rock when he stopped. He couldn't just leave the others behind no matter how bad they had treated him. He needed to help the other boys. He could have made the same mistakes they had and been tied up in the back of the cave with no hope of finishing the competition. He couldn't stand back and do nothing just as he had done when the soldiers had captured Gale.

Evan ran to Alec and quickly untied his hands. He then ran to the water's edge to get water to splash in Alec's face, but when he turned around Alec was already at the pile of rocks.

"You were faking?" Evan whispered, astonished.

"I figured they would leave me unattended if they thought I was unconscious. I wasn't sure how I was going to get untied though."

"How can we free the others?" Evan asked, thinking Alec would want to help.

"It's a competition Evan. You didn't need to save me and you shouldn't worry about the others."

Evan heard movement from the back of the cave, the soldiers were coming back.

"Every boy for himself," Alec said as he dove into the water and disappeared.

Evan couldn't believe it! Weren't the others Alec's friends. Evan quickly stepped back into the shadows, just as the soldiers appeared.

"Where did he go?" the skinny soldier asked.

"He must have been faking that he was unconscious and untied himself. He couldn't have gone far." Both men dove into the water to chase after Alec.

Evan didn't waste any time. He quickly ran back in the direction the soldiers had just come. The cave got darker the further back he went. By the time he reached the small room at the back of the cave he could barely see the three boys who were tied and gagged.

Evan removed Thomas's gag first.

"What are you doing here Evan?" Thomas asked.

"I don't have time to explain, we need to hurry." Evan quickly untied the boys and together they ran to the cave's entrance. Each boy grabbed a rock from the pile and were about to jump into the water when the soldier's heads appeared.

"Look what we have here," the skinny soldier said as he climbed out of the water.

Simon and Thomas picked up the clubs the men had left behind.

"Simon, you wouldn't dare hit your uncle," the older soldier said, trying to appeal to his nephew.

"It didn't stop you from almost knocking me out earlier!" Simon said.

"It was nothing personal."

"I guess I can say the same thing," Simon said. "Nothing personal."

Simon and Thomas stepped forward. Without weapons and being out numbered four to two, the guards decided that since this was only a competition that no one should get hurt, especially them, and they surrendered without a fight.

"Where did Alec go?" Barrett asked as he finished tying up the last soldier.

Evan picked up a rock and put it into his pocket. "He left after I untied him."

Barrett, reached down and picked up his own rock, "I guess I would have done the same thing," he said looking a bit rejected.

"We all would have," Simon said.

"You could have left us all here and escaped without the soldiers even knowing you were here. Why did you help us?" Thomas asked.

"I'm not sure," Evan said. "I just couldn't leave without at least trying to help."

"You're a complicated orphan?" Thomas said as he slapped Evan on the back and then dove into the water with Simon close behind.

"It must be almost light," Barrett said as he prepared to dive into the water. "Whatever happens don't stop running." Without another word Barrett disappeared into the water.

"You're never going to make it to the clearing," Simon's uncle said as Evan prepared to follow Barrett.

"Yeah, the Captain will make sure of that," the skinny soldier said.

"We'll see," Evan answered as he dove into the cold water.

■ ·· ■ ·· ■ ·· ■ ··

Evan ran through the forest as fast as he could, not bothering to conceal his whereabouts.

When he had re-surfaced at Reflection Pool, he was surprised at how light it was. He didn't know exactly what time the sun would rise, but he knew he didn't have long.

Evan hadn't seen any of the other boys since they had split up after leaving the cave. It was true what Alec had said, it was every boy for himself. Evan's lungs were on fire as he raced the sun. The clearing was close, but the fact that he hadn't seen any soldiers worried him. Were they all waiting to ambush the boys outside of the clearing?

Movement caught Evan's eye. He stopped running and moved off the trail. Barret was sneaking in the shadows towards the clearing. He must have sensed a trap as well.

Suddenly a soldier sounded the alarm by yelling at the top of his lungs.

"Get him! Don't let him get away!"

Barret bolted from the edge of the clearing as soldiers from all directions jumped out from their hiding places in pursuit.

Evan picked up a stick about the size of a baseball bat and ducked down into the bushes. Barret and two of the soldiers were heading straight for him. Every boy for himself, Evan heard Alec say again in his head but he couldn't let the soldiers catch Barrett, he had to help.

Barrett didn't see Evan as he ran past Evan's bush. Evan sank deeper into the thick brush to conceal himself. Just as the first soldier ran past the bush Evan stuck the stick in between the soldier's legs. The soldier yelled as he crashed to the ground. The second soldier, who was following too closely, tripped over the first soldier. The men landed in a tangled mess a few feet from Evan.

"Barrett, this way!" Evan yelled as he got to his feet.

"Barrett turned and sprinted back towards the clearing with soldiers closing in.

Evan followed at full speed.

Barrett ran into the clearing with hands held high above his head in celebration. Evan felt like doing the same. He couldn't believe that he was going to make it, he was going to complete the Gauntlet.

Just as Evan was about to break out of the trees, he was struck in the chest by a staff, completely stopping his forward progression. Evan's legs swung into the air and he landed on his back on the hard ground, knocking the wind out of his lungs. Evan was dazed. What had hit him? He was sure the path had been clear. He had been right behind Barrett.

Captain Curtis stepped over Evan, holding a staff in his hand. "You didn't think I would let an orphan finish did you?"

Evan's eyes moved from Captain Curtis to the horizon. The sun had just peaked. He looked into the clearing. Alec and Barrett stood in the center of the clearing. Thomas, Simon and Gale were all tied up next to a group of soldiers. Just like Evan, they had failed.

Chapter Twenty

A Warrior's Task

The royal stable was deserted. Only the sound of hooves pawing at the ground and an occasional snorting from a horse could be heard. Evan's ability to tell time using the sun was shabby at best and he hoped he was not late for his warrior task especially because he was to perform this task with Alec.

It had been two days since Evan had attempted to run the Gauntlet. Even though he had not completed the Gauntlet successfully, Captain Curtis had seen warrior potential in Evan. He was now attending warrior training and doing warrior tasks instead of working in the fields at night. Evan had avoided Emma the past two days, embarrassed because he had failed. She had been so sure that he would finish the Gauntlet and be invited to participate in the Crossover. He guessed that she wouldn't want anything to do with a failure and so Evan avoided the awkward rejection by avoiding her. The worst part of failing was that Evan now realized how much he had wanted it. It had been his one chance to really belong.

Tonight was a celebration where they would select the two champions who would perform the Crossover. Since Barrett and Alec were the only ones to finish the Gauntlet, Evan guessed it was really only a formality. Evan didn't want to go, but was required to since he had participated in the Gauntlet. He was sure Emma would be there too, but wasn't sure if she would talk to him, now that he was considered a failure.

"How about a carrot?" Evan asked trying to entice an old brown stable horse as he entered her stall.

The mare moved toward Evan's outstretched hand, her head reaching forward excitedly. There weren't many horses on The Ledge and since Evan wasn't the best rider, he wanted to take an older, more predictable horse. Evan tied a lead rope around the horse's head and then grabbed an old battered saddle.

"You know how to shoot, don't you?" Alec approached from the courtyard, leading his large black horse, Crescent. He threw a bow and several arrows in a quiver at Evan's feet.

"Yes," Evan answered, glad that Emma had taught him that skill.

"You're not thinking of taking that horse are you?" Alec asked annoyed.

"Why is that a problem?"

"Yes, I'm not even sure that one can run anymore" Alec said. "I don't want this task to take all night. I don't know if you've heard, but there's a celebration in my honor tonight."

"I've heard?" Evan said.

"Take Smokey, Emma's horse. That way we might finish the task before tomorrow.

"What are we doing exactly?"

"The easiest warrior task there is. Which is fitting for you."

"What's that supposed to mean?" Evan asked defensively.

Evan's question was answered with a smirk. "My job is to ensure the border is safe. Your job is to keep up and try and learn something."

"We're riding the entire border of The Ledge?" Evan asked excitedly. He had never ventured that far into the forest.

"Some of the border," Alec corrected. "Just make sure you keep up. I don't want this to take all night. I have to accept my Crossover medal tonight at the celebration."

"What's a Crossover medal?"

Alec jumped on Crescent. "Something you will never have to worry about." Without saying another word, he kicked the stallion into a full gallop, leaving Evan in a cloud of dust.

Evan led the old mare back into her stall and then walked over to Smokey's stall.

"You're stuck with me tonight," Evan said as he quickly saddled the gray mare.

Evan fastened his bow on his back and jumped onto Smokey. Without any prodding, the powerful gray mare lunged forward.

— ·· — ·· — · — ··

The dense forest blocked out the evening sun as Evan followed a trail at the base of the jagged cliffs. He looked back toward the direction he had come and could still see the tallest towers of the castle glistening in the last rays of the sunlight. The evening air felt cool as it whipped through Evan's hair. There was still no sign of Alec and Evan hoped he had picked the right trail.

Smokey slowed her gallop to a trot as she rounded a corner in the trail. "About time you caught up," Alec taunted. Grabbing Crescent's lead rope, Alec stood up on the log he had been sitting on and jumped onto the stallion's back in one fluid motion.

"Try and keep up this time." Alec said as he kicked Crescent to a full gallop.

Prodded by Evan, Smokey matched the stallion's speed as the path plunged deeper into the forest, the bushes and trees tightening their grip on the narrow trail. Evan had previously only been allowed to ride Smokey in the clearing where he met Emma every morning, but now that he was allowed to train as a warrior, he had more freedom. Instead of being confined to the fields he was on the other side of The Ledge guarding the safety of the kingdom. For the first time since coming to The Ledge, Evan felt like he belonged. He felt like he was part of something greater than himself.

Lost in thought, Evan forgot to control Smokey and when the trail split Alec went one way while Smokey chose the other which turned out to be nothing more than an overgrown path. Evan raised his hands in front of him to try and block the tree branches that were hitting him in the face.

"Stop!" Evan yelled at Smokey. "Whoa!" he yelled again as he inhaled a mouth full of leaves.

Smokey burst into a clearing and skidded to a stop in the soft, white sand, almost throwing Evan over her head.

"What's gotten into you?" Evan asked with disgust as he dismounted.

White sand surrounded a deep blue pool of water. The mist from a towering waterfall dropped the temperature a few degrees, and Evan shivered slightly. Stairs had been chiseled into the solid rock leading to an overhang that looked perfect for cliff jumping. Green moss covered the cliffs and vines hung down from the trees which surrounded the water.

"This place is," Evan stopped, as he tried to think of the right word to describe his surroundings.

"Too nice for an orphan," Alec finished, seeming annoyed as he came into the clearing behind Evan. "You took the wrong trail."

"Smokey took the wrong trail. I just came along for the ride," Evan clarified. "And I was going to say this place is beautiful." Evan admired the vines, which dropped from the tall trees down to the water's surface. "Have you been here before?" Evan turned to look at Alec.

"Not that it's any of your business, but yes we come here to swim sometimes," Alec offered as he dismounted. "That's probably why Smokey took the trail. We jump off those cliffs into the cool water." Alec pointed to the cliffs on the far side of the pool.

"We?" Evan asked, surprised that Alec was sharing this with him.

"Yeah, me and Peter. Sometimes Emma comes, too. It's somewhere we can go to get away from the castle. Everyone expects us to be perfect inside its walls. But out here, we can be ourselves,"

"I understand," Evan said.

"You understand? I doubt anyone expects an orphan to be perfect!" Alec mocked.

"No, I understand expectations!" Evan shot back. "Everyone expects me to fail and hates me before they get to know me because I am an orphan. The expectations people hold you to are different than mine, but no more severe."

Alec grabbed a flat rock and skipped it across the water. "I never thought of it like that."

"Why would you?" Evan said as he turned back towards Smokey.

Alec watched Evan for a moment as if deciding whether or not to share something with him. "The day we found you, we were coming here."

"You found me nearby?" Evan gawked. This was the closest he had come to finding the spot where he had first entered The Ledge.

"Just down that trail." Alec pointed to a path that disappeared into the thick underbrush, following the stream. "You can imagine how shocked we were to find anyone else out here, so far from the castle that is."

"Is that why you threw me into the dungeon, because you didn't want me to find your special spot?" Evan asked, still annoyed.

Alec chuckled. "Maybe that did have something to do with it." Alec's look then turned serious.

"The night before we found you, we discovered a man within the castle. If it hadn't been a full moon that night, the man in his dark hooded cloak would have gone unnoticed. A guard from one of the towers spotted him in the moonlight, emerging from behind one of the large oak trees in the courtyard. "That guard sounded the alarm, signaling several other guards who all converged on the courtyard, blocking all exits. There was nowhere for him to run. He was trapped, but when the guards arrived, the man had disappeared. They searched the courtyard for hours, and eventually the entire castle was searched, but the hooded man was never found."

"How did he escape?" Evan asked.

"We don't know," Alec responded, looking at the ground uneasily. "The next day we found you in the forest."

"Alone," Evan added. "Just like the man."

"Yes, so now you can understand why we threw you in the dungeon and I'm still not sure if we should trust you or not."

The sun had disappeared behind the cliffs and night was approaching. The pine-scented air felt chilly, as a slight wind picked up from the north.

"We need to finish our task," Alec stated.

"Do we have far to go?" Evan asked.

"Not far." Alec jumped on Crescent.

They left the small piece of paradise in a cloud of dust and traveled deeper into the forest. The forest filtered most of the fleeting light from the night sky, but the horses knew the way, which allowed Evan's mind to drift to the overgrown path, which followed the stream. A sense of excitement overcame him as he released all tension on Smokey's reins, giving her freedom to speed up. Now that he knew where to start looking, Evan hoped he could find some answers. Suddenly, Alec pulled Crescent to a skidding stop. Smokey followed suit.

"What's wrong? Why did you stop?" Evan asked.

But before Alec could answer, Evan could see for himself. On either side of the trail, the bushes and small trees had been crushed under the weight of an unseen force. Alec dismounted and surveyed the trail, which was littered with tree limbs.

"There's blood here," Alec whispered as he rose from the trail, two of his fingers glistening red from where he had touched the ground.

The silence of the forest was shattered by a single long howl. The sound echoed through the darkness.

"There haven't been wolves this close to The Ledge for years," Alec mumbled as he looked up to the top of the cliffs.

"There's no way someone could have survived that fall," Evan said, staring up at the wall of rock.

"Maybe not someone, but possibly something," Alec shrugged as he moved closer to the edge of the path, examining a crushed sapling.

There was a loud snap in the dark forest adjacent to their path. It hung in the air ominously. The horses moved restlessly and Evan quickly dismounted and grabbed their lead ropes to keep them from running off. Evan stared into the darkness, trying to see beyond the thick undergrowth. Not far from the path, he heard labored breathing. Something was out there. Evan ran through options in his head. He had seen mountain goats a few weeks ago scaling the large cliffs. Maybe one had slipped from its perch high above their heads and fallen. Looking around at bushes and trees, Evan doubted a mountain goat could have caused so much damage.

"Maybe a boulder dislodged from the cliff," Evan hypothesized to Alec, unconvincingly.

"Maybe, but that doesn't explain the blood," Alec countered cautiously, his eyes fixed on the forest.

Evan stared into the dark trees again. He felt as though they were being watched.

"There's a print in the mud," Alec whispered. He was now on the edge of the path, kneeling again and examining the print in the darkness.

Evan heard a twig snap in the forest and then another. This time louder. Something was moving toward them. Alec arose from the path and looked back at Evan, terror in his eyes.

"Run!" Alec called in an urgent voice as he started to draw his sword. He quickly stepped away from the forest, as it came alive.

It all happened very quickly. The beast sounded like a freight train smashing through everything that stood in its path as it moved directly towards Alec. The horses bolted in the direction they had just come, throwing Evan to the ground as he attempted to hold onto them, their lead ropes burning his hands as they slipped through his grip. Evan rolled onto his back as a large bear charged through the underbrush at full speed. Its fur was matted down with dried blood. The bear let out a roar that silenced the entire forest, its giant white fangs glistened in the moonlight.

Alec held his ground, trying to draw his sword, but the bear charged too quickly. The beast collided with him at full speed, his teeth sinking deeply into the Alec's shoulder. Alec screamed as the bear flung him like a small rag doll into a large, jagged bolder.

Alec's screams silenced as his body smashed into the rock, knocking him unconscious.

"No!" Evan screamed.

The bear ignored Evan, as he walked towards Alec.

In one fluid motion, Evan swung his bow from his back and took an arrow from his quiver. He pulled the bow string back with all his strength, and then clearing his head, took careful aim at the base of the bear's head and released. The bear let out a roar of pain as the arrow made contact, tearing through the bears thick hide just below his giant skull. The bear turned toward Evan, abandoning Alec's lifeless body.

Evan tried desperately to load another arrow as his hands trembled. Finally, he pulled back again, this time to save his own life. He aimed directly between the bear's eyes and released the second arrow. The arrow flew straight, but to Evan's horror, the thin piece of wood shattered on impact.

The furious beast charged Evan at full speed, Alec's blood now staining its teeth. Evan turned to run but tripped over a branch from one of the smashed pine trees that had been crushed when the bear had fallen from the cliff. He fell hard to the dusty path as the angry bear closed in.

Evan knew he only had seconds. As he tried to raise himself from the ground, his hand caught hold of one of the sharp, shattered tree limb he had just stumbled over. In desperation, he raised the limb with both hands and faced the bear. The bear hit the jagged pine limb and then Evan knocking him backwards into the cliff wall, smashing his head. Evan fell to ground again, this time unconscious.

— ·— ·· — ·· — ··

Evan slowly opened his eyes. It took him several moments to figure out where he was and what had happened. He was still alive. He sat up quickly as he remembered the charging bear. A large mound, inches in front of him, moved. Startled, Evan backed away from the bear until his back was up against the cliff. The giant beast didn't attack but laid on the ground, gasping for air. The bear took one last breath and then laid motionless, the pine limb protruding from its chest.

Evan stumbled over to Alec, who was still lying next to the boulder. Evan lowered his face to Alec's mouth and waited for signs of life. He watched Alec's chest slowly rise and then lower. He was alive but had lost a lot of blood from where the bear had bit his shoulder.

"Help!" Evan yelled at the top of his lungs, but his voice simply disappeared into the empty forest.

Realizing that he was Alec's only hope, Evan focused his energy on saving Alec's life. He took his cloak off and tied it tightly around Alec's shoulder, to try and stop the bleeding. He then looked down the dark trail in the direction the horses had fled. Evan debated for a moment about leaving Alec unguarded in the forest, but realizing what little precious time Alec had left, Evan made the only choice he could. He needed to leave Alec and find the horses. It was the only way to get Alec back to the castle.

Still light headed from being knocked out, but driven by desperation, Evan sprinted down the path in the direction the horses had run, praying that they hadn't gone far. Evan's lungs were on fire as he pushed his body through the pain. He had never run this fast before, the adrenaline propelled him forward through the darkness. After about a mile, Evan's legs started to give in to exhaustion. No matter how much oxygen he inhaled, it was not enough. He pushed himself around another bend in the trail, knowing that if the horses weren't there, all hope for saving Alec would be lost.

Smokey raised her head ever so slightly as Evan burst into the small clearing. Crescent was nearby, lazily grazing, appearing to not have a care in the world. Evan felt like yelling for joy but stopped. He didn't want to scare the already-spooked horses, so he eased forward slowly, calling Smokey by name. It seemed like an eternity, before he reached the mare and was able to grab hold of her reins. He then walked towards Crescent.

"Alec needs you," Evan encouraged, stepping towards the wary stallion. Crescent bucked his head violently and trotted away from Evan as Evan barely missed the reins. Of course, Alec's horse wouldn't trust him.

"We're wasting time," Evan hissed under his breath. He knew that they would travel much faster with two horses. Evan picked up a handful of lush grass and held it out.

Smokey followed Evan, as he again walked towards Crescent, his free hand outstretched. The stallion took a step toward Evan.

"That's right. Come on, Crescent, just a little, closer." Evan grabbed the reins as the horse reached for the grass. Not wanting to waste any more time Evan jumped on Crescent's back and pulled Smokey alongside the larger stallion, he kicked the horse into a full gallop back down the trail.

Alec was still lying next to the rock, his skin pale. Evan quickly dismounted and led Smokey near Alec.

"Down, girl," Evan called as he pulled the mare's lead rope towards the ground. He had seen Emma do this trick many times, but it was the first time Evan had attempted it.

"Down, girl. Down!" Evan repeated with more intensity. The horse dropped down on her knees. Evan grabbed Alec and lifted him over the mare's back. He then tied Alec's arms tight around Smokey's neck.

"Up! Up, girl." The mare rose to her feet. Satisfied that Alec wouldn't slip from the horses back and be trampled, Evan jumped on Crescent and still holding Smokey's lead rope, he nudged the horses into a fast trot toward the castle.

— ·· — ·· — ·· — ··

"Help, we need help!" Evan yelled as he pulled the exhausted horses to a skidding stop in the courtyard of the castle under the giant oaks. "Help, the prince has been injured!" Evan yelled as he dismounted.

Using his knife, Evan cut the rope from Alec's arms and slowly lowered him to the stone ground. There was a flurry of activity as people filled the courtyard from the Grand Hall where the celebration was being held. Several guards rushed into the courtyard. Evan had made it. He felt the adrenaline, which had spurred him on, leave his body as he knelt beside Alec. Evan sensed movement around him, but his hearing was muffled and his vision blurred. He felt weak and dizzy. Emma had moved in front of Evan.

"Evan, are you okay?"

Evan tried to answer but couldn't speak.

"They are both hurt!" Emma said.

Did she say both? Evan thought to himself.

"No Emma, just Alec. You need to help Alec," Evan mumbled weakly. He wanted to lie down. He wanted to sleep. Then everything went black, and Evan toppled to the ground.

— ·· — ·· — ·· — ··

Evan opened his eyes and found himself in a room with a small fire. The warmth felt nice. There were several people around the bed next to him.

"Alec has lost too much blood, and we can't stop the bleeding," a man stated, a sense of finality in his voice, as if they were ready to give up.

"Get out!" the Queen yelled as she pointed to the door. "All of you, get out!" Evan heard quick footsteps leave the room before the door snapped shut.

The Queen and King stepped close to Alec's bed as the door shut. The King gave his wife a nod, and she pulled out a small object, wrapped in a white cloth, from a bag she had been holding at her side. The Queen unwrapped the object and pressed it hard against Alec's shoulder. Alec didn't react, but laid lifeless, his eyes closed. She then turned to Evan.

The Queen stopped abruptly, noticing Evan's eyes fixed upon her. She had obviously not realized Evan had regained consciousness. She motioned to the King who walked briskly to the opposite side of Evan's bed and rolled him onto his side away from the Queen. Evan heard the Queen step close and then felt an ice cold object placed on the back of his head. The cold quickly engulfed Evan's head and then his entire body as it intensified to the point of excruciating pain. Evan lifted his head slightly and tried to yell out, but the pain of having the warmth ripped from his body was too horrifying for his mind to comprehend and quickly the darkness returned and Evan's head fell back to the bed.

Chapter Twenty-One
The Mysterious Memories

Evan woke up to find himself under several heavy blankets in a room he didn't recognize. The room was dark. The thick drapes drawn shut over the windows. Small embers crackled in the fireplace. Evan moved his stiff body slightly, but his efforts were met by a sharp pain pounding on the back of his head. Evan carefully reached his trembling hand to the back of his head. The spot was cold to the touch, as if he had been using a block of ice for his pillow. Evan shivered under the heavy covers and pulled them up to his chin. The room was warm, but his body felt ice-cold, as if he was experiencing chills that normally accompanied the flu.

Confused, Evan tried to navigate through the fog that normally accompanied the first few moments of consciousness after waking. But on this particular morning, the fog lingered ominously. He started to ask himself simple questions, trying desperately to remember anything at all. Why was he lying in this room? What had happened yesterday? Why was the back of his head ice-cold? With every question he couldn't answer, Evan's panic grew. He closed his eyes and tried to chase the growing panic from his mind, searching for one familiar thread that would tie his thoughts together.

Another sharp pain pounded in his head. He closed his eyes tightly, a groan escaping his lips. Instantly Evan found himself in a forest, almost as if he were in a dream but much clearer than any dream he had ever experienced. It felt as though he were actually in the forest. The dark room had been replaced by trees and the dense forest undergrowth. He had to shield his eyes from the bright rays of the sun as they penetrated the thick trees high above his head. Sounds echoed through the forest, shattering the silence. Something was moving toward him. Evan looked for a place to hide. He didn't know who or what was moving in his direction, but he didn't want to get caught in the open. Evan quickly dove behind a bush at the edge of the clearing and waited.

Two hooded figures burst into the small clearing running at full speed. The smaller of the two collapsed to the ground in a heap, as their legs gave way to exhaustion. The larger, a boy not much older than Evan, skidded to a stop next to his fallen companion. He was breathing heavily as he knelt down. He was calm, but Evan could see urgency in his eyes as he pulled his fallen companion to their knees.

"We have, to keep moving," he warned between deep gulps of air. "They are close." He looked back nervously in the direction they had come.

Long brown hair fell out of the fallen traveler's hood as she raised her head to meet his gaze. "I can't, go on. I don't have any energy left. Go without me, I shouldn't even be here. They will stop chasing you, once they have me."

"You don't know what you're saying," the boy shot back with concern.

"There's no time to explain and even if there was, you wouldn't understand," the girl argued.

"I won't leave you," the boy said defiantly. He looked up and turned his body to shield the girl from an unseen, approaching danger.

Evan strained to see or hear what had alerted the boy.

The sound of crunching dead leaves on the forest floor confirmed something moving towards them.

"We have to go," the boy pleaded, turning to his exhausted companion.

With great effort, using every ounce of strength she possessed, she began to stand. In one fluid motion, while she wasn't looking, the boy removed a small rock about the size of a baseball from his bag. After looking at it for a brief moment, he carefully placed it into the girl's leather satchel.

A deep growl from the clearing's edge snapped Evan's attention away from the travelers. A grey wolf had entered the clearing, its curled lips revealing razor sharp teeth that looked capable of biting through bone. The beast's back stood as tall as the boy's waist, and they looked equal in weight. They eyed each other, neither moving.

"Run," the boy commanded in a low tone that Evan barely heard.

"No! I won't leave you," the girl whispered, panicked.

"Run and don't look back!" he yelled more forcefully.

The girl held firm.

"RUN!" he yelled, and in one motion he drew his bow, which was slung around his back.

The girl started to run, spurred on by fear. The snarling wolf charged the boy, who was waiting with his bow at full draw for the wolf to get close enough. Two other wolves broke through the underbrush, following the charge of the first one. It all happened in slow motion. The lead wolf leaped for the boy's throat. Evan feared the boy had waited too long. With the wolf only feet from the boy, he released his arrow. The wolf yelped and fell to the ground, skidding to a stop inches from the boy's feet, dead. The boy wasted no time. He loaded a second arrow and let it fly. Without even waiting to see if the arrow found the second wolf, he dove to the side just as the third wolf leaped for him. The wolf missed his prey, but recovered quickly, charging the boy again. As the boy dove to the ground he pulled out a knife and threw it at the charging wolf, catching it in the neck. The wolf staggered for a moment and then crashed to the ground. The girl had already disappeared into the forest, but even with the wolves dead the boy did not follow. He stuck his remaining arrows into the dirt in front of him and waited.

Evan heard men yelling in the distance. They were close and moving fast. The boy didn't move. He just waited. Within moments, several armed men entered the clearing. The men looked weary from the chase. All four of the men were much larger than the boy and by the positions they took in a semicircle around their victim, Evan could tell they were seasoned warriors. Two of them gripped large swords with razor sharp blades, and a third held the leashes of two giant, snarling beasts, just like the three wolves the boy had just killed. A fourth man remained at the edge of the clearing, standing under a large pine tree in the shadows. Most of his face was concealed, but Evan could tell that he was smiling slightly as he watched the other men move closer to the boy.

"Where is she?" a man in the center of the dangerous group snarled in a raspy voice, as his eyes fell on the dead wolves.

"You'll never find her. She has probably reached The Ledge by now," the boy bluffed. "King Lewis will be on his way shortly.

"You're lying!" the man spat.

"You won't live long enough to find out," the boy stated with complete soberness as he pulled his bow back.

The man stepped back cautiously and gripped his sword. After a moment, the man began to chuckle softly, his mouth forming into

219

an evil smile. The man looked away from the boy to both of his companions, not threatened by the arrow. With pure evil in his voice and without any hesitation, he addressed his companions in a low tone, "Kill the boy, and then find the girl!"

The forest behind the men started to blur, and Evan realized the trees were fading away. He concentrated, trying to stay in the clearing with the boy, but it was no use. The forest, the men, and lastly, the boy disappeared and Evan was no longer in the depths of the forest.

Evan laid in his bed, reacquainted once again with the small, dark room, perspiration falling on his pillow. The pain returned again with such force that Evan wondered if it would split his head in two. He closed his eyes, trying to absorb the pain, resisting the temptation to scream.

Suddenly, Evan found himself in the forest again, another dream engulfing him. The light from the sun, which had already dipped well below the cliffs, was dim, and Evan struggled to make out anything more than twenty feet away. The cliffs looked familiar and he realized that he was somewhere on The Ledge, but where he didn't have a clue. The night air was blowing in from the coast. He was on the bank of a small stream, standing on a beach of soft sand next to an old log, bleached white by years of weather. Evan remembered this beach. He walked over to the large log on the edge of the beach. His shirt and socks he had been wearing the night of the dance at Wellsford Academy were lying on the log, exactly where he had left them before he walked to the stream to wash the blood from his head. This was the first place he had remembered being on The Ledge. Thinking that this was his memory, Evan jumped onto the log thinking he would see Emma riding through the forest just as he remembered it.

At first glance, Evan assumed the forest was empty. He didn't see Emma anywhere. He was about to jump down from the log when movement caught his eye a few feet in front of him. A person wearing a hooded cloak, stared motionless at a small pine tree. Evan found this odd. This person was not part of his memory. Evan didn't move for fear he would disturb the dream. After a moment the person stood and left the pine tree and walked away from Evan through the thick underbrush in the direction of the trail where Evan had met Emma for the first time.

Evan jumped over the log and stared at the ordinary tree. He was about to turn and follow the person when he noticed something wedged under a bush next to the pine tree. Bending down he reached under the bush and pulled out a book. Turning the book over in his hand he read the cover. Evan's head started to spin out of control, he couldn't breathe as he read the cover again, "Advanced Calculus." The book fell from his hands and he rushed after the person through the underbrush. He had to find the person in the cloak, they were the key to helping him find his way home.

"Please wake up," a familiar voice encouraged in the distance.

Evan ran faster, as the dream started to blur, just as the last one had.

"Please, you must wake up."

Darkness was closing in around him and then he felt someone's hand embrace his own. The warmth of the touch pulled him out of the darkness and all at once the forest and the person were gone.

"It's all my fault," Emma sniffed in between her soft cries. "If I hadn't pushed you so hard, you would have been farming, and none of this would have happened."

Evan found himself back in the dark room, but this time he wasn't alone. Evan was surprised to find Emma sitting on his bed, her head resting on Evan's chest. He thought Emma wouldn't care about him because he had failed to complete the Gauntlet. Why was she here? Was he still dreaming or was this real? Awkwardly he reached his hand up to Emma's head.

Emma stopped crying and slowly raised her head from Evan's chest. Her eyes were red and puffy and her cheeks wet from crying, but she was smiling as she embraced Evan without saying a word.

"You're, you're awake!" Emma whispered, breaking the silence.

Evan was still confused. "What happened to me?" He muttered.

"You don't remember?" Emma asked cautiously.

Evan reached deep into his mind, trying desperately to remember what had happened. "I remember riding off into the forest with Alec to patrol the border." Evan stopped. His mention of Alec brought back a flood of memories.

"Alec!" Evan blurted out, remembering the bear attack. "How's Alec? Did he survive the attack last night?"

"Last night?" Emma repeated, confused.

"Yes, after the bear attack," Evan continued.

Emma paused for a moment, collecting her thoughts. Slowly, she stood and straightened her dress. "Alec survived the attack, thanks to you, but the attack happened seven days ago, not last night. You have been lying in bed motionless since the attack. The physicians thought you were dead, but mother assured them you were not. She was convinced that you would wake up. She knew that you would, and now you have."

"I've been lying here for seven days?" Evan asked, feeling weak again.

"Yes, and your body was ice-cold, just like Alec's was. He woke up, however, and you stayed asleep. I have to tell them that you woke up. Everyone will want to know." Emma said excitedly.

"Everyone?" Evan repeated, confused.

"That's right. What's wrong?" Emma asked seeing the look on Evan's face.

"I didn't think anyone cared about me," Evan said plainly, still confused. "I didn't think you cared about me anymore."

"Why would you say that?" Emma said.

"Because I failed to complete the Gauntlet."

"I don't care about that."

"But I'll never be able to perform the Crossover," Evan said.

"That doesn't matter to me. From what I heard from Alec and Barret, they would have never been able to complete the Gauntlet without your help," Emma stated.

"But Alec hates me," Evan said still very confused. "Why would he say that?"

"Alec has been different since he woke up," Emma said. "I guess almost dying changes a person."

Evan didn't know what to say, but he was sure Emma was mistaken.

Emma quickly moved toward the door.

"Where are you going?" Evan asked.

"I told you already, I have to tell everyone that you are awake. Gramps has been here every day since the attack. And of course, Francis will want to know. And my parents. And the rest of the royal family. And naturally the entire kingdom will have to be informed."

Evan was overwhelmed by Emma's list. "Why would they care about me?" Evan asked, completely confused.

"You saved Alec's life! Saving a member of the royal family doesn't go unnoticed," Emma exclaimed as she opened the door to rush out.

"Emma, wait!" Evan quickly said before Emma could leave.

"Yes."

"This may sound like a stupid question." Evan feared he would sound crazy, but he had to ask, he had to know. "Have you ever heard of a King Lewis?" Evan asked holding his breath.

The mention of King Lewis in his dream was the only thing that might prove to Evan that his dream was more than just a dream, because if the first dream was somehow a memory of things that had happened then maybe the second dream was a memory as well and there might be a chance for Evan to return home.

Emma looked at Evan confused for a moment, but then without hesitation she answered. "I only know of one King Lewis," Emma said matter of fact. "He was my grandpa."

Evan laid back down on his pillow as Emma shut the door. He had so many questions, and absolutely no answers, but for the first time in almost five months he had hope. The dreams had given him reason to believe that he wasn't crazy and that he might actually see his family again.

Chapter Twenty-Two
Honoring the Orphan

Evan sat on a patch of tall grass near the cliff's edge outside of the city wall, watching ships of various sizes enter the sanctuary of the bay from the rough waters of the open sea. The floating docks far below were busy with all manner of trade and business as the late morning sun rose over the cliffs and touched the waters of the bay.

Evan tugged at his tight collar to allow for more breathing room. This is worse than wearing a tie, he thought as he made a soft choking sound.

Evan was wearing a brilliant white shirt, the collar rose half way up his neck, strangling him. His pants, a soft tan leather, were surprisingly comfortable. His dark blue cloak was sewn from the warmest imported fabric, and the soles of his shoes were filled with the finest tree sap Gramps had ever collected. Evan assumed he looked "sharp," as his mother had often referred to him when he was dressed up. He missed his mother. It had been almost five months since he had seen her and two weeks since the bear attack.

The dreams he had experienced after the bear attack had given him a reason to believe that he wasn't crazy after all. Although he couldn't explain how the dreams had come to him, or what they meant, he knew one thing for sure, he had to find the small pine tree by the stream he had seen in his dream and he knew exactly where he needed to start his search.

225

Evan breathed in the salty air as he watched an osprey lazily soar over the bay looking for fish. Nestled in the tall grass was the only place he could truly be alone. Since the bear attack two weeks ago, he had become something of a celebrity on The Ledge. Everyone wanted to hear about the attack and how a boy had managed to slay the giant bear. He tried to explain to everyone that he had tripped over a sharp pine tree as he was backing away from the terrifying bear. It had been dumb luck. He had explained time and time again, but nobody listened to him. He was a hero for saving Alec from certain death and should be treated as such. That's what the ceremony today was all about and why he was dressed up. He was to be personally honored by the King and Queen for services rendered to the kingdom or something like that.

Why couldn't they just say thanks and be done with it? Evan thought. He didn't like all of the extra attention he was receiving.

"There you are," Francis called, out of breath and looking relieved to have found Evan's hiding spot. "You know the ceremony is starting soon?" Francis sat uninvited in the grass next to Evan.

"Oh, is that today?" Evan joked, pretending to be surprised.

"You joke, but Emma is ready to kill you. She actually thinks you won't show up today," Francis warned as he pulled a long piece of grass out of the ground and started to suck on the flavorful root.

Evan laughed to himself. Francis truly looked like a farmer with the long piece of grass hanging out of his mouth.

"I mean, you've got to learn to accept your new-found fame."

"It was luck, Francis," Evan seethed, frustrated that he needed to explain this again to his friend for the twentieth time.

"You don't think that people who do amazing things get lucky in some way or another?" Francis shot back. "Look, answer one question. Would Alec be alive today if you hadn't been there to intervene?"

Evan tried to think of a quick retort, something that would end this discussion once and for all. But as much as Evan didn't want to admit it, Francis was right.

Knowing he had won the argument, Francis put his hands behind his head and laid back in the soft grass with a smug look across his boyish face, "That's what I thought."

The two friends sat in the grass for a while saying nothing, simply enjoying the last days of summer until Francis sat up. "I guess this is one of the last days we will get to spend together," Francis said, the joy of winning the argument now faded.

"What do you mean?" Evan asked, slightly alarmed.

"I'm heading back home before the Crossover celebration," he admitted. "My father sent word just after the bear attack that I'm needed back in our kingdom."

"Why didn't you tell me?" Evan asked, feeling a sense of despair growing in the pit of his stomach. Evan didn't have many friends on The Ledge and no family, besides his adopted Gramps. Francis had been his friend, someone who was always there.

"I didn't want to ruin your moment of fame, being a hero and all," Francis mumbled with a slight chuckle.

"I'm going to miss beating you during Emma's training sessions," Evan joked.

"You can come with me, you know."

"You mean, leave The Ledge?"

"What future do you have here?" Francis asked. "You will always be an orphan."

"What about Emma and Gramps?"

"You don't have a future with Emma. She's the princess and you, you will never be anything more than just a lost boy who can't remember where he came from." Francis looked directly at Evan. "Things are about to change on The Ledge. Come with me!"

"What do you mean change?"

"Nothing, I'm just saying," Francis paused for a moment. "I'm just saying, you can have a life in my father's kingdom. Just tell me you'll think about it."

"Okay, I'll think about it," Evan answered.

"Great," Francis exclaimed, jumping up and pulling Evan to his feet. "We should get moving. If I don't get you there early, Emma will kill me. Do you think they will have some good food at this thing?" Francis asked as he started in the direction of the castle.

"Always thinking with your stomach," Evan laughed as he followed his friend.

— ·· — ·· — ·· — ··

Evan spotted Emma waiting at the main gate looking less than pleased as they skidded to a stop, out of breath from the run. Evan wanted to say he was sorry, but the words would not come out. Emma looked like she was dressed for a fancy ball. Her hair was adorned with wild flowers and she wore a small silver crown. The blue fabric of her dress brought her eyes to life. The butterflies in Evan's stomach were doing cartwheels, and Emma's cheeks flushed a light pink color as she noticed the attention the boys were giving her.

"Honestly, it's like you're trying to miss the ceremony," she scolded as she straightened Evan's cloak that had fallen to one side.

"Well, to tell you the truth, I was kind of, ouch!" Evan yelped as he looked over at Francis, who had just jabbed him with his thumb sharply in his side.

"What's wrong?" Emma asked with concern.

"Nothing," Evan mumbled as he rubbed his side, the sharp pain subsiding.

"We just lost track of time. That's all," Francis assured as he shot Evan a warning look.

"Well, I guess that's okay. The ceremony hasn't started yet, so no harm done," Emma commented as she turned to lead them into the castle.

"What was that for?" Evan whispered as they followed.

"This is a great honor. The royal family doesn't hold a ceremony for just anybody. You need to at least pretend to be appreciative."

The Great Hall was almost completely empty, leading Evan to wonder if Emma had gotten the day of the ceremony wrong, but she didn't look concerned at the lack of people. The noon day sun illuminated the bright colors of the stained glass window at the head of the room, producing rays of colored light which danced off the polished stone. The ball of light being handed from deity to man depicted in the masterful glass creation reflected an especially bright round circle in front of the expertly carved wooden thrones. The spacious room was silent as the three of them made their way past the giant stone columns and bright tapestries.

The greatness of the room reminded him of his last visit with the King and Queen when they had released him after being held in the dungeon. He had been an outcast, but today he was to be honored by the royal family. Francis was right, this was a big deal and Evan silently cursed himself for his sour attitude.

They approached a small group of people silently facing the empty thrones. Evan was surprised to see that everyone in attendance held a special place in his life on The Ledge. Gramps shot Evan a wink and a sly smile as Evan glanced in his direction. Evan had never seen him out of his stained, old leather apron. On this occasion, he wore a light grey cloak and dark pants that had been patched. He had attempted to slick his unruly white hair back on his head, but some of it had broken loose and was sticking straight up. Evan smiled back at him.

Rosalina was standing next to Gramps. She had a smile so contagious, Evan couldn't help but smile back. She was wearing a light green dress, which Evan guessed she kept tucked away for special occasions. Rosalina reminded Evan of his mom, not in the way she looked, but more by the way she made him feel. She always wanted to hear about his day and tried to solve all of his problems with good food. Looking at her now, Evan felt slightly selfish. She knew all about his life on The Ledge, but he didn't know anything about hers. Was she married? Did she live in town or with the orphans? Evan was surprised by how little he knew, and he made a mental note to ask her about her life during their next early morning breakfast together.

Peter and Alec were standing on the other side of the half circle wearing dark cloaks of different shades and silver crowns, similar to Emma's, but not as ornate. Evan had spoken to Alec several times since the attack, but neither had brought up the night in the forest. They had almost died, an event that had formed a strong, unbreakable bond. Alec no longer called him "orphan" and had spent the last week, to Evan's complete embarrassment, introducing Evan to all his friends as "the boy who saved his life." Peter towered over Alec, standing at least a head taller and looking noticeably more mature than his younger brother. He already held himself like a king. A glimmering sword hung at his waist as he waited patiently for the ceremony to begin.

Evan noticed, after looking around the intimate circle a second time, that the King and Queen weren't in the room. He looked over at Emma and Francis, unsure as to what he was supposed to do next. Sensing his confusion, Emma gave him a comforting smile, letting him know that nothing was expected.

No sooner had Evan looked away from Emma then he heard the sound from a single trumpet. Evan looked around to find its source, but saw nothing as the blast of the trumpet lingered, echoing from the floors to the towering ceiling overhead. The regal sound of the trumpet was replaced by the sound of footsteps marching in unison. The royal guards had entered the back of the room in their full armor, marching in two columns. Captain Curtis marched in the front, carrying the royal colors. The men looked impressive, stone faced and dressed for battle. Evan had seen these men around The Ledge. They protected the royal family and, from what Emma had told him, were the best, most loyal warriors on The Ledge, proven on and off of the battle field.

The two lines of warriors, upon reaching Evan's small semicircle of friends, fanned out on either side of the thrones, creating a larger, more impressive semicircle. After reaching their designated spots, the guards drew their swords in unison and placed the tips of their swords on the floor in front of them. They kneeled down on one knee and bowed their heads.

The trumpet sounded a second time and, as the echoes diminished, the King and Queen entered the room. They wore royal robes that trailed behind them. Their golden crowns glistened from the sunlight filtering through the windows as they walked into the bright circle illuminated in front of Evan. Everyone in the semicircle followed suit with the guards and bowed to one knee. The King quietly raised one hand in the air signally everyone in the room to stand. The King stepped forward and stood directly in front of Evan.

"Are we not all equal?" the King asked as he looked around the semicircle.

No one responded to this question, and Evan wondered if they were waiting for him to answer. He was about to open his mouth, not knowing what he should say, when the King continued.

"The Ledge is a sanctuary from the outside world, a place where we are protected. We look after one another, and we step into the roles that best fit our talents. Whether your talent leads you to be the best cook this kingdom has ever known," the King smiled at Rosalina. "Or an innovator who has mastered the art of shoemaking," The King motioned to Gramps, who bowed his head. "From the Captain of the Guard, who defends our cliffs, to our Queen who started a school to teach our children and build relationships with the neighboring kingdoms," The King made a point of looking at Curtis and then fondly at his wife. "We all have a place on The Ledge, and we support each other. When you bow to the royal family, you are not bowing to us. You are showing respect for what we have built together, to our way of life. As the stable boy serves the King, the King must also serve the stable boy. We care for one another, but we do not expect others, those not from The Ledge, to do the same. We learn from what the past teaches us, and we do not take lightly the responsibility of deciding whom we should trust. The kindnesses that Evan showed to Alec during the bear attack and to the other boys running the Gauntlet proves his trustworthiness. We are here today to honor him in the only way we know how."

The King pulled a silver medallion from his pocket, and Evan heard Emma gasp. The medallion was the size of a silver dollar and was engraved with a design Evan couldn't decipher. It was attached to a braided leather strap, which the King held in his hand, allowing the medallion to dance in the bright light. Alec stepped forward and took the strap from the King's hand before turning to face Evan.

"Because you saved my life, you are now one of us. You are no longer an orphan, destined one day to return to your homeland. You are now one of us, part of The Ledge family," Alec announced as he fastened the medallion around Evan's neck. "Those chosen to participate in the Crossover are given this emblem. You have been chosen by the King and your peers to take part this year. The decision was unanimous," Alec returned to his spot in the circle.

Evan's mind was racing. He didn't know whether to thank Alec or to give the medallion back. He didn't know much about the Crossover, but he knew enough to have serious doubts as to whether he could perform such a dangerous task.

"We have also added your story, while we don't believe it is finished yet, to one of our tapestries. The tale of your role in saving the Prince from certain death will become legend," the King instructed as several guards came forward and unrolled a colorful tapestry telling the story of the bear attack in detailed pictures.

The rest of the ceremony was a blur to Evan. He heard Alec recounting a slightly exaggerated version of the details depicted on the fabric of the tapestry, but besides that Evan's mind fixated on the Crossover. He had only been on The Ledge for nearly five months, and the little training he had was going to be tested in the most grueling and dangerous way possible. Gramps had told Evan that people died on the Crossover, people more experienced than he.

Chapter Twenty-Three
Emma's Short Cut

After the ceremony, Evan sat alone in the shade under one of the large trees in the courtyard, staring at the medallion. The sun was high overhead and the day had turned into a beautiful warm fall day. Evan looked up into the branches of the great oak trees in the courtyard high above his head. Some of the leaves were starting to change color. He had spent the last hour accepting congratulations from everyone in the room. Apparently, being chosen for the Crossover was a great honor, but he wasn't so sure he agreed. Emma and Francis had gone with Alec and Peter to see the tapestry hung. Evan said he would join them in a moment but was enjoying his time alone in the shade. The medallion was heavier than he expected it would be, given its size. It was made of pure silver. He expected it to be engraved with an inscription of some sort, explaining its significance. There was no writing, however, just a series of cutouts, where silver had been removed, so that Evan could see through the medallion. Evan was holding it up to his eye, looking through the cutouts at the tree leaves high above him, when someone grabbed him from behind, causing Evan to cry out.

"You should see your face," Alec laughed as he plopped himself down next to Evan.

"Yeah, and that squeal! I don't think Emma could have screamed higher," Francis snorted, lying down on his back with his hands behind his head.

"You're right, Francis. I can't even make a sound that high pitched," Emma joined in as she sat down right next to Evan.

Evan's face turned red. He didn't get embarrassed often, but it seemed all the more likely to happen when Emma was around.

"Ha, ha. I'm glad I could provide you with a show," Evan joked, smiling awkwardly.

"I can't believe you get to participate in the Crossover," Francis gawked, noticing the medallion in Evan's hand. "Why are there holes in it?" Francis asked.

"I have no idea," Evan shrugged.

"Let me see it," Alec requested as he grabbed it from Evan.

Evan had completely overlooked the possibility that Alec had not been invited to perform the Crossover.

"Have you," Evan paused for a moment, wondering how he should phrase his next question. "Have you ever seen one up close?" Evan asked as he watched Alec close one eye to look through the medallion.

Emma and Francis looked at Alec with concern, the significance of what Evan was asking hit them now as it had Evan moments earlier.

"A Crossover medallion?" Alec asked as he looked down at the grass, exhaling deeply.

The four of them sat in silence for a moment, none of them knowing what to say.

"You can have mine," Evan offered, breaking the silence.

Alec looked up, "You can't give away your Crossover medallion. You have been chosen by the King and validated by your peers. Besides," Alec paused for a moment, "I have my own." He pulled his own medallion from under his shirt, laughing so loud that an older woman on the other side of the courtyard looked over at the group with alarm.

"You toad!" Emma called, smacking him hard on the arm.

Putting his medallion back under his shirt, Alec stood up. "We should celebrate!" He began walking away.

"Where are we going?" Evan called after him.

"Last one to reach the waterfall is a slimy slug," Alec yelled over his shoulder as he started to run.

"No fair. I need to change out of my dress," Emma whined as she raced in the opposite direction.

"We will wait in the stable," Evan called after her.

"You will wait in the stable, while I'm swimming in the cool water," Alec called back to the group.

"He always has to be first, doesn't he?" Francis stated as he slowly got to his feet.

"We wouldn't be able to keep up with his horse anyway," Evan said as he and Francis started toward the stable.

"Francis, about your offer earlier," Evan started to say.

"You don't have to say it," Francis interrupted lowering his eyes to the ground. "I understand, you're one of them now. Look, I'll catch up with you later." Francis ran off in the other direction, before Evan could say anything more.

Evan had already rounded up the horses by the time Emma came running into the stable.

"Alec left a few minutes ago," Evan offered as he handed her Smokey's reins.

"That's okay," Emma shrugged as she jumped on Smokey and kicked her into a full gallop. "I know a short cut."

"It looks like it's not only Alec I have to try and keep up with," Evan acknowledged as he mounted a large, dark brown mare used to fetch supplies from the floating docks.

The day had turned into a perfect fall afternoon, with blue sky as far as the eye could see. Most afternoons on The Ledge, dark clouds would appear carrying afternoon thunderstorms. They wouldn't last long, but you didn't want to get caught outside in one. Evan hoped he could catch up to Emma, but the old mare was no match for Smokey's powerful strides. The trail Emma chose seemed familiar to Evan, but he didn't know why. It was overgrown and not much more than a game trail in some places.

Something in the forest caught Evan's eye. He turned his head, straining to see what had shimmered in the trees. All he could see, however, was green undergrowth, shaded by the large pine trees. Evan looked back to the trail, just in time to see a large tree branch looming in front of him. Evan flinched sideways and raised his hands in panic, knowing there was no way to avoid the collision. The branch hit Evan across his chest and ejected him from his horse with such force that he landed flat on his back, knocking the wind from his lungs. He laid sprawled on the ground for several minutes trying to regain normal breathing while waiting for the pain to subside. Finally, he was able to draw in the deep forest air, which cleared his head and allowed him to assess his situation. He moved his legs, then his arms, and slowly raised himself to a sitting position. He could hear his horse still running down the trail as if nothing had happened.

"Stupid horse! She will probably go on for a mile before she realizes I'm gone," Evan muttered as he stood up and brushed off his clothes.

Evan looked around the forest and saw the fleeting reflection of light again in the distance. As Evan looked back in the direction he had come recognition finally dawned and he remembered meeting Emma for the first time in this very spot five months ago. Tentatively, Evan stepped off of the trail into the thick undergrowth, in the direction of the reflection. The bushes were well over his head, and it was almost impossible to see more than a foot in front of him as he made his way through the thick undergrowth. He could hear water flowing and decided to head in that direction to keep from walking in circles.

Evan finally broke through the undergrowth and landed on a white sandy beach on the bank of a stream. Evan froze when his feet touched the soft sand. He had been on this beach before. The beach, the stream, the log. Evan recognized all of it. This was the first place he remembered on The Ledge. This was the place where he had first met Alec. Evan found his shirt and the socks he had been wearing the night of the dance at Wellsford Academy lying under the log. They were dirty and faded, but they were his shirt, socks and shoes. Evan's heart started to beat faster. He jumped up on the log. He remembered seeing Emma galloping down the same trail that Evan had just been riding on. Evan's eyes then fixated on a small pine tree sitting in a small clearing a few feet in front of the log. He remembered the dream he had experienced after the bear attack. He had seen someone standing in front of that tree, looking at something.

Evan jumped down from the log and slowly walked towards the pine tree. He knelt down and reached under a bush next to the small tree. His trembling fingers wrapped around a book. Slowly Evan pulled the book from under the bush. He stared at the cover and even though its pages were soaked from the last rain storm and it looked like a rodent had been chewing on the cover it was the same book he had seen in his dream. His book from Wellsford Academy.

"Advanced Calculus," Evan read out loud. He never thought that he would be so excited to see his Wellsford math book again. The dream had been more than a simple dream. It had been a memory, something that had actually happened and if that was true what had the hooded figure been looking at. It hadn't been his math book.

Evan stepped in the same spot where he had seen the hooded figure stand in his memory. He stared at the small tree for a moment, seeing nothing at first and then all at once he saw it. Something reflected the light, inches in front of him. Startled Evan quickly stepped back. Evan could see the tree in front of him as if nothing existed between him and the tree. But as the sun's rays reached the forest floor through tree limbs high above his head, the rays were reflected by something in between him and the pine tree.

"Is this what the cloaked figure had been staring at in the memory?" Evan asked himself as he tried to understand the reflected light suspended in the air. Evan felt dry, cool air coming from the reflection, as he inched closer, now only inches away. Mesmerized by the reflection, Evan raised his hand and reached out. His hand disappeared into the reflection. It felt cool inside the reflection. He pulled his hand back. Something was drawing him to move towards it. Maybe he would find the answers he was searching for inside. Evan took a deep breath and then slowly with his text book in hand he walked into the reflection.

Evan saw slivers of light inches from his face. He could hear people in the distance, the sounds of a party perhaps. The confined space smelled musty, a hint of mold in the stale air. Extending his hands tentatively to each side, he touched cold metal. Evan looked down, but couldn't see anything in his dark surroundings. He turned around and tried to return to the small pine tree, but he ran into a metal wall. He would have started to panic, but his confined tomb felt familiar, even though he was sure he had never been locked in a metal box before. Evan reached forward and pushed on the wall in front of him and to his surprise the wall moved. Evan pushed harder and the door in front of him opened and he stepped out of his locker onto the fourth floor hallway of Wellsford Academy.

Evan stood outside his open locker door, listening to his fellow students three floors below. He was confused and didn't know how this had happened. Only moments earlier, he had been riding through the forest trying to catch up with Emma, and now he was here. He was back home.

The reality of the situation started to stir emotions within him. He was excited to be back, excited to be able to see his family after five months of being lost, but at the same time, he couldn't bring his legs to propel himself forward away from the locker. He couldn't take that first step. How would his family receive him after being gone for such a long time? They would ask questions of course, but how could he answer them? Could he simply walk down the stairs and ask to use the phone to call his parents?

Instead, Evan leaned against the locker and slid down to the floor. He placed his weary head into his trembling hands. The worry that they must have experienced. The search parties, the flyers, the unanswered questions. Evan knew the drill. He had seen more than one family search for a lost child on the evening news. Would they think he had run away? He was angry when they had moved, but he would never run away. He would never want to cause his family that much anguish. Still, Evan was frozen on the floor. He thought of Emma and Gramps. How long would they search for him? What would they do when they couldn't find him? Evan felt so conflicted about the loyalties he felt to both his family and his friends on The Ledge.

Finally, Evan's desire to see his family again won the tug of war warring inside of him. Even if his parents didn't believe his story and thought their son was crazy, he had to at least try. As he slowly stood up, Evan realized that he was still wearing his cloak and shoes from The Ledge. This would warrant unnecessary attention from the other students. Wanting to be as discrete as possible, he changed into the clothes he had left in his locker the night of the dance, five months earlier. With his Wellsford jacket on and his cloak safely hanging in his locker, Evan hesitantly moved toward the stairs. There were no students on the third floor, but as Evan reached the balcony on the second floor, he cautiously peered over the railing.

Students were filing out of the ballroom dressed in their absolute best. It didn't hit Evan at first, not until he saw Brad and his two goons walking down the stairs. They looked unusually proud of themselves as if they had just done something impressive. A pit formed in Evan's stomach so large that he feared it would swallow him. His head started to spin, as he watched students come out of the ballroom, dressed in the same fancy clothes they had worn the night of the dance, the night he had found himself on The Ledge. But how was this possible?

Evan saw Phillip, Janelle and Cooper by the front door waiting for him. Had no time elapsed since he left the school?

Evan turned away from the students, not able to comprehend how time had stood still. Was he truly crazy? Had he imagined his entire experience on The Ledge? Evan walked to the window overlooking the ocean. He was not looking at the waters in the darkness beyond the window, but at his reflection. His hair was longer, his skin tan and judging by the length of his pants, he had grown at least an inch. Time had passed. He had matured while living on The Ledge. The work had hardened his muscles. He was no longer the skinny kid who had been shoved into his locker five months earlier, or five minutes ago. He didn't know which.

Turning around, Evan slowly followed Brad and his thugs down the stairs. No one looked in his direction as he joined the other students on the bottom floor.

"It's about time," Phillip exclaimed as he saw Evan coming down the stairs.

"How long have you been waiting," Evan asked tentatively. He half expected Phillip to say five months, but without hesitation Phillip answered.

"At least 10 minutes."

"Did you get lost?" Cooper asked.

"It's a big school. You never know what might happen," Evan responded as he looked over at Brad and his thugs.

At the sound of Evan's voice, Brad spun on his heels so fast that he almost fell to the ground.

"How did you?" Brad gawked.

"Get out of my locker so quickly?" Evan finished. He had expected Brad to not be so surprised. If anyone knew anything about what had happened to Evan he figured Brad and his thugs would know something, but they looked as confused as Evan was feeling.

"You look different," Janelle observed looking closer at Evan.

"Almost like you haven't seen me for five months?" Evan prodded.

"No, I saw you 10 minutes ago. There is just something different.

"Well I did change back into my Wellsford jacket," Evan chuckled. None of this was making sense.

"It's not just that. There's something else," she continued, her impenetrable gaze starting to make Evan uncomfortable.

"Janelle, give the kid a break. He just got shoved into his locker. I want the whole story," Cooper encouraged, as he stepped in front of Janelle.

"Maybe later, Coop. Right now, I need to get home. I don't want to keep my mom waiting," Maybe Evan's mom would be able to help.

The cool air felt refreshing as Evan led his small group of friends out into the winter night. Amid the fancy SUV's and foreign cars, Evan spotted his parents' battered, rust-colored SUV. He wanted to run to his mom, to tell her everything, but he held back. What if she didn't believe him?

Evan slammed the door shut against the cold air, the old heater rattling as it produced a steady stream of warmth.

"How was the dance?" Evan's mom asked as she pulled the car onto the road.

He couldn't believe it. First his friends and now his mom. How was it possible that for him, he had been gone for months, but to everyone else, it was like he had never left? Evan found himself staring at his mom's familiar face, his eyes welling with tears. He couldn't formulate a response for several moments.

"Evan, did you hear me? How was the dance? Is everything okay?"

"Oh yeah, the dance," Evan finally found his voice, trying to recall anything about the dance. After all, it had been five very long months ago.

"Did you dance with that girl you like? What was her name? Mandy, Mindy, Madison. That's right Madison. Did you dance with Madison?"

Evan thought hard, "Yeah, I think so."

"What do you mean, you think so? And I thought my memory was getting bad."

It was great seeing his mom and hearing her voice again. Evan had forgotten what it was like to have these discussions. Rosalina had been great, but she wasn't his mom.

The rest of the drive home was filled with endless questions about the dance. What band played? What were people wearing? Evan answered the questions as best he could remember, but his mind was on The Ledge. Several times, he almost told his mom about the experience, but decided against it. Maybe he had imagined the entire thing, or experienced a hallucination after hitting his head. He needed to figure things out before he told his family. He needed to figure out what had happened. For the first time since the family had bought the rusty old car, Evan was glad the interior lights didn't work. He didn't know how he was going to explain his physical changes to his mom. Coop saved him from Janelle's questions, but there wouldn't be anyone to save him from his mom's questions.

Chapter Twenty-Four
The Math Problem

The next morning Evan stared at a small lump under the covers in Jackson's room. His kid brother was lying on his bed backwards with his feet on the pillow where his head should have been. Jackson was motionless. Only the occasional snort confirmed that there was life under the giant mound of blankets. Evan slowly inched closer, a loose floor board let out a low creak, protesting the added weight. The noise wouldn't have been noticed during the normal family traffic of the day, but at this early morning hour, the intrusive squeaks shattered the silence of the room. Evan paused, hoping he wouldn't be detected. He held his breath as Jackson shifted under the covers, rolled over, and yawned.

Evan stayed motionless for at least a minute. His muscles ached, begging him to move, but Evan remained still. Jackson stopped moving. Evan stayed in his position for a few more agonizing minutes, making sure it was safe before slowly moving his foot from the loose board and stepping forward again toward his prey. His victim rested only a foot away. Evan could hear breathing and see the blankets rise and fall with each breath. He positioned himself for the attack. It would be over quickly. Jackson was still fast asleep and would not see Evan advance.

Disregarding any last attempt at secrecy, Evan launched himself at Jackson, relying on the element of surprise to tip the odds in his favor. He spread his arms wide as his body hit Jackson under the covers with more force than Evan had intended, causing both of them to fall off the bed and hit the floor with a loud crash.

Jackson tried to free himself from Evan's death grip, but it was of no use. Five months of training on The Ledge, had given Evan the upper hand. After a couple of futile punches, Jackson finally laid motionless, seeming to accept defeat.

"Say it," Evan demanded.

"Never!" Jackson screamed back.

Evan applied pressure with his elbow to Jackson's back and said again, slightly louder, but completely calm and in control, "Say it!"

Jackson paused for a moment, contemplating options. "Uncle," Jackson answered from beneath the covers.

"Say it louder. I have to hear it," Evan demanded again.

"Uncle," came a soft whisper.

"What?" Evan taunted, pushing his elbow down harder.

"Uncle, Uncle, Uncle," Jackson surrendered from under the covers.

Evan jumped away and took a fighting stance. "Remember, you said uncle," he teased.

Slowly, Jackson rose to his full height. Without warning, and faster than Evan had anticipated, the down comforter flew in his direction. Evan tried to anticipate the attack, but Jackson's charging form was obscured by the moving blanket until it was too late. Jackson's shoulder caught Evan under his arms, lifting him from his feet and propelling him onto Jackson's bed. Evan attempted to throw Jackson off of him, but he was tangled in the blankets and couldn't get a good grip on his brother.

"I give up! I GIVE UP!" Evan yelled, feeling very claustrophobic, pinned under the blanket by Jackson's weight.

"Say it," Jackson chuckled, knowing he had won the battle.

"Uncle," Evan mumbled, barely audible.

"Good enough for me," Jackson announced, jumping off the bed. He grabbed a pair of jeans hanging on the back of a chair.

Evan sat on the bed breathing in deep gulps of fresh air as he looked at his brother. Somehow he had expected Jackson to have grown the same as he had, but Jackson had not aged a day during Evan's five month absence.

"Did you get a haircut?" Jackson asked as he turned to face Evan.

"I can't get anything past you," Evan responded, trying to hide his smile.

"No, seriously. Something is different," Jackson said, examining Evan.

Jackson sat down on the bed next to his brother. Evan had always been able to tell Jackson everything, but this time he couldn't speak. He wanted to tell him about The Ledge, the bear attack, and the ceremony, but he couldn't. His younger brother would never believe him. If a land had existed like The Ledge, wouldn't it be documented somewhere or still exist? Evan thought to himself. Shouldn't I be able to find information about it?

"You aren't going to tell me, are you?" Jackson asked, looking annoyed.

"Tell you what?" Evan inquired, acting dumb.

"Boys, time for breakfast!" Evan's mom called up the stairs, as the aroma of cinnamon French toast and buttermilk syrup reached Jackson's bedroom.

The boys launched themselves toward the open doorway as if fearful the first one down would eat the entire breakfast before the second one arrived.

"Evan, are you wearing a wig?" his mom asked, puzzled. She paused mid-way through flipping the French toast on the griddle, as the boys stormed into the kitchen.

Evan stopped running. Jackson was already loading a full stack of French toast onto his plate.

"Didn't you get your hair cut two weeks ago?" she asked, a puzzled look on her face.

Evan had anticipated the questions about his hair and had thought of several explanations, but none sounded plausible, so he went with the truth.

"I can't believe no one noticed that I have been growing my hair out for the past five months," Evan fumbled as he walked over to the table and grabbed a couple pieces of bacon.

"No, I remember taking you to get your hair cut," his mom countered.

"Sorry, Mom, I don't know what to tell you. You wouldn't believe my hair grew over night, would you?" Evan forced an unconvincing laugh as he looked away from his mom's puzzled expression to the French toast that was making his stomach growl.

"I like it," Evan's dad admitted, looking up from his breakfast. "I mean, you're only young once. I wish that I had grown out my hair when I had the chance." Evan's dad rubbed his hand over his balding head.

"I must be getting old," Evan's mom shrugged as she looked down at the burnt pieces of toast.

— · · — · · — · · — · ·

Evan's mom finally stopped asking questions about Madison and school, when she noticed that his mind was elsewhere. The family's SUV wound its way up the road leading to Wellsford

Academy the Monday after the big dance. He had wanted to tell his family about his locker and The Ledge all weekend long, but he didn't know where to start. This was something he needed to figure out first before he tried to explain the unlikely story to others.

Evan waved to his mom as she drove out of sight, leaving him alone in front of the deserted school. His excuse was that he needed to arrive early to study, that reason seemed to suffice.

The hallways were empty. A janitor looked up as he mopped the marble flooring. He glanced at Evan in his blue blazer and returned to mopping, paying little attention.

The fourth floor was dark and deserted, just as Evan had hoped. He paused for a moment as he reached his locker. What did he expect to find inside? Evan's heart raced as he entered the first number.

What if the back wall doesn't open to The Ledge, Evan thought to himself. Would he then have to admit that he had lost his mind?

His hand trembled as he turned the lock to the last number. He paused for a moment and slowly opened the door.

The locker was exactly as he had left it the night of the dance. He reached in and grabbed his cloak, which hung from the single hook in the middle of his locker. Tentatively, he reached toward the back of the locker and pushed on the back wall. To Evan's dismay, the cold metal held firm, no matter how hard he pushed. Evan ran his hand along the back of the locker, attempting to locate hinges or a gap, anything that would allow it to open.

"Something has to be here," Evan muttered to himself.

Stepping back from the locker in frustration, Evan decided that he needed to replicate the events from the night of the dance, the night he was transported to The Ledge.

Evan entered the locker, the space was small, and he started feeling claustrophobic. He distorted his body to rotate toward the back wall. Again, he pushed on the wall, but nothing happened. He pounded harder starting to panic, as he realized the back wall was just that, it was a wall and not a door leading to The Ledge. Exhausted, his pounding slowed, until a single hit was all that he had left.

"I must be crazy," Evan whispered to himself as he tried to back out of his locker. In Evan's haste to breathe fresh air again, he tripped on the bottom lip of the locker and fell out onto the floor, flat on his back.

"What are you doing?"

Evan looked up to see Phillip's confused expression.

"Phillip! Good to see you. I was just looking for my math book," Evan lied. He swallowed hard and wondered how much Phillip had witnessed.

"Your math book is right there on the floor," Phillip pointed to Evan's open backpack with the book falling partway out.

"So it is. It's a good thing you came along. I might have torn apart my entire locker looking for it. Why are you here so early?" Evan asked, rising to his feet and dusting off his blue blazer.

"I always get to school early. My driver drops me off before he starts running errands for the day. I saw you walk past the library and couldn't wait to hear the story of how Brad shoved you in the locker."

"Well, for starters, it wasn't just Brad, he had help."

"Were his goons there as well?"

"Yep, it was three against one." Evan grabbed his backpack and closed his locker door. "Let's head back downstairs and I'll tell you the entire story." Evan wanted to steer Phillip's thoughts away from the locker and what Evan had been doing inside of it.

"Yeah, okay, sounds good."

As they started down the stairs, Evan glanced back at his locker. It had been his last hope of proving his sanity. Brad and his goons must have dressed him in the cloak and shoes as a joke, trying to confuse him. Maybe Evan had not traveled back in time. A feeling of sadness engulfed him as he realized his friends and The Ledge did not exist, the bear attack had not occurred, and Emma was simply a figment of his imagination.

— ·· — ·· — ·· — ··

"Evan. EVAN!" Phillip repeated louder the second time, jolting Evan from his thoughts.

After Evan had told Phillip the entire story from the night of the dance, they had decided to catch up on some last minute homework. The harder Evan tried to study, however, the more difficult it became for him to believe that The Ledge didn't exist. It had seemed so real.

"We had better get to class. You know how Dr. Parkinson will react if we're late." Phillip grabbed his bag and followed a group of students out of the library as Evan gathered his things.

Evan slowly rose to follow but stopped, shocked as he stared at a painting on the wall near the history section of the library. Evan had passed the painting before but had not noticed it until today. He walked closer to get a better look as the morning sun pierced the library through the large windows, illuminating every brush stroke. He scanned the details of the painting, every color painstakingly placed in a deliberate location to create the most beautiful sight Evan had ever seen.

"You have a good eye," Ms. Flinders, the old librarian interrupted, as she moved next to Evan. "This is my favorite painting."

"What is it a likeness of?" Evan asked, not removing his eyes from the canvas.

"Now, that is a mystery. You see, no one knows where it came from or what it represents. It has been hanging in this very spot since before anyone can remember. Several years ago, we had all the paintings in the school examined. We have more paintings hanging on our walls than many museums have, and some pieces are considered priceless. But this painting," she said shaking her head back and forth, "This painting has puzzled all of the experts who have viewed it."

"Why?" Evan asked, his sad feelings starting to lift.

"The canvas, the type of paint used, and the artist's technique are an older style, but the painting itself actually dates back only a few decades.

"Does the painting have a title?" Evan inquired.

"Why, of course. It's written on the bottom of the frame," she answered as she bent down to take a closer look at the metal plaque on the wooden frame. "Hang on a minute." She used the sleeve of her sweater to wipe the dust away.

Evan's heart leapt when he read the words, "The Ledge."

"Funny name for a picture, I don't see a ledge in the picture," Miss Flinders stated.

The bell rang for the start of first period. "Oh no, Dr. Parkinson is going to be livid." Evan grabbed his backpack and scurried to the library exit. "Thanks, Ms. Flinders," Evan called over his shoulder as he rushed out of the door.

Evan was breathing heavily as he rushed into math class, a full minute late. Every student in the class stared at him. Dr. Parkinson looked up from the roll, a cruel smile forming on his face.

"Second tardy this term," he announced to the entire class as he made a note on his roll. "A full grade point lower."

Evan didn't say a word as he sat next to Phillip, Janelle and Cooper.

"What took you so long?" Phillip whispered.

"I was talking to Ms. Flinders," Evan shrugged, his mind still on the painting.

"It must have been a good conversation to throw away all of the tutoring I have been doing with you. I don't know how you are going to recover from this," Phillip admitted, frustrated.

Evan, however, was no longer listening to his friend or Dr. Parkinson for that matter. He was staring at the blackboard. Posted on the far-right corner was the math problem Dr. Parkinson had written on the board at the start of the term.

"Whoever can solve this problem with a unique solution will receive an instant A," he recalled Dr. Parkinson's offer on Evan's first day of class.

Evan stared at the problem. The numbers and symbols started to align themselves differently. The problem was simplifying itself right before his eyes. He was not looking at the problem as a whole, but as individual pieces that needed to be solved. Just like the puzzles Evan's family worked together on Sunday evenings, the solution was starting to form in his head. He had not learned this from Dr. Parkinson or from Phillip's tutoring sessions. He had learned this on The Ledge. Emma had beaten it into his head during their study sessions. He had mastered the basics and learned how to apply the simple concepts to complex problems, just like the problem written on the board in front of him.

"What are you doing?" Janelle whispered as Evan stood and walked to the front of the room.

"Young man, I don't know what you think you are doing, but you need to take your seat," Dr. Parkinson demanded.

Evan ignored him and walked directly up to the blackboard. He picked up a piece of white chalk, then paused for a moment. Was this what a breakdown felt like? Evan thought to himself. "No," he muttered under his breath, determined to not let his doubts get the better of him. First, the picture and now this. The Ledge existed, Emma was real. He had traveled back in time.

"Brad, go and get the headmaster. We might rid ourselves of Mr. Myers today, saving me the time of having to fail him at the end of this term," Dr. Parkinson commanded.

Brad jumped to his feet and rushed out of the room.

The metal plaque on the painting had said it all. It wasn't a coincidence. The letters jumped back into his mind as his mouth formed the words he had read on the painting of a long forgotten kingdom, "The Ledge"

Evan raised the chalk to the board and pressed down a little too hard. A screeching noise pierced the air. All the students plugged their ears to block out the unpleasant sound. Evan adjusted the chalk in his hand, beads of perspiration cascaded down his forehead. He carefully reached up to the blackboard again and started to write.

He simplified the equation first, dividing it into ten parts. He then divided those ten parts into even simpler equations. The class was silent, and Dr. Parkinson sat down at one of the desks on the front row, as if he was a student. Evan worked for ten minutes, until he was interrupted by the abrupt arrival of a breathless Brad and an angry headmaster.

"You're coming with me young man," the headmaster ordered triumphantly.

Brad beamed as though it was his birthday.

"Wait, wait," Dr. Parkinson interrupted as he stood up. "Let the boy finish."

"But he disobeyed you," the headmaster challenged as he stepped toward Evan, who had continued writing during the disruption.

"We have rules at this school, Dr. Parkinson. We can't allow a scholarship student to rob us of our order," he confirmed.

"Yes, yes, but look at his work on the board," Dr. Parkinson motioned toward the equations Evan had written.

Evan finished with one board and moved onto the next one. The headmaster looked amazed and slowly sat next to Dr. Parkinson.

"What about expelling Evan?" Brad whined.

"Be quiet, boy," Dr. Parkinson hissed, as he motioned for Brad to move out of the way of Evan's work.

Evan continued for the entire hour until the bell rang. The students remained in their seats, fascinated by what was unfolding in front of them.

Finally, as the next class gathered outside of the door, anxiously waiting to take their seats, Evan put the chalk down on the tray. His work covered four large blackboards and his hand was cramped from writing for the entire hour, but he had done it. He had successfully solved the equation. Without waiting for Dr. Parkinson to confirm the solution, or the headmaster to drag him off to his office, Evan walked to the desk, where Phillip sat staring at the board, and grabbed his backpack.

"That was brilliant," he barely heard Phillip say as Evan squeezed past the waiting students and headed straight for his locker.

Chapter Twenty-Five

Destruction

Evan sprinted up the stairs to his locker moments after the bell rang, ending math class. Evan took two steps at a time. He threw his backpack in front of him, and it slid across the hallway, finally coming to a stop next to his locker. He steadied his breathing and then carefully entered his combination and opened the door. The inside was unchanged, but Evan wasn't deterred. He hadn't expected anything to be different.

He dropped to the ground and started pulling books from the floor of his locker into the hallway.

"It's got to be here," Evan insisted, tossing the last book onto the pile.

With the locker empty, Evan slowly ran his hand along the bottom of the locker, feeling every contour and groove, his eyes scrunched up in concentration. The bottom of the locker was the only place he hadn't checked earlier. The locker had transported him to The Ledge, he was sure of that now. If only he could find something that unlocked the door to The Ledge. Evan smiled as his fingers found a metal lever on the bottom of the locker floor that he could engage with his foot when he was standing in the locker. The lever made sense. He must have pushed it when he was trying to stand after Brad and his friends had shoved him into the locker.

Quickly, he got to his feet and looked down the hallway. He wasn't concerned with the mess he was leaving behind. He was sure he would return at the exact moment he left, just like the last time. Evan quickly dressed in the clothes he had worn when he left The Ledge and stepped into his locker. Closing the door, he stood in the darkness for a moment. The locker was cold, and the air smelled stale. He turned his body, faced the door and then, taking a deep, anxious breath, he pushed his foot forward, engaging the lever.

He heard a clicking sound coming from underneath his feet, as though some contraption had just engaged. Looking down for the source of the sound, he saw a light mist rising from the bottom of the locker. Evan remembered that his vision had blurred when he had been thrown into the locker the first time. As the mist engulfed the inside of the locker, Evan resisted the urge to open the door and run. He could breathe freely now, the air smelled fresher. No longer feeling confined to the cramped locker space, he extended his arms and, instead of touching cold steel, he felt only warm air. Still facing where there had once been the locker door, Evan carefully turned around and stepped out of the mist, into the forest.

Evan squinted as his eyes adjusted to the sun. The shimmering light, in front of a pine tree, had reappeared, suspended in the air. Evan had been with his family the entire weekend. Two full days must have passed on The Ledge as well. His friends must have searched for him. He wondered if they had given up, thinking he was dead. Evan wondered. Had it only been a couple of days? Something felt different.

He examined the forest more closely. New flowers and grasses were poking out of the ground, the trees surrounding him were filled with buds. It was not late summer, but early spring. Evan wondered how much time had elapsed during his absence. He needed to reach the castle and locate Emma. How would he explain that he wasn't dead without telling her the whole truth? Evan's thoughts were all over the place as he rushed through the thick underbrush to reach the path that would lead him to the village.

The cool air and adrenaline fueled him forward until he reached the last hill blocking his view of the kingdom. He slowed to a walk, as he climbed the hill, emerging from the forest. Evan gasped at his view of The Ledge.

"What happened?" Evan stuttered, not believing his own eyes. He felt weak. His legs buckled, and he fell to his knees, never taking his eyes off the horrible scene below him.

The once grand, impenetrable castle was in ruins. The glistening walls were blackened by the scars left from a massive fire. Several towers laid in rubble in the palace courtyard. Only one of the majestic trees remained. Evan saw no movement. No guards stood watch at the castle gates. No town's people roamed the grounds. The castle looked deserted. Cautiously, Evan followed the overgrown trail down the hill and into the once-beautiful village. The main street was badly overgrown with grass poking up through the cobblestones. Black rubble was all that remained of some of the buildings. Evan stopped at the giant stone building where he had been taught. He looked through the entrance. The roof's giant wooden beams had collapsed and were blackened from fire.

"Hello!" Evan yelled into the building. His voice echoed off of the stone walls. There was no reply.

Evan could see the remains of the large stone globe in the center of the room. It was broken into two pieces, which were now lying on the floor under pieces of the roof. Evan left the building and continued down the main street of the village. He stopped and stared at a large brick oven standing tall in the location where the bakery once stood. Evan longed for the smell of fresh breads and pastries that he remembered. The smell of smoke was gone, but as Evan walked he left footprints in the remaining ash which still covered the ground. He stopped in front of Gramps' leather shoe shop, now a hallowed out building covered by green overgrown vines. He stepped into the remains and picked up a small piece of leather poking up from under the blackened timber which had fallen from the collapsed roof.

"Who did this?" Evan forced the question through gritted teeth, burning anger replaced his grief. In frustration, Evan threw the piece of leather back into the rubble and slowly left the building and continued on. The giant gate at the end of town, which had once protected its people, had been smashed and burned, reduced to burnt wooden splinters. The tall stone towers flanking each side still stood, but were scarred black, just like the castle had been.

Evan heard movement from the docks far beneath him. He moved closer to the gate, careful not to be seen. He assumed that the people down below were not his friends. They must be the intruders who destroyed the kingdom. A hatred started to burn deep down within him. Evan moved forward, wanting to get a closer look at the activity down the cliff, when he heard someone speak.

"Who goes there?" came a weak voice from the shadows of one of the towers.

Evan jumped back defensively, not realizing that he wasn't alone. He frantically searched for a weapon, expecting to be attacked at any moment. Hastily, Evan picked up a piece of wood from the destroyed gate and turned to face his unknown assailant.

Evan stared toward the tower. There wasn't any movement.

"Show yourself," Evan ordered, sounding more authoritative than he felt. There was no reply. Finally, a hunched man hobbled forward. He was covered with an old, soiled blanket, his pants were torn, and his white hair was unkempt. He timidly approached Evan, avoiding eye contact.

Recognition dawned on Evan, dropping the stick, he ran to the old man, taking him into his arms.

"Gramps, is that you?" Evan asked, tears welling up in his eyes at the sight of the man Evan considered to be family. "What happened to you? What happened to The Ledge?"

"Evan, is that you?" Gramps asked cautiously, raising his eyes to meet Evan's for the first time.

"Yes! Yes, it's me!" Evan cried, tears streaming down his face.

Gramps embraced Evan. His eyes looked tired, and part of his face was scarred from a bad burn, but he smiled at Evan.

"How is it that you haven't aged a day since you disappeared?" Gramps asked, stunned by the impossibility.

"I..." Evan paused for a moment. "I don't know."

"You are real, aren't you? I mean you're not a figment of my imagination."

"No, I'm real. I, I just can't explain why I haven't aged."

Gramps was silent for a moment, as he looked at Evan suspiciously and then he shrugged. "I guess there are harder things to explain in this world, like why the sun rises every day, and why my rabbit stew smells so good," he chuckled as he said this. "The important thing is that you are safe." Gramps paused again, a faraway look in his eyes. "If only Emma had known. Come, come, you must be starving," Gramps encouraged, coming out of his trance and pulling Evan into one of the towers.

The tower was small. The only pieces of furniture were a chair and a log that served as a table and held the tools Gramps used for working leather. A few blankets piled in the corner served as a makeshift bed. Gramps walked over to a small fireplace and stirred the stew in a pot which was suspended over a small fire.

"Why are you living here?" Evan asked as he looked around the makeshift room.

"The cottage burned to the ground the night of the attack, along with everything else," he answered matter-of-factly. "And the woods," he paused for a moment, searching for the words, "well, the woods aren't safe anymore."

"Who attacked The Ledge?" Evan finally blurted out. "And what happened to everyone?"

Gramps let out an exhausted sigh as he continued stirring the stew. Evan's heart ached to see Gramps suffering. His clothes hung from his skinny body. Slowly Gramps turned back toward Evan.

"I guess I should begin with the day you disappeared. Everyone on The Ledge turned out to look for you. We searched for three days, but besides the horse you had been riding, we found nothing. Emma never gave up hope. I saw her go into the forest every night to search for you. But every night, she returned, her eyes red from crying. Two weeks passed, and the King decided to keep your spot on the Crossover vacant, as a tribute to you and what you had done for the kingdom."

"So Alec left alone on the Crossover?" Evan said as he realized how many people he had let down.

"Yes, and we were anticipating his return three nights later for the festival. But as we prepared for the feast an army attacked." Gramps shuffled to the chair and slowly sat down, looking very frail. With a faraway look in his eyes he simply said, "Alec never did return from the Crossover."

"How did the army get onto The Ledge? I didn't think anyone could get past the cliffs." Evan said, trying to make sense of how the once mighty Ledge could be destroyed.

"They attacked from the bay," Gramps answered. "We fought back, of course, but this attack was different than any previous one. They were ready for every counter attack we launched. They knew where to hit us and when. It was almost like they knew what we were going to do even before we did." He shuddered as he lowered his eyes to the floor. "We didn't have a chance," his shoulders slumped as he said this.

"I wish I had been here. I could have helped," Evan said, tearfully.

"No, no. There was nothing you could have done." Gramps reassured. "The village went up in flames as we ran to the castle for protection. We watched as they killed those who remained to try and defend the bridge and those who couldn't outrun the enemy. I can still hear their screams as they begged for their lives. The army killed without mercy. We could have defended the castle, that was our plan," Gramps continued, his voice trembling with emotion. "However, in the middle of the night as we slept, someone from inside the castle lowered the bridge, someone from within betrayed us. Once inside the castle, the true massacre began," Gramps words were barely audible and he had a look of despair in his eyes. "Those who survived," he attempted, searching for words. "The few of us who survived, were beaten and enslaved. Some of the survivors are forced to work on the docks, while others were killed as they tried to escape. Those of us who are still here are trapped between the floating city and these towers. They don't need to guard us. We have nowhere to go. Most of the "leftovers," that's what they call us, live in makeshift shelters. They allow me to live here because of my skills with leather. If I repair their shoes and don't cause any trouble, they leave me alone."

"But if they don't keep you here, why don't you leave? Why don't you run for it?" Evan challenged.

"Some have tried, but none have succeeded," Gramps responded. "The pack always catches the ones who run."

"The pack? What are you talking about?"

Gramps had stopped talking. It was as if he didn't want to recall the painful memories anymore.

Evan pressed, he had to know. "What happened to the royal family?"

Gramps looked at Evan, with tears in his eyes. "They fought to the bitter end."

"What about Emma?" Evan asked, his eyes filling with tears as the full realization hit him all at once.

"They all fought to the bitter end," Gramps said, as he stood up and walked back to tend the stew.

Evan suddenly felt claustrophobic, as the walls of the small room closed in around him. How could they all be dead? He had seen them just two days ago. They couldn't be dead. They just couldn't. Evan needed fresh air. He ran from the tower but only made it a few feet before collapsing to his knees.

Gramps followed Evan out of the tower and placed his hand on his shoulder.

"Who did this?" Evan raged, anger filling the emptiness he felt.

"Revenge won't bring her back Evan," Gramps assured.

"Who?" Evan demanded.

Gramps paused for a moment and then answered. "It was a combined effort by many kingdoms to bring down The Ledge." Gramps moved from Evan's side, taking several steps to look down the path which led to the floating city.

"Come quickly, inside," Gramps ordered.

Evan hurried back inside the tower behind Gramps, not understanding what was going on.

"You must hide under here," Gramps instructed, as he held up the blankets from his bed. "No matter what happens, stay hidden. Do you understand?" His tone was sterner than Evan had ever heard. "I need you to promise that no matter what happens you will stay hidden."

"I promise," Evan muttered.

No sooner had Evan settled under the blankets, then he heard voices at the door. Three men strolled uninvited into the tower.

Evan peered through a small hole in the blankets.

"What's for dinner?" a man asked, pushing Gramps roughly out of his way so he could see what was in the pot.

"Rabbit stew," Gramps answered.

"Smells good," the man commented as he took the spoon, dipped it in the soup, and took a sip.

"It's not for you," Gramps warned.

Something seemed familiar about the man. Evan had not previously seen the other two, but the man tasting the soup, reminded Evan of someone he knew.

"You're not very hospitable today, are you?" the man taunted. "I just wanted to know if my shoes were done."

"Come back tomorrow," Gramps replied curtly.

"Well now, that's a problem," the man spat. "You see, I leave in the morning to return to my father's kingdom and I need those shoes. Maybe if you spent less time making stew and more time working on my shoes, we wouldn't have this problem." The man tipped the pot over, spilling the stew onto the fire. The other two men laughed.

Evan was furious and almost stood to defend Gramps, but he remembered his promise and remained hidden.

"I will finish them tonight and bring them to your barge before you leave," Gramps assured, ignoring the spilled remnants of his dinner. "Now leave," Gramps ordered.

"You can't talk to the prince that way," one of the men warned, stepping forward to grab Gramps by his shirt, lifting him off the ground.

"It's okay, Nicholas. Put him down," the prince consoled, as he patted Gramps on the shoulder. "Gramps and I go way back. Isn't that true Gramps?" Then without warning, he backhanded Gramps across the face sending him roughly to the stone ground. "Sometimes, the old man just needs to be reminded where he belongs. I leave at dawn. You had better have the shoes ready by then."

As quickly as the three men had entered the tower, they were gone.

"Gramps!" Evan whispered as he rushed out from underneath the blankets. "Are you okay?"

"I'm all right," Gramps replied a little shaken.

Evan helped him sit up. Taking a handkerchief from his pocket, Gramps held it to his nose to stop the bleeding.

"Who were those men?" Evan asked.

"You didn't recognize the prince?" Gramps inquired, looking surprised.

Evan stood and walked over to the fire, where he stayed for a moment in silence. He did recognize the man's voice but couldn't bring himself to believe it.

"Francis?" Evan mumbled in a low, disbelieving tone.

"You sound surprised," Francis exclaimed, as he returned through the doorway. "I have to admit, I'm the one who is surprised. I thought you were dead." He chuckled as he drew his sword. "I'm glad I came back for this little reunion, and to think I

266

almost kept walking back to the docks. There was something different about the old man today. It was almost like he had something to live for again."

Francis was not the same scrawny kid Evan had known five years earlier. His thin frame had filled out. Other than his flaming red hair, the boy Evan had once known had changed into a man who Evan didn't recognize. Instead of adventure and a joy for life, the man standing before him had only darkness in his eyes.

"You haven't changed at all," Francis observed in confusion. "How is that possible?"

Evan ignored Francis' question. "How could you do this Francis? Emma was our friend?"

"Oh yes, Emma. Now that was unfortunate, but I was never her friend."

"What do you mean?" Evan's eyes discreetly searched the room for a weapon.

"The reason I came to The Ledge was to uncover its weaknesses, to find the best way to destroy it."

"You may be able to lie to yourself Francis, but I know that you cared for Emma," Evan called his bluff.

"I didn't care for that spoiled brat!" Francis responded. "But you. You were my friend. I even gave you an offer at a better life in my father's kingdom, a real chance to be someone, but you turned me down."

"Francis, I'm sorry," Evan said. "But it wouldn't have been right for me to leave The Ledge after the honor they gave to me."

"And how did that work out for you Evan? The Ledge has been destroyed and your rotten princess is dead," Francis said in a mocking tone.

"Don't talk about Emma that way," Evan threatened.

"Or what?" Francis taunted Evan, holding his sword dangerously close.

Evan backed up towards the fire.

"You're right, Francis," Evan admitted as he reached down and placed his hand on Gramps' shoulder. With his other hand, he reached behind his back and wrapped his fingers around the handle of the heavy cooking pot. "You were never our friend. Emma and I felt badly for you. You were so pathetic. Looks to me like you haven't changed a bit." Evan grinned as he said this.

Francis raised his sword and rushed at Evan with the speed of a lion, all of his strength concentrated on the attack. Evan had spent an entire summer fighting against Francis and expected this move. His anger always got the best of him and caused him to advance recklessly. Evan stepped to the side, avoiding his friend's charge, and with the pot in his hand, he swung it at Francis. The pot found the back of Francis's head, and with a loud cracking noise, Francis fell to the cold stone, his sword falling from his hands with a loud clank. Evan dropped the pot to the floor and bent to the ground. Francis wasn't dead, just unconscious.

"You must go before the sun sets!" Gramps warned. "They will send men to find Francis, and if they catch you," Gramps stopped for moment. "You can't let them catch you."

"What will you do?" Evan asked, grabbing Francis's sword off of the stone floor.

"I'll be okay. They need me to make shoes, and besides, I didn't knock Francis out, you did," Gramps reassured, forcing a smile.

Evan embraced his old friend, who was trembling. "I'll make this right," Evan promised as he released Gramps and ran out of the tower, heading for the forest.

The sun had just dipped below the cliffs, and a cold, ocean breeze started blowing. Evan fastened the front of his cloak as he remembered the words from Gramps, "The forest isn't safe anymore."

What did he mean by that? Did they patrol the forest? Evan shivered. Something seemed to be lurking in every shadow of the ruined village. He wanted to return to the school. He wanted to find a way to undo the destruction scattered around him. He needed to find a way to save Emma.

As he reached the top of the hill, Evan looked back at what remained of the castle and the village. The breeze had grown into a steady wind, and black clouds moved in from the coast, promising rain within the hour.

"It won't be long before I'm back on the fourth floor," Evan muttered to himself as he turned and started into the forest.

Evan stopped. He heard something in the distance, but he wasn't sure what it was. Was it the wind blowing through the trees? Evan didn't know. Maybe his imagination was playing off the warning Gramps had given him. Evan strained to listen for the sound again, but all he heard was the wind whipping through the pines.

Evan's heart started beating faster as he picked up the pace carrying him deeper into the forest. After ten minutes, he heard the terrifying sound again, but this time he recognized the high pitch call as it echoed through the trees. He knew something was in the forest with him. It wasn't the wind or his imagination. He now knew what Gramps had meant when he said that the pack catches the ones who run. Evan picked up speed down the pine-covered trail, fueled by fear and the motivation to leave this place behind.

He heard the sound again. It was closer now but coming from a different direction.

There's more than one? Evan thought to himself.

A new level of fear spurred him on faster. Branches tore at his cloak and face. In the fading light, he tripped several times over logs on the trail. Evan was finding it harder to control his breathing as he ran recklessly deeper into the forest.

Evan stopped and fell to his knees after almost an hour of running. He struggled to catch his breath. The forest was silent now. As his breathing slowed, Evan raised himself to his knees, his lungs no longer on fire. He listened to the silence. He no longer heard the terrifying sound that had spurred him on. Maybe they had moved to another part of the forest. Maybe they weren't hunting him. Evan stood cautiously to his full height and started walking forward slowly, Francis' blade in his hand.

He was close to the pine tree, close to the doorway that would lead to his safety. He slowly moved off the trail and into the brush. He could see the pine tree and the inviting shimmer of light in front of it. He was going to make it.

A twig snapped behind him. Evan quickly whipped around. He saw nothing. Evan turned back to the pine tree once more and froze. A large wolf stood in the shadows, just beyond the pine tree. The wolf's huge head was lowered slightly, his white teeth glimmered in the fleeting light as it growled. Evan heard movement behind him and another to the side. He had only one choice and no time to think. The staring match would end soon enough, and the attack would begin. Rain started falling, and almost instantly Evan's cloak was soaked.

Evan screamed a war cry, as he ran directly at the wolf, his sword held high. He could hear the other wolves join the chase. The entire forest came alive. He didn't look behind him or to the side. He knew they were close, he could hear the dead leaves crunching behind him. He knew he couldn't hesitate for even a second. He didn't take his eyes off of the lead wolf, who still hadn't moved, surprised by Evan's reckless charge.

The shimmering light was only ten feet in front of him, but the lead wolf was now charging, challenging Evan's move. He was closing the distance between himself and Evan. Evan threw his sword in the wolf's direction, causing it to swerve and allowing Evan just enough time to jump headfirst into the light.

Evan instantly felt the wolves sharp teeth clamp down on his foot, as his body was pulled back toward the forest floor. Evan looked for something to grab, his torso was now in the locker, but his right leg was still on The Ledge. He cried out in pain as he realized what was happening. The wolf was dragging Evan back to the forest. Evan struggled to find anything he could use for a weapon, but he had emptied his locker before traveling to The Ledge, and the space provided no weapons to hurl toward the aggressor. He had to do something before one of the wolves decided to move into the shimmering light. He had to close the door to The Ledge. Evan cried out again as the wolf's sharp fangs dug deeper into his foot. Grabbing onto the walls of the locker, Evan pulled his leg toward him until the black head of a vicious, snarling wolf, emerged through the light. With all his strength, Evan kicked the wolf's head with his left foot, causing the wolf's teeth to rip free. He screamed in pain, as he pulled both legs into the safety of the locker with such force that he somersaulted through the locker door and onto the hallway floor. The doorway to The Ledge closed immediately.

Evan laid in the hallway, trembling uncontrollably, his eyes moving from one end of the hallway to the other, looking for any sign of a continued attack by the wolf. He was alone, his locker door still open. The rain had stopped, and the violent attack was over.

Evan let out a sigh of relief as he sprawled on the floor, all of his energy exhausted. His right pant leg was ripped, but as he inspected his leg for further damage, a wave of relief passed over him. The wolf's sharp teeth had not penetrated his thick leather shoes. His leg had been scratched, and his foot throbbed, but it could have been worse. Much, much worse. Evan quickly changed into his school clothes, and placed his books back on the locker floor. Slowly, and limping slightly, Evan headed to his next class, his mind on Emma and Gramps.

Chapter Twenty-Six

The Message

Two weeks had passed since Evan had seen the destruction on The Ledge. He sat in the library after school with Cooper, Janelle and Phillip cramming for their biology exam. His friends had been discussing the meaning of a complex scientific theory for the last half hour, but since his return from The Ledge, Evan just wasn't motivated to learn anything at school.

"You're not even trying to understand what I'm saying," Phillip explained to Janelle.

"I understand, I just think you're wrong!" Janelle shot back.

"Cooper, Evan, will you please explain to Janelle that I am right and she is wrong!" Phillip pleaded.

"I'm staying out of this one," Cooper said throwing his hands in front of him in a defensive motion.

"Help me out Evan," Phillip asked.

"What?" Evan asked, not having followed the argument.

"Tell Janelle that she is interpreting the theory completely wrong."

"Um, what was the theory again?" Evan asked.

"I give up," Phillip said in a frustrated tone as he leaned back in his chair and threw his arms in the air.

"Told you I was right," Janelle said, understanding Phillip's gesture to be a sign of surrender.

"I'm sorry," Evan apologized to Phillip. "My mind is somewhere else."

"Well you need to bring your mind back to reality if you're going to pass our biology exam tomorrow."

"I know, you're right of course. I've just been wondering about…" Evan stopped.

He had been thinking of asking his friends about something for the last couple of weeks, but hadn't known how to bring it up without them thinking he was weird.

"Wondering about what?" Cooper prodded.

"Do you think it's possible to change the past?" Evan asked.

"How can you change the past?" Janelle asked rolling her eyes. "And what does this have to do with our biology exam tomorrow."

"What do you mean?" Phillip asked Evan. He was still mad at Janelle and welcomed an opportunity to talk about something she didn't want to talk about.

"If there was a way to go back in time," Evan said. "Do you think the past could be changed?"

"Hypothetically," Janelle said. "Because we all know that traveling back in time is impossible."

"Impossible!" Cooper shot back. "Time travel is not impossible."

"Here we go," Janelle said.

"Just because you haven't traveled back in time doesn't mean it's impossible." Cooper said.

"And you have traveled back in time?" Janelle asked.

"No, but I have read tons of books about it. Back me up Phillip." Cooper asked.

"I'm staying out of this one," Phillip said throwing his hands in front of him in a defensive motion just as Cooper had done when Phillip had asked him for help.

This conversation was not going as Evan had planned.

"Let's just pretend for a moment that time travel is possible," Evan said hoping to bring the conversation back to something that could help him. "Could someone change the past?"

"In one of the books I read," Cooper explained. "It talked about everything being predestined to happen."

"You mean that no matter what we do, we can't change the past or the future?" Janelle shot back. "That's a load of crap."

"I have to agree with Janelle on this one," Phillip said. "If time travel were possible and that's a big if. I think someone could change the past if they did something big enough to alter the events they wanted to change."

"I don't know," Cooper said. "The guy who wrote the book seemed pretty smart."

"Do you believe everything you read?" Janelle asked.

"I don't believe everything I've read in this biology book," Cooper said holding up his textbook.

"That's because you haven't read your biology book," Phillip said.

"True, but after listening to you two argue about theories all night I think I've learned enough to pass the exam tomorrow."

"Can we pick this back up tomorrow morning?" Evan said exhausted. He couldn't handle one more debate. "I'm sure we will all be refreshed and ready to learn more by then."

"Sure, but you better get a lot of sleep tonight," Phillip said looking at Evan, "You can't afford to fail this exam tomorrow." Phillip, Cooper and Janelle gathered their notes and shoved them into their bags. "Are you coming?" Phillip asked Evan as they stood to leave.

"In a minute, I want to look over my notes for a little while longer, besides I don't think my mom is here yet." Evan pretended to look through his notes as his friends started to leave.

"Okay, we will see you tomorrow," Phillip said.

"Don't study too hard," Cooper called back to Evan.

"See you in the morning," Janelle said as she followed Cooper and Phillip out of the library.

Evan sat back in his chair and sighed. The truth was that he expected to fail his biology exam in the morning, just as he had his English exam earlier in the day. He couldn't pull his mind away from the destruction he had seen on The Ledge. He wanted to help, but didn't know how. He had been called a hero when he had saved Alec from the bear attack and when he had saved the little girl at Niagara Falls, but as he sat in the library he didn't feel like a hero. A hero would know what to do.

"Studying late tonight?" Ms. Flinders asked as she moved towards his table.

"No, I was just packing up. Not sure last minute cramming will help me pass my exam tomorrow," Evan said as he stood.

"Before you go," Ms. Flinders said. "I need to show you something."

Evan hesitantly sat back down. "What is it?" Evan had no idea what Ms. Flinders would need to show him.

"I wasn't completely honest with you when we talked about the painting on the wall. What I mean is, I didn't tell you everything," Ms. Flinders said as she fidgeted with something behind her back. "The truth is that I have never told anyone what I am about to tell you."

Ms. Flinders was clearly nervous and Evan wondered what was so important that she had to share it with him.

"Almost 30 years ago, an old English gentleman visited the school. I thought that the man was here to deliver a lecture to the students and he needed directions to the lecture hall, but to my surprise he had come to see me. He started by telling me a story about a kingdom he had discovered when he was a young man. He told me that there wasn't much left of the castle or the village, but because of its remote location there were still some artifacts to unearth. While exploring the ruins, he overturned a stone and found a message sketched on the underside of the rock. It had been remarkably well-preserved, and, with a little bit of cleaning, the message was legible."

"What did it say?" Evan asked, his excitement growing.

"Apparently," Ms. Flinders said slowly, "the message was addressed to me."

"How could that be?" Evan asked. "The message must have been written before you were born."

"Exactly, I instantly suspected that the man was lying. I believe he suspected that I didn't believe him because immediately after giving me the photo of the rock with its inscription he left and I never heard from him again. I would have thrown the photo away, but something else the man said intrigued me."

"What did he say?" Evan asked.

"He told me that the ruins where he had found the rock were on a giant ledge."

Evan's jaw dropped and he wanted more than anything to see that photo.

"For almost 30 years I have kept this photo, still questioning its authenticity, until you came to me to get your library card on your first day of school."

"Why would that stop you from questioning the photo?"

Ms. Flinders took a deep breath, "Because you are mentioned in the inscription as well." Ms. Flinders placed the photo in front of Evan.

The rock looked no larger than a dinner plate. The shallow scratches on the rock's surface were faint and Evan had to squint to make out the letters.

"Is this a joke?" Evan asked after reading the message twice.

"That's what I thought, too," Ms. Flinders said. "He told me that he had been waiting 50 years for an Abigail Flinders to join the faculty at Wellsford Academy. He waited, without showing anyone the inscription on the rock. When I received the photo, I wrote it off as something too impossible to be true and threw it into the bottom of my drawer. I had forgotten about it until you entered my library. Evan, I don't know if this is an elaborate hoax and I'm not saying that you should do anything about it. In fact, I'm telling you the opposite. I would recommend that you don't waste your time at Wellsford Academy worrying about this photo. You should not put energy into things that you can't explain. It's better to stick with things that you can explain. But I felt," Ms. Flinders shifted her weight uncomfortably. "I felt that it was your decision to make and not mine." Ms. Flinders left Evan sitting at the table with the photo lying in front of him.

Evan read the message again.

"Abigail Flinders
Wellsford Academy
Evan Myers
Save Us"

The etchings on the stone could not have been clearer to Evan. With renewed urgency Evan turned back to his notes for his exam in the morning. He wouldn't be able to save anyone if he flunked out of Wellsford Academy.

Bryan Loveless grew up loving adventure and storytelling.
Whether on real life adventures hiking in the red cliffs of the desert,
skiing down the slopes of the Rocky Mountains or creating bedtime
stories for his four kids, Bryan is always seeking out new
experiences and stories. While receiving a master's degree in
mechanical engineering and serving as an officer in the United States
Navy, Bryan never lost his excitement for life. The stories Bryan
creates at Wellsford Academy are filled with excitement and
unlikely heroes who will inspire his readers to seek out adventures in
their own lives.

Made in the USA
Monee, IL
05 December 2020

51041884R00166